HOUSE OF DOLLS

Book One

By Harmon Cooper

Centralian Power

Classifications

Power Classifications Cheat Sheet
Created by Kevin Blackbook

Type	Class
• Type I - Severely Dangerous	• Class A - Telepathy
• Type II - Dangerous	• Class B - Shifter/Absorber
• Type III - Moderately Dangerous	• Class C - Elemental Mimicry/Organic Manipulation
• Type IV - Non-Dangerous	• Class D- Kinetic/Energy Related
• Type V - Unknown God-like Power (Rare)	• Class E - Intelligence-based
	• Class F - Teleportation
	• Class H - Healer

Chapter One: I'm Going to Jump

"I'm going to jump!" Kevin shouted over his shoulder. The overweight man stood on the ledge of the Centralian Immigration Office's rooftop, a magnificent building at least thirty stories high.

No one moved a muscle aside from Roman, who took one step closer to Kevin.

"Easy, buddy," he called to the middle-aged immigration advisor. Roman didn't particularly like Kevin, but seeing someone melt down and/or commit suicide was a terrible way to start a Monday.

"It's his first attempt, right?" Nadine, the woman standing next to Roman, asked.

"Yeah, he's been struggling lately," Roman told her under his breath, the tone of his voice indicating that he was looking for sympathy. He hadn't spoken to Nadine often, but he'd definitely noticed her—the new employee in the Immigration Inspection for Fast Travel Powers Department.

"Really?"

"I should know. He sits in the cubicle next to me. Come down, Kevin!" Roman shouted, without taking his eyes off Nadine.

It was a long way down, and it was technically illegal to commit suicide. The paperwork Kevin would leave his family to fill out alone would put fear in the eyes of any middle-of-the-road administrator.

But Roman wasn't focused on the details now. If his shorter, more robust counterpart wanted to end it all, that was his problem.

Truth was, Roman had been trying to figure out a way to introduce himself to Nadine for months now, ever since she'd started at the Centralian Immigration Offices.

And Roman was the type of guy ready to seize any opportunity presented to him.

"I try to talk to Kevin—you know, be friendly," he said coolly. "I invited him out once. It was just for lunch, but I definitely would've split the bill with him. Definitely."

For a non-exemplar, Nadine was as fit as a super.

Lean, thin, with green eyes and blondish-brown hair she usually wore in a bun, there was an exotic beauty about her, something Roman couldn't quite place. Another thing he liked about her was the fact that she always wore tight dresses, even on casual Fridays. He appreciated Nadine's attention to detail, and was just about to compliment her on her earrings when Kevin shouted.

"I'm going to jump!" A breeze whipped up, and Kevin nearly lost his balance. The top-heavy man regained his composure, snorting as he yelled, "I'll do it! I'll fucking do it!"

There were about twenty people on the rooftop now, all murmuring as they waited to see if Kevin would do it or not.

"Anyway, like I was saying, I tried to be friends with the guy. Hell, I even gave him a donut a few weeks back. Well, I brought the whole office donuts."

9

Roman raised an eyebrow at her. "You didn't happen to get one, did you?"

Nadine thought about it for a moment. "Are you sure it was you that brought them? I thought they were a gift from management for making us work through the last holiday."

Roman maintained his grin. "On the surface, yes, but who do you think wrote to HR and suggested it?"

"I'm going to jump!"

Roman considered his next options carefully. He could try to talk his officemate down from the ledge, which would be the right thing to do; or he could continue to talk to Nadine, which would be the smart thing to do.

He chose the latter.

"You're new here, right?" Roman asked her as more people gathered behind them.

What Nadine didn't know was that Roman had been quietly collecting as much info on her as he could. Nothing stalker-like, just asking if anyone knew her and, more importantly, if she was single. All he'd needed was an in, and it had come to him as a surprise that this happened to be Kevin's attempted suicide.

"That's right, I'm new around here. Or newish. Nadine," she said, shaking his hand. He held her hand for just a second longer than he should have, judging its weight.

"Roman Martin, Immigration Advisor."

"I think I've seen your signature on a few of the documents I've processed. A big signature, right? A little messy."

He shrugged. "I was going for avant-garde, but messy will do."

"Nice to meet you, Roman."

"Same, Nadine."

"Do you think he'll do it?" the green-eyed woman asked, returning her focus to Kevin, who was all but flapping his arms like wings at this point. There was a glint on her right hand, a peculiar silver ring that Roman hadn't noticed before.

"Kevin has threatened to do it before, which reminds me…"

Everyone loved a hero, and even though Roman wasn't a super, that didn't mean he couldn't save someone. So, after giving Nadine the dashing smile he'd perfected over the years, Roman strolled over to Kevin and started speaking to him as casually as possible.

"Hey, pal, any chance you'll come down from there?" he asked, "I could really, and I mean *really*, use a little love in that regard."

"Love?" Kevin sobbed, snot dripping from the tip of his nose. The wind pressed through his thinning hair, tossing his cowlick around. "What do you know about love?"

"Relax, Kevin. What's got you so angry and upset, anyway?"

"My wife left me for a super, an old college fling of hers. A fucking Type III Class D. A flyer. I caught them fucking in my living room. Fly-fucking."

"Fly-fucking?"

"Suspended upside down, midair. Fuck! I'm jumping, dammit—everyone stay back!" Kevin called over his shoulder. "Screw this world! To hell with Centralia!"

12

"Cool it," Roman said, inching just a little closer. "Hey, remember Nadine? The one I told you about? You know, the inspector for Fast Travels?"

"She's here too?"

Roman threw his thumb over his shoulder. "Everyone's here. Well, everyone aside from Selena, but that's fine. No one likes her anyway. Look, Kevin, point is, we're with you. We're here to support you."

"Fucking jump already!" someone from the back of the crowd called out.

"Hey!" Roman barked to the man. "Don't listen to him, Kevin. I think that was a warehouse guy, anyway. Those guys suck. I don't even know why Centralian Immigration has a warehouse."

Kevin rolled his eyes. "To house older documents. All paper files must be kept!" he said, pointing a finger over his head. "Now step back, Roman, I'm saying goodbye to this shitty life."

"Kevin." Roman laughed in a fake way. "Come on, pal, you don't want to jump. Talk about a way to go. Do me a solid here—Nadine is watching. Besides, you don't want to leave your family with the paperwork. You know what I mean. Lots of paperwork…"

"My family? All I have is my wife, and look what she's done to me! She cheated with a super! They were going at it floating horizontally in my living room. I saw it!"

"You already told me that."

"She was orgasming when I walked in. Ever see someone orgasm upside down? Fuck him! Fuck her! And fuck Centralia!" Kevin threw his arms wide, preparing to jump.

"Do it!" one of the warehouse guys called out.

Roman turned and pointed at the man. "Keep your mouth shut."

The warehouse worker bit his lip and slipped back into the crowd, not able to match his bark with his bite.

"Wasn't it an arranged marriage anyway?" Roman asked, looking back to Kevin.

"What? Don't be ridiculous. How long have I known you?"

"Two years? Has it really been two years? Damn, it sure has. That's depressing. Got room for me up there? Ha! I'm kidding; please come down."

"Two years? I bet you don't even know my wife's name."

Roman considered this for a moment. "Jane? Was it Jane? Or no—it was something with a K. Kathy? Kathy and Kevin? At least that sounds good together."

"Screw you, Roman." Kevin lifted his chin high and looked at his coworker over the bridge of his nose.

"Ah, don't be like tha—"

With a deep breath in, Kevin bent his knees and jumped backward.

Chapter Two: Heroes Anonymous

"I am not a superpowered individual. I am not an exemplar. I have never had a superpower. I am not a hero, nor will I ever be a hero," everyone said simultaneously. "I am not a superhero. I am half-powered. I will always be half-powered. I am a non-exemplar."

Roman frowned as they recited the next part.

"There is nothing about me that is extraordinary. I am not a hero. I am not a superhero. I am half-powered. I will always be half-powered. I am a non-exemplar."

He sat at the front of the room, next to the beautiful non-exemplar he'd been eying for weeks. The woman's name was Paris, and she was just about the hottest female he'd ever encountered at one of these meetings—dark hair, busty, pencil skirt, dimples too.

They'd made eye contact last week, but that was about it.

"Roman, would you like to begin?" the Heroes Anonymous session leader, Bill, asked.

Bill was a monster of a man, practically a Type II, with a shaved head and an earnest look in his eyes.

Roman cleared his throat as he made his way to the podium. "Hi, everyone, my name is Roman and I'm a non-exemplar. Um, it's been tough, I'll say that. The last few weeks, *whew*." Roman glanced at Paris, the brunette in the second row.

Better turn it up a notch, he thought as he continued. "So, just last week—and I swear I haven't even suggested to anyone I'm a hero for six months…"

"No need to justify anything. Just tell us what happened," Bill the sponsor said.

"Last week I broke the code. I lied about who I was." Roman gulped. "I masqueraded as a super and I knew it was wrong. It wasn't a big deal."

"Now, Roman…"

"It was small, Bill, that's all I'm trying to say here. I was at the grocery store, and what can I say? I'm a sucker for people in trouble." Roman winked at Paris, who crossed one leg over the other, showing a bit of flesh in the process. "Anyway, there were some exemplar kids outside, you know, just raising money for their super trials. Lucky kids, and you all know as well as I do that they aren't allowed to use their powers. And some of those kids, damn, they take that seriously."

Someone in the back of the room coughed.

"Anyway, a guy tried to hassle them for the candy they were selling. What kind of guy does that, right? Who steals candy from a bunch of kids? This asshole— sorry, Bill—this guy grabs a bag, and I'm talking a big bag of candy here, and takes off. So I took off after him."

"And?"

"And I start making noises with my mouth, pretending I'm a super. What do you expect, Bill? I'm not proud of it."

"Hey, no judgement here, brother," a guy in the third row said. Roman recognized him; he was always here, sometimes in a cast due to a misguided attempt at heroism.

"Hey, I may be a non-exemplar, but that doesn't mean I don't have stamina," Roman said, locking eyes with Paris. "I can go all night, if you all know what I mean. I used to be a fighter; some of you know that as well. So I'm running after him, and he's a fast one too, also a non-exemplar but maybe he's got more speed than me. Not strength though, and eventually, he trips and…"

"You didn't." The guy in the third row gasped, looking for confirmation from a chubby woman next to him who was always knitting a sweater.

"I did. I hopped right on top of him and we start rolling around, candy flying everywhere, and I felt like I had a superpower moving through me, activating, slowing down time—"

"Roman, you know that type of fantasizing isn't tolerated here. We are half-powered, non-exemplars. There is nothing unique about us," Bill reminded him.

"Yeah, I know, but okay, you asked and I'm telling you what happened. It wasn't my idea to come up here and say what's on my mind. I'm just a man, Bill—a man who wants to help people," Roman said, again locking his orange eyes on Paris, who now had a thin smile on her face. "So I overpowered him. I took the

19

bastard down, and I would have—I would have taken him to central booking too if..."

Bill waved his hand in the air to signal that Roman should wrap it up. "If what, Roman?"

"One of *them* showed up and took it from there. A Type II Class A—sorry, I work in superpowered immigration, so I usually refer to them this way. 'Type Two' means the woman that showed up had a second-tier power, while Class A signifies she was of the psychic variety. Anyway, you guys know the rest from there. I had to pay a fine for impersonating a hero, and they added three more months of mandatory Heroes Anonymous to my tab."

"I don't remember seeing that," Bill said, suspicion painting across his face.

"Yeah, it takes a little time for the paperwork to process." Roman smirked at Paris. "Government, am I right? Anyway, that's my story, and I'm sorry. I'm sorry I broke my promise to all of you and that I went against our creed. It would be nice, though..."

"I think that's enough, Roman," Bill said, ushering him off the stage. Roman had lied at the podium multiple times, and tonight was no different. Bill had heard Roman's real story once or twice, but no one was going to hear it today, or even this week.

The real reason he was at H-Anon was something that haunted Roman every day.

"Thanks, everyone." He took his seat in front of Paris, and as the next speaker made her way to the podium, he felt a tap on his shoulder. He turned to find Paris holding out a slip of paper.

Bingo, Roman thought, and he relaxed into his chair.

"I hope this isn't too sudden," Roman said after he'd met Paris at the corner of 11th and 19th. He wouldn't normally contact someone so quickly after getting their information, but something told him this was what Paris was expecting and, sure enough, here they were.

"It's fine," Paris said, her voice sweet music to his ears.

Roman had to work in the morning, which he wasn't looking forward to because of Kevin's messy departure. It was too bad that Kevin had decided to jump, and what had happened after the heavy man had gone over the side of the building was one of the more ironic things Roman had seen in a while.

But he would think about that later—probably tomorrow, when he took on Kevin's workload.

For now, he was all eyes on Paris, who wore a different pencil skirt and a matching blouse.

"So tell me about yourself." He stuffed his hands into his jacket and turned toward 12th Street. They'd already agreed on a bar called Peace of Mind, which was known for its mixed drinks. It was a good spot to pick up non-exemplars, too, something Roman did occasionally if he was going through a dry spell.

"Paris Renara, and I know I should speak at H-Anon sometime, but I will later. Bill keeps pushing me, but I'm a little shy in front of people."

"It's fine," Roman told her, running his hand through his white hair. Even though Roman was two years shy of thirty, he'd had white hair his entire life. It contrasted with his orange eyes, something that always caught the attention of the opposite sex.

"So, more about me: I work as a real estate agent. Have you heard of the new development in Northern Centralia, the one called Waterfall Heights?"

"I read about it in the paper."

"Those are the ones I'm currently working with. I have other agents I work with, but the commission is great." Paris continued speaking about the realty business, eventually steering the conversation back to Roman. "I really liked your story today. That must have been embarrassing with the Type... what was it?"

"Type II, Class A and D. She was a female telepath who used kinetic energy. I didn't mention that last part."

"Ah, that's right. But you got the kill," she said, turning to Roman and smiling. "And by that I mean you were the first to take down the candy thief. You shouldn't forget that."

"I'll try to remember it."

Paris looped her hand around his arm, pulling her body closer to his. They continued down the street until they reached Peace of Mind. Roman wasn't nervous per se, but his ears did perk up when they entered. He was hoping to avoid contact with any past flames.

Luckily, it was a weekday, and the bar known as Peace of Mind was pretty much empty.

Once they were seated, the conversation kicked into high gear, the alcohol loosening Paris's tongue a bit and making Roman feel the familiar comfort that came when things were going his way.

He told Paris his partially fabricated backstory, his struggles with heroism, his practiced stories from start to finish, and after the third round of drinks, he knew he had this one under wraps.

And it wasn't that Roman was cocky. Rather, like anyone who'd done the same thing multiple times, he knew the dance—knew how to lead, knew when to retreat and most importantly, knew how to steer.

Two hours later and the two were on the couch in his living room, Paris with her top off, her hands pressed into his shoulders as she gyrated her hips against him. She still had her skirt on, but it was hiked up over her ass, revealing her thighs and panties.

Roman was in heaven, and it was only when anger flashed behind her eyes that he knew something was wrong.

Paris's tongue shot out of her mouth and wrapped around his neck, and soon, Roman had lost consciousness.

Chapter Three: Hogtied Treason

From what Roman could recall, he'd been slammed into the wall by Paris's powerful tongue.

Definitely a Type III Class B Exemplar, he thought as he tried to steady his vision, the taste of blood at the back of his throat. *Maybe a Type II...*

He was belly down on his living room floor, hogtied, his lower back and chest screaming with pain. Paris sat before him in her blouse and pencil skirt, one leg crossed over the other as she looked through a small notebook.

"Good, I'm glad you could join me."

"You're an exemplar..." he spat, feeling the strain from his muscles pulling tight across his chest.

She snapped her small notebook shut. "What gave it away? Was it my tongue?" she asked, licking her lips.

Paris squatted before him. "I really should have killed you. Not that there aren't people willing and ready to take your place. But that's what shifters are for. It's too bad we couldn't have at least finished what we started."

"Who said we can't?" Roman asked, doubling down. When it came to deceit or trying to get his way, Roman *always* doubled down.

Paris raised an eyebrow at him. "You're serious?"

"Why the fuck not?" he asked, ignoring the strain in his muscles. "If you're going to kill me, I'd at least like to go out with a bang, and by 'bang' I mean…"

A smirk formed on Paris's face. She dropped her hand to his side and slowly stroked her fingers down the muscles on his arm, to his waist and then to his nude hip. From there, she traced her fingers along a vein that pumped blood to his penis, and flicked his growing erection.

"Nope, that's not what I came here for." She stood. "I have two options for you: One, I kill you and we replace you with a shifter."

"They'll know," Roman barked. "We do checks for that."

"Not to worry. We have a new way to replace you with a shifter, and it's quite painful."

"Damn."

"Two, you become my informant on the inside. The Western Provinces have questions about Centralian immigration."

Roman tried to contain the look of realization on his face. *She's a Western Province spy.*

"You answer these questions, collect data, and provide it to me. I may also need you for other matters, such as a future processing concern I have. Do a really good job, and I just may find the time to finish what we started earlier, with or without my tongue, if you get my drift."

Roman swallowed hard. He'd never been loyal to the state, and while he may have worked for Centralian immigration, he treated it just as he would any other day job.

No, Roman had loyalty to one person, and one person only—his dark secret something only a few people would ever know.

"Fine," he told Paris. "What information do you need?"

Chapter Four: Super Cheating

There was a reason Kevin Blackbook had decided to commit suicide.

Kevin had never been the happiest of guys, but he'd been happier than usual over the last few years, after he'd married a widowed non-exemplar named Susan who was way out of his league. They'd met at one of the coffee shops on 15th Street (not far from Roman's place, actually, although he and Roman never discussed this), and it hadn't quite been love at first sight, but it did bloom into something of the sort.

Love at tenth sight? It may have been the eleventh or twelfth time they'd met—Kevin never could get it right—that he'd mustered up the courage to ask her on a date. The rest was history, Kevin's history, and Mrs. Susan Blackbook had been the love and sole purpose of his life ever since.

This was before Kevin knew Roman—hell, before any of the newer employees had become immigration advisors. And Kevin and Susan had been happy enough, vacationing to the Southern Alliance when given a chance and even purchasing a timeshare in Lower Centralia.

Kevin suspected that Susan was up to something when he came home one night, just a few weeks back, actually, and found the furniture toppled over. At first, he had assumed it was a burglar, but then Susan emerged from the bedroom in the flowing kimono she wore as a house robe with cherry-red cheeks and just about the biggest smile he'd ever seen on her face—a pleasure smile if he'd ever seen one.

"Sorry," she'd said at the time, "I got carried away cleaning."

Kevin had believed her, and that had been that.

In fact, if Susan had been more careful, Kevin would never have figured out what she was up to.

But like many non-exemplars who'd had affairs with exemplars, the temptation to experiment was too great, and it was yesterday that Kevin had come home to find a Type III Class D—a fucking Class D!—

floating on his back in the living room while Kevin's wife rode him reverse cowgirl, her feet pressed into his lower back, her hands pinching her nipples as she always did when she was orgasming.

So that was what led Kevin to want to jump.

And before he did, like he had done for years, Kevin Blackbook purchased a single Hero Ticket at the local corner store.

This was mostly out of habit; he knew he didn't have a chance to win. And besides, he'd be dead before they announced the winner anyway.

Chapter Five: Nadine

After the hospital visit he made every morning, Roman took the trolley to the Centralian Immigration Offices.

He had a lot on his mind as he stared outside the window, watching the city blaze by, the morning sun reflecting off the smooth glass surfaces of tall buildings.

One of the things on his mind was the fact that his day had just gotten a lot busier. Instead of sitting at his desk and looking busy or going to the break room hoping to see Nadine, as he normally would have on a Tuesday, he now had to take all of Kevin's appointments.

And judging by the piece of paper he'd received from Selena, their bitchy department manager, Kevin had a full caseload.

Kevin always had a full caseload; the middle-aged immigration advisor was still under the impression that if he worked harder, he would get noticed and be able to advance in the agency.

Truth be told, the only way to advance was to know someone, and if you didn't know someone, you could be good looking and fuck your way to the top.

At least that was what Roman had seen, which explained how someone like Nadine, who had come in just recently, was already at a higher salary rank than Kevin.

Not to say that Nadine had fucked her way to the top, but she was definitely hot, young, and had a way with words—all things chubby Kevin did not have. So maybe she had seduced her way to the top.

Roman had seen opportunities to do this, a couple times actually, but he'd never really taken them. He liked his current position as an immigration advisor because he had some power, yet not enough to let it go to his head. Plus, he never had to work overtime.

This fact didn't stop Kevin from working overtime, which was why he had so many appointments today. And tomorrow.

Appointments that now belonged to Roman. There were exemplars from the Northern and Southern

Alliance, as well as the Eastern and Western Province. A worldly caseload if there ever was one.

"Dammit, Kevin," Roman whispered as his thoughts jumped from the stack of work that lay ahead to late last night, when he'd nearly been strangled by the powerful tongue of a Western Province spy.

Now Roman was supposed to be some type of informant, but the information Paris had asked for wasn't that classified.

She simply wanted numbers, and possibly favors, which made no sense to him as he had absolutely no authority here.

What Paris had done seemed like a lot of trouble to go through just to get some numbers, especially attending Heroes Anonymous, which must have been boring and pathetic as hell for an exemplar.

Once Roman arrived at work, he took his sweet time walking from the train station to the entrance, something he did every morning, and made it to his desk ten minutes *after* he was supposed to be there.

Selena had caught him doing this before, but every time she did, he told her he had a stomach sickness that was triggered by coffee, which he had to drink to stay awake, so he'd spent a little more time in the bathroom than he'd hoped to spend.

His manager grumbled every time he used this excuse, but Selena had bigger fish to fry, those fish being upper management and their constant need for metrics.

"Hey Nadine," he said as the slender woman passed by his cubicle.

As always, the hotbody from the Immigration Inspection for Fast Travel Powers Department wore her dirty-blond hair in a bun, and this time, she had a hair clip in it that matched the green of her eyes. Her dress seemed tighter than yesterday too, something he noticed quickly and then tried to unnotice as she approached him.

"Are you okay?" she asked.

"Why? Does something look wrong?" Roman smiled at her.

"I mean about Kevin. Did you hear?"

"No, what happened to Kevin? I mean, aside from the fact that he tried to commit suicide yesterday and

36

just so happened to be saved by the same goddamn flying exemplar that was boning his wife."

Her eyes went wide. "That's who saved him?"

"I'm sorry, I thought everyone here knew. Call it the ultimate irony. He jumps, and that asshole just happens to be flying by. It's too bad, too. He used to sit right there." Roman nodded toward Kevin's cubicle. "I talked to him a bunch about it yesterday morning, before he jumped. I wish I'd been able to say more."

"That's so sweet of you," she said as she took the seat in front of him.

"It was the least I could do."

"Well, I guess it's my turn, then, to tell you something you don't know."

Roman raised an eyebrow at the pretty blond sitting before him. "Go on," he said, leaning back in his chair to seem relaxed.

"Kevin died last night."

He gasped. "You're serious?"

"Yes, he died."

"How?"

Selena, the chunky middle manager, came around the cubicle and stopped in front of Roman's workspace.

"You're late, and you still have time to chat?" Selena rolled her eyes at Roman. "I don't know what's happened to this place, I really don't, but it's employees like you that make it hard for me to do my job. Have you ever thought about that? Have you ever thought about how hard it is to manage all these people like you?"

"Not really," Roman admitted.

"You know what? Never mind. You're not going to change your ways, and you aren't the worst employee we've ever had, so there's no reason for me to discipline you because then I'd eventually have to hire someone else that knows all the things you know, and that would require training, and training would require more unpaid overtime for me."

"Sorry to, um, hear that."

Selena threw her hands in the air and stormed away, only to return five seconds later. "By the way, Kevin died, and his first appointment should be here soon. Good luck."

"Thanks?"

Nadine waited for Selena to leave before she continued. "Kevin was in the hospital when he disappeared."

"He disappeared? I thought you said he died."

"No, he's definitely dead. They had some Type III Class Es scope out the area and, yeah, whoever took him killed him first."

Roman's eyes darted to the handy chart pinned to his cubicle.

Power Classifications Cheat Sheet
Created by Kevin Blackbook

Type	Class
• Type I - Severely Dangerous • Type II - Dangerous • Type III - Moderately Dangerous • Type IV - Non-Dangerous • Type V - Unknown God-like Power (Rare)	• Class A - Telepathy • Class B - Shifter/Absorber • Class C - Elemental Mimicry/Organic Manipulation • Class D- Kinetic/Energy Related • Class E - Intelligence-based • Class F - Teleportation • Class H - Healer

"Class Es make great detectives."

"So I've heard."

He paused briefly to admire Nadine.

It wouldn't be easy, but if he put just a little more work in, he'd probably be able to hook up with her. There was a spark between them, but he could tell she was modest. Call it intuition, or call it two years in the game since the incident that had changed his life for the worse.

Point was, Roman could sense it.

"It's been rough," he lied. "I've been thinking a lot about Kevin and how I wish we'd connected better. It would be nice to connect with more of my coworkers, actually. I mean, we all work together forty hours a week, yet I hardly know some people, especially the new ones."

"I'm new," she volunteered. If she got the hint that Roman was asking her out, she didn't let on. This led him to believe that Nadine, like Roman, knew what she was doing. It made sense, too, as Nadine had worked her way up the ranks pretty quickly.

"I should be going." Nadine stood. "We have a meeting this morning."

"Not another one," Roman joked, and sure enough, Nadine laughed.

"How did you know we have so many meetings?"

"A hunch."

He dropped both elbows onto his desk and clasped his fingers together. If Nadine could have seen the hamster wheel turning in Roman's mind at that very moment, she would have seen it working overtime as he tried to think of another angle.

"How about coffee today?" she asked, throwing him a bone. "After work. I know a spot on 19th Street. It's quiet, low key. Called the Proxima Cafe."

Roman casually leaned back in his chair, made an effort to check the calendar posted on his cubicle wall, and turned back to Nadine. "Yeah, today, I'll meet you after work. 19th Street, right?"

"Yeah, that's right," she said as she left his cubicle. "See you tonight."

Chapter Six: The Hero Ticket

The super known as Hazrat scowled at Roman Martin.

"I know it's not what you wanted to hear," Roman told him, "but your wife is here in Centralia on an S2 Visa. Which means she is your dependent. Because she is your dependent, and not here as an immigrant worker, she is not allowed to work."

"But my wife is a Type III Class E, and the job she has is working with a science lab directly affiliated with the Centralian government."

Roman, sitting at Kevin's desk, sighed as a frown took shape on his face. He had been arguing with Hazrat for ten minutes now, and the guy just didn't seem to get it.

There was nothing Roman could do for him.

It was out of his control—just like most, if not all, immigration-related laws.

Hazrat, who was clearly from the Southern Alliance, was used to a different way of government. Bribes, forgery, nepotism, privilege. It wasn't that Centralia didn't have these things, but the exclusive Southern Alliance was known for them.

It struck Roman as ironic that a rich man from the south would be arguing immigration with him; the Southern Alliance had some of the strictest immigration laws on record.

And Roman wasn't stupid enough to think Hazrat wasn't dangerous.

The muscular man was a Type II Class D. His records indicated that he could manipulate shadows into weapons, which was why Roman was keeping an eye on every shadow cast in Kevin's cubicle office.

He'd already seen a few of the shadows tremble.

"I don't think you understand how talented she is," Hazrat said, his long mustache lifting back as he revealed his teeth.

"Sir, with all due respect, my understanding of your wife's ability has nothing to do with her current visa status. If she wants to switch to a W visa, that's fine, but she'll need to do what's called a Change of Status, which can take up to one year to process, and during that time she cannot work, *period.*"

"But if it takes a year, she'll lose this job opportunity!" Hazrat's nostrils flared. He was a light-skinned guy with tattoos and markings running along the sides of his head and down his spine. Not everyone in the South looked like this; from what Roman could tell, Hazrat must have had somewhat of a rebellious streak in his youth.

"I am well aware of that, but again—and I can't emphasize this enough—this situation is out of my hands. There is no one you can appeal it to, and as I told you five minutes ago, you have two options: One, you can file for a change of status. This would mean she goes from an S2 Visa to a W Visa. Two, you could go back to the Southern Alliance and then come back on the correct visa. If you did this, you would have to go to the Centralian Embassy again, go through the entire application process of getting a W Visa, and come back that way. Personally, I suggest the second option, as it is faster and she could probably start working sooner."

"But she wants to start working now," Hazrat growled. Roman noticed the shadows cast by the books on Kevin's desk start to grow.

"Intimidating me isn't going to get you what you want; it will just end with you either going to jail or being forced to leave the country after going to jail," said Roman, his voice firm. He wasn't visibly scared of Hazrat, regardless of the man's powers. "And I'm sorry to be the bearer of bad news here, but all this information was made available to you when you came here on a Student Visa."

Shadows from beneath Kevin's desk tore through the wood paneling, sending pens, pencils and loose papers into the air.

The corner of the cubicle collapsed, causing some commotion as they also brought Kevin's neighbor's cubicle wall and Roman's cubicle wall down. Every available shadow now floated in the air, barbed, occasionally stabbing at items around them.

Roman had already kicked over his chair at this point, and, realizing he was pinned, he kept both arms at the ready, poised to spring into action as soon as the opportunity presented itself.

Security was already on the way, evident by the siren that was going off.

"I will fucking kill you," Hazrat said.

"Then do it," Roman said, his fists in front of his body. He'd fought an exemplar before. It hadn't been easy, and he'd ultimately lost, but after all the battles Roman had been in, he wasn't the type to go down without a fight.

Besides, there hadn't been a moment in the last few years in which Roman hadn't been ready to die. And this wasn't the first super who had blown up at him.

A tendril of shadow pulled back, and just as it was about to whip at Roman, Hazrat began choking. He fell to his knees, his face turning red as his eyes bulged.

Standing behind him was one of the security supers, her eyes white as she held her hand out.

Roman had to laugh.

Coco was a Type I class D, someone not to be fucked with. He should know; he'd helped do her paperwork for some relative she had in the North Alliance.

"You okay?" Coco asked.

"Yeah," Roman said as his heart lowered from his throat back to his chest.

Just because he was accustomed to dealing with angry supers did not make him any less nervous when accosted. "I will, um, go ahead and get the paperwork for this filled out and bring it down for you to sign."

"Okay, I'll take him down to holding and we'll go from there." Coco grabbed Hazrat by the back of his shirt and dragged him away.

"Geez," Roman said as he examined the mess.

They were going to need to get a new desk—that was certain. And looking over to his cubicle, he saw his desk had been partially destroyed as well.

As he'd done when this had happened previously, Roman began going through some of the debris, waiting for the cleanup team to arrive. He just needed to grab a few of the papers to file his report, and he was picking up the last of the paper when he noticed the shimmering end of a Hero Ticket.

Roman rolled his eyes.

He couldn't believe Kevin was stupid enough to play this stuff, and having gone through his own spell of trying to win exemplar status, he knew just how big a waste of money it was.

Still, the Hero Ticket was there, and Kevin wasn't going to be around to see if it was a winner.

So Roman slipped the ticket into his stack of papers, figuring he could check the number later.

Chapter Seven: Soul Speed

Nadine held her smile until she got back to her desk.

Her desk was the last in a line of cubicles in the Immigration Inspection for Fast Travel Powers Department, which was a fancy way to say they vetted teleporters and others who could move rapidly. She'd had an out-of-office meeting with a team from the Centralian Diplomatic Corp, so she had no idea about the attack Roman had experienced just twenty minutes ago.

Nadine knew when she had the upper hand, and she was willing to hold off on celebrating until she was sure no one was watching. It hadn't been easy for Nadine to get a job here—nor for any of them, so it was amazing to her that they had chosen some of the people they had chosen—and while it wasn't frowned upon for one to date a coworker, it also wasn't encouraged.

But that wasn't the reason she was smiling.

"Hey, Nadine, any chance you can take my 10:30?" a voice asked from the neighboring cubicle. "I've got a doctor's appointment—well, my wife does, so I promised I'd be there."

"Sure, Sarah, I'm fine with that," Nadine told her coworker. Her coworker, Sarah, never stopped gushing about her wife. Maybe all newlyweds were this way; maybe it was a Centralian thing.

Nadine heard Sarah's chair squeak. The middle-aged fast transport advisor came around to her cubicle and smiled at Nadine over the rims of her glasses.

"You probably don't want to hear what's going on with her, but I can tell you if you'd like."

"No, that's fine, medical situations are a private matter," said Nadine, who had grown tired of hearing about Sarah's wife. Her coworker seemed to always be going on about her significant other, and always managed to shove her into the conversation.

Sarah sat down as if she owned the cubicle. In a way, she did—or at least she had. Nadine worked in Sarah's former cubicle, and Sarah had been here for ten years, so she'd seen everyone come and go, and had seen the entire process change at least three times—four if you asked her, but three if you actually looked at the documentation.

"Well, it all started out with an ache she was having in her lower back."

"Really, Sarah, you don't have to tell me anything."

Sarah let out a sigh that eventually turned into a burp. Nadine had seen her do this before, and it was absolutely disgusting to watch, let alone hear.

"Excuse me, I've been meaning to have that checked out. You know, it's funny, we really are like trains."

"Why are we like trains?"

"Well, I guess that's not a good analogy. We aren't like trains at all. With trains, you can keep the shell and just change out the insides—you know, keep things fresh. You could theoretically keep one going forever if there weren't changes in government regulations on size and things like that. But us? You can't just change out our parts. Well, some exemplars can, and the rich can pay for a super to do it for them, but you get what I'm saying."

"No. I mean, yes, I do. Well, I have a lot of work to do, so…"

"Yeah, but back to the conversation we were having about my wife. So she had this pain in her lower back, always had it as far as I can remember, but things really took a turn for the worse yesterday."

"Sorry to hear that."

"She had gone down the street to get the mail, and, well, you can't blame young supers, but they really should learn to control their abilities better than they do. Anyway, a few of them were play-fighting and when you have a fifteen-year-old who has the ability to control vector fields and turn his arms to steel chasing after another kid—equally talented, at least a Type II— well, that's a recipe for disaster."

Nadine began shuffling papers on her desk. "I'm sorry to hear that."

Sarah snorted. "So these young supers were play-fighting, and sure enough, my wife got in the crosshairs. She didn't get hit by anything, but there was a small quake that caused her to fall, and she threw her back out. So now she's in the hospital again. Third time she's been in the hospital this month, actually, but they never seem to heal her up. I mean, she's on a waiting list to meet with the healer, but you know how that goes. People like us, half-powereds, we never get to meet the healers."

"I'm sure things will change one day," Nadine said.

"Huh! That really is something. You said that with a genuine tone of hope in your voice. I have to commend you on that. I haven't had hope in years—not since the guy who used to sit in my cubicle left. What was his name? Was it Bobby? No, maybe it was Joel. No, that wasn't it either. Anyway, he was a good guy. Stinky, but nice. Okay, thanks for taking my 10:30."

With that, Sarah stood and shuffled out of Nadine's cubicle.

Nadine didn't have much time to prepare for Sarah's 10:30 appointment, and Sarah, always being the type of person who wanted to arrive early, had left minutes after their very one-sided conversation.

Nope, Nadine would have to wing it.

"I need to see some ID," Nadine said in place of a greeting.

The young woman standing before her, Sarah's next appointment, handed Nadine her ID.

Lisa Painstake was a Type IV, Class C & F, which meant she was a teleporter who also had some sort of elemental mimicry/organic manipulation ability. The young exemplar was incredibly fit, and a pink bouffant with blond bangs made her seem just about as young as she actually was, nineteen—and already in trouble with the law.

There was a note on her ID that led Nadine to decide she actually needed to see her case file. This kind of hidden note was only visible to administrators and advisors.

Every administrator had gone through a process in which a telepath had imprinted on them the ability to see hidden codes on people's IDs, and for Nadine and anyone else in the immigration building, this meant notes based on their immigration status, as well as more detailed notes regarding their abilities.

"Stay here; I'll be right back."

Nadine moved over to Sarah's desk, ignoring the cutesy picture of Sarah and her wife at some park in the Northern Alliance. While she was a little gross and always took over every conversation, Sarah was incredibly organized, and this was evident in the fact that all her files were in order.

It only took Nadine about twenty seconds to find the young super's file.

"Okay, Ms. Painstake, to confirm, go ahead and tell me where you think your case stands?"

Nadine had her files open now, back at her own desk, and she knew very well where Lisa Painstake's case stood. The girl was close to getting deported, and she would have already been deported if not for the fact that she had a relative in a distant embassy.

Lisa had been caught smuggling, so she was facing deportation or jail.

The thing was, since she was from the Southern Alliance, Centralia didn't have jurisdiction to actually jail her. This was one of the things that benefited immigrants in Centralia.

Due to a prisoner exchange law that all five countries practiced, and the fact that there were supers all around, it was very hard to police certain types and classes. Most jurisdictions preferred to let their home state take care of exemplars like Lisa. It was fairly difficult to actually get arrested and stay in jail in a foreign country, not that it wasn't possible.

There were holding cells—and other, more secretive government prisons—where supers who severely violated laws were kept for years on end as their paperwork was processed, but for the most part, it was easier to transfer them back.

The only thing was, at least for Lisa, she had a pretty good case as to why she should stay.

Or so she thought.

"I can't go back there. I have a brother there, and... let's just say, it was all his idea, this whole smuggling thing, and, um... we're kind of not on good terms now. I don't think I would be safe if I went to my home country."

The look in her eyes did not match her demeanor as Lisa spoke of her brother and her fear for her life.

As Nadine listened, the young exemplar with the pink bouffant laid out more issues regarding her family and why it would be very dangerous for her to go back.

Nadine had heard these types of stories before, and since she really didn't care what happened in Centralia much anyway, she was going to approve her paperwork, saving the poor girl from having to deal with Sarah, who loved to schedule dozens of meetings just to arrive at the same conclusions.

But approval would come at a price.

And as she continued to look over the file while Lisa gave Nadine her life story, she realized that a person with Lisa's ability in her pocket could prove useful. The thing was, Lisa wasn't exactly a teleporter, nor was she a traditional fast-traveling super who relied on physiology and stamina to travel long distances.

Lisa had a power known as Soul Speed.

It was a rare variation of enhanced speed that allowed the person to project their astral body forward and travel anywhere while their physical body stayed in one location.

Nadine had read about it, so she knew that someone who traveled this way had advantages over a teleporter, namely in the fact that astral travel didn't trigger teleportation detection devices.

Out of courtesy, and to show the young woman she was on her side, Nadine let her finish her spiel.

Once Lisa was done, Nadine closed her case file and smiled at the young exemplar. "I believe we can work something out."

Chapter Eight: Cat Girls

Kevin awoke with a gasp, finding himself on just about the biggest bed he'd ever seen, easily twice the size of his cubicle.

There were four posts on this bed, like something Kevin had seen in a picture book about kings and queens in the Southern Alliance. The posts were covered with translucent drapes that matched the sheets, the cover, and the large number of fluffy pillows.

It was a great place to be, definitely much better than the hospital he'd fallen asleep in.

With a yawn—and the realization that life wasn't as bad as it had been when he'd been standing at the top of the immigration administration building contemplating suicide, nor was it as bad as being rescued by the same douche-bucket who was boning his wife, only to be whisked away to a hospital against his will—Kevin placed both hands behind his head and sighed deeply.

He looked down at his belly, which was large, but not as large as some he had seen in Centralia. Perspective was key for Kevin; while he may be a fat man, at least he wasn't as fat as other people, and on the scale of things, those other people would probably be envious of someone with a body like his.

"He's awake," said a soft, female voice.

"Who's there?" he asked.

The drapes surrounding his bed parted, and a petite woman no taller than five feet hopped onto the mattress. She had furry cat ears, and her dark-black hair was cast into two pigtails at the sides of her head. Her skin was a few shades away from light brown, flawless and hairless.

She was topless, her breasts perfectly formed. Better than any exemplar, better than any woman at one of the secret strip clubs in Centralia, better than anything he had seen in a comic book.

The cat girl standing before him was in a league of her own.

She turned and revealed her bottom half, which was barely covered by a pair of panties. A black tail jutted out just above her thong, its end lightly curling in the air.

"Where are we?" he asked, the realization that he definitely wasn't at the hospital blooming.

"Hello, Kevin."

"A Type III Class B? Beast-morphing?" Kevin whispered to himself.

The petite feline female pretended to claw the air and then stopped, giving Kevin a moment to look her over once again. With that, she pressed the heels of her feet together and lowered her knees to the side, now sitting in a variation of a cross-legged position.

Kevin's eyes naturally gravitated towards her panties, which barely covered her mound. She was clean-shaven, no fuzz sticking out the sides, and while her panties may have been black, there was an emblem on the front. A dark-blue emblem he could barely make out.

"Glad you're here," said another, sharper voice.

The other side of the bed curtain parted and another petite feline female, this one with turquoise hair and a yellow clip near one of her ears, crawled into the bed.

"Who are you two, and what do you want from me?" Kevin demanded as he took the second one in, noticing the minor differences between the two. While the dark-haired cat girl had larger breasts, the turquoise-haired cat girl had a larger ass, which she accentuated by sitting on her knees and looking over her shoulder at Kevin, her turquoise tail bobbing up and down.

There were other similarities as well, namely in their overall height and their facial features, which were soft, oval, their skin the meeting place between white and tan, like the pages of a journal but softer, creamier, classic.

"He's a little too big," the black cat girl said to her counterpart. "But I kind of like it."

"He has bigger breasts than I do," the other said with a chuckle.

"Who are you?" Kevin asked, kicking his feet.

"Obsidian," said the one with black hair and pigtails.

"Turquoise." The turquoise-haired cat girl spun around, putting her weight on Kevin's shins so he could no longer kick his feet. Kevin tried to move away, but only found himself against the backboard.

"Mmmm, he's so feisty," Obsidian said as she pressed nearer to him. She placed her clawed hands on the blanket that covered his lower half and whipped it away, exposing Kevin's nude body.

"Look what I found…" The black-haired cat girl took in Kevin's rather large erection.

It was his only selling point, and probably the reason his wife, Susan, had married him in the first place. Kevin may have been a tub of lard, but he was a tub of lard with a nine-inch cock, practically a superpower to most men in Centralia, the Eastern and Western Provinces, or the Northern and Southern Alliances.

Obsidian clasped her hand around it, admiring its girth.

"Please, I'm not trying to offend anyone. It's just— I'm sorry!" Kevin blabbered.

Obsidian let go of his member and moved up his body so that Turquoise could move up as well. She now sat with her legs clasped around one of his thighs, her knee inches away from his gonads. She placed her hand just below his naval and began slowly drumming her fingers.

A bead of sweat appeared on the side of Kevin's head.

"They really are like a woman's breasts," Obsidian said as she squeezed his man-tits. The black-haired cat girl now sat to his immediate right, a curiously mischievous look on her face.

"Do they taste like them too?" asked Turquoise.

Obsidian lowered her head to Kevin's nipple and licked it with her sandpaper tongue.

"Oh my!" Kevin gasped as she did it again.

"What do you think?" Turquoise asked her counterpart. Kevin's heart was beating faster than it had ever beat before. Never in his wildest dreams had he imagined there would be one—not to mention two—beautiful, clearly foreign exemplars in bed with him, each of them dangerously close to his throbbing penis—and licking his nipples at that!

"Please," he said, his brain barely able to maintain control over his lower half. "Just let me go."

The black-haired cat girl bent forward and licked Kevin's other man-tit, considered the taste, and turned to her counterpart. "I think it tastes almost the same."

"Kevin," Turquoise said without looking away from his throbbing erection, "are you ready to tell us what we need to know?"

Kevin felt a furry appendage wrap around his penis and he knew immediately, without a shadow of a doubt, that it was one of their tails. Sweat dripped from his hairline, his heart beat against the inside of his rib cage, his nerves tingled—Kevin had discovered the blurred, intoxicated line between pleasure and fear.

"What... what do you mean?" he finally asked.

"You know exactly what we mean, and you're going to tell us everything we need to know."

"About what?"

The black-haired cat girl laughed. "About your job, silly," she said as her tail lifted from his cock and into the air again. "That's why we brought you here. You tell us about your job, and we pleasure you. Don't tell us about your job, and we pleasure ourselves, using you."

"Pleasure yourselves *using me*?"

Obsidian brought her hand back and slapped Kevin's face, leaving four fresh scratch marks across his beefy jowls.

"Hey!" He winced at the sting of the cuts. "I don't know what you're talking about. And I don't know why you want to know about my job. I work as an immigration advisor!" Kevin cried, sobbing now, even though he still had a raging boner on the verge of bursting. "I'm just a normal guy, just working to help exemplars come here from other places. I swear! That's what I do; that's all I do."

Turquoise sighed. "He's lying to us."

"I really wish you wouldn't lie to us."

Kevin looked with true fear at Obsidian's predatory grin.

"I'm not lying," he finally managed to say, his voice quivering. "I promise this is really who I am!"

"No, no, Kevin. We know exactly who you are," said Turquoise, a sinister frown forming on her face, "and you are going to tell us everything we want to know. There are worse things than torture…"

"There are?" Kevin asked, a strange glaze painting over his vision.

"Poor thing, he's already starting to feel it." Obsidian ran her claw down Kevin's arm, drawing more blood. "It's only downhill from here."

Chapter Nine: Roman's Lucky Day

The urge to check the Hero Ticket swelled in Roman's chest.

He was on a busy trolley heading toward the place where he was supposed to meet Nadine. The Proxima Cafe was pretty easy to spot, on the corner of 19th just like she said it would be, set on the bottom floor of an old building. A sidewalk sign pointed to the entrance and advertised the day's special, which was a simple soup and half a grilled sandwich.

Roman wasn't hungry, but he didn't want to look like he was just sitting in the cafe waiting for someone.

So he ordered a cocktail.

Nadine hadn't said if they were going for drinks or not—only to meet her here—so he made sure the cocktail was coffee-based, something he could easily cover up if he'd mistaken her intent.

The caffeinated cocktail was good, a little bitter, but it put him in the right mood—somewhere between feeling excited and sensing a newfound mellowness.

A woman passed by in a skirt that reminded him of what Paris had been wearing last night.

Roman shook his head, remembering the assignment given to him by the strange woman from the Western Province—a spy. A goddamn sexy spy, but a spy nonetheless.

Treason wasn't a word that had ever crossed Roman's mind. Now he was on the verge of committing treason and he knew there was little he could do, especially since he'd agreed to help her. That would only complicate his case.

He didn't want to get drunk before Nadine came, so he sipped his next cocktail slowly, trying to enjoy it for once, to separate the bite of the alcohol from the robust coffee flavor.

Roman closed his eyes, and a couple thoughts came to him that he didn't want to examine.

Rather than explore the bits of his past he'd chosen to ignore, aside from his morning visit to the hospital, he opened his eyes and watched the waitress' hips sashaying in front of him.

The waitress was cute, but Roman was at the point in his life where he could find something attractive about most women. The only thing that turned him off was a terrible personality, like his boss Selena had.

It was never too hard for Roman to convince a woman to go home with him. He was fit, and while his white hair wasn't unique to Centralia, his orange eyes were, something that led many to assume he was an exemplar.

And that was it, wasn't it? Convince a woman he was an okay enough guy to sleep with, not a creep, a responsible citizen.

Roman, I'm sorry, I can't make it now.

Roman recognized Nadine's voice in his head almost immediately. Nadine wasn't a telepath, but she'd sent the message to him through a popular telepathy service used for personal communication.

It was pretty easy to use, too.

In this case, since she had started the dialogue, Roman simply thought back a reply.

Really? That's too bad. I'm here now, and the atmosphere is great. Is everything okay?

Part of him was annoyed she had bailed at the last minute; the other part of him knew better than to let these thoughts show—which was strange when he really thought about it. How did the telepaths that transferred these personal messages truly know which messages to send?

Nadine's reply came a few moments later:

Everything is fine. Well, I guess everything isn't fine, because I'm not there. We had to stay late, or should I say I had to stay late, because my colleague left for the hospital. Something happened to her wife. Anyway, I have to stay another two hours, and after that I had plans with some girlfriends, so how about a rain check?

Roman nodded as the thought spilled from his brain. *Sure, rain check, no big deal at all. Have fun with your friends, and let me know if I can do anything.*

You're too sweet. I'll make it up to you.

No need, he thought back to her as the waitress approached.

"Waiting for someone?"

"Funny you asked that…"

The woman was at least five years younger than Roman, her skin soft, her eyes wide apart and her hair cut short. It was a particularly slow night, evident by the fact that there were only two other patrons in the bar and two waitresses, so Roman figured he'd give it a shot.

"How long have you been working here?" he asked, striking up an easy conversation. "I've never seen you here before."

She laughed. Her pad went into the front of her apron and she tucked the pen behind her ear. She had a long, elegant neck, with her head almost perched on the end of it like an exotic animal.

"I've been here for a year," she said. "So maybe it's me who has never seen you."

"Do you work most shifts?"

"Usually work the days," she said, "but I just switched to night."

"Ah, that's why I don't recognize you," he lied.

"You usually come at night?"

"Occasionally. I don't live very far from here, and I like the walk. What's your name, anyway?"

"Harper. You?"

"Roman, but everyone calls me Roman."

She raised an eyebrow at him.

"It's a joke."

A smirk took shape on her face. "And what do you do, Roman?" Harper asked, sitting down across from him.

Roman smiled at her, his charm radiating from every pore.

Roman was good. He knew he was good, and he'd perfected the art of talking to someone on two levels. This self-taught power had different incarnations. With supers, he used it to put double meanings in the advice he gave them. For women, almost everything he said had a flirty nature to it.

"I help people," he said, reading Harper like a book.

"Are you a doctor or something?"

Roman grinned. "No, nothing like that. I don't know where you stand politically, but I'll just come out and say it. I help immigrant exemplars come to Centralia, find work, get an education, help build our great country."

"That's sweet," Harper said, her eyes softening.

"You know, it's a government job, and there is a ton of bureaucracy, but it's not bad. At the end of the day, I want to help Centralia become a better nation. Maybe it's selfish; maybe by taking the best from the other nations to better ours, I'm actually a type of patriot. Don't know. That's not for me to decide; I just do my job to the best of my ability, and try to help as many as I can."

"That's incredible."

"It isn't easy. Hell, today I was actually attacked by a Type II, Class D."

"A what?"

"Sorry, immigration talk. It's how the Centralian government classifies supers. So this guy, I probably shouldn't say his name, but I'll say it anyway: Hazrat."

Harper's brow furrowed. "That's a scary sounding name."

"For a scary guy. He was a Type II, which means dangerous, and the Class D means his power is energy related. He can manipulate shadows." Roman pointed to a shadow to the right of the bar. "For example, he could turn that shadow into a sharp dagger and hurt someone."

"He can make the shadow tangible?"

"He can. Odd power. He should probably be classified as a Type I, but anyway, that's enough about me. What about you?"

"Me?" She looked around. "I work here, go to night school. Not tonight, though. I have the night off."

"That brings me to my next question," he said, his eyes lifting from her lips to the bridge of her nose until finally, their pupils locked—Harper's green and Roman's orange.

"Yes?" she almost whispered.

"When do you get off work?"

Roman lay in his bed, Harper next to him. There was a half-empty bottle of wine at the side of the bed and when he sat up, he reached for it and took a chug.

He glanced over his shoulder at Harper, who was resting on her side, the curves of her body outlined by the city lights peeking through his blinds.

Roman never knew what to expect from a one-night stand, but Harper was definitely someone he'd like to turn into at least a three or four-night stand. She was fierce, much fiercer than her soft and trusting personality put on.

She'd pretty much taken charge once they'd started up, which Roman liked.

It was Harper who'd told him to put his fingers in her mouth, to bend her over the side of his bed, to go harder, to lift her and do her against the wall. Hell, after he'd come, she'd continued to suck him off for a good minute, keeping Roman in a state of bliss that was almost painful.

She was great. And now Roman was restless.

The bottle of wine gripped tightly in his hand, he walked to his living room and found his pants. He wanted something to eat, and there was fuck all in his pantry, so he figured he'd head downstairs to the bodega, which was open twenty-four hours.

Grab a snack, head back, eat it.

Easy.

Brush his teeth, get back to bed, and hopefully get some morning sex going in a few hours.

Not wanting to go back into his bedroom and disturb Harper, Roman put his pants on without underwear. He put on the jacket he'd been wearing earlier and slipped out of the apartment, placing his keys in the jacket pocket.

Roman had forgotten Kevin's Hero Ticket was in his pocket, and as he headed downstairs, he figured he'd check to see if it was a winner. The odds were against him, but then again, the odds were generally against everyone.

Out into the cold streets Roman went, a breeze carrying up from the Southern Alliance, where it was always cold.

He swung around the corner and headed straight into the bodega, where he saw the usual woman reading a popular comic book behind the counter.

"You're in late," she said with a yawn. She'd been here for over a year and that was just about all she'd say to him.

"Hey, you don't happen to have the results from today's superpower lottery, do you?"

"You know, you could have just asked a telepath."

"Yeah, I know, but I wanted to get out of the house for a minute. So anyways, do you have them?"

The woman set her comic down. "Fine, I have them. Got your Hero Ticket? I didn't think you were the type to play this game, to be honest. It seems like only desperate non-exemplars try to win the super-power lottery."

"I was feeling lucky," Roman said. "Just tell me the numbers, if you don't mind."

She thumbed through a notebook near the register and came to a page in the back. "The numbers are as follows…"

"Wait," Roman said as he reached in his jacket pocket for the ticket. "Okay, got it."

"Eight, sixty-seven, five, thirty, nine."

"Thirty-nine or thirty, then nine," Roman asked, his hand shaking.

"The number thirty, then the number nine."

Roman wiped his brow and placed the Hero Ticket back in his pocket, barely able to contain his excitement.

"Well?"

It took a lot of willpower for Roman not to freak out right then and there. "Nothing," he finally said, excitement boiling in his chest. "Didn't win this one."

He spun on his heels and exited the bodega, making a beeline for his apartment.

Chapter Ten: Derailed

Nadine sighed. The part about her staying late wasn't a lie; she really did have to cover for her coworker, Sarah. But the part about meeting her girlfriends that night was definitely bullshit.

Nadine didn't usually have time to go out.

While her passport and birth certificate said Nadine was from Centralia, she was actually from the Eastern Province, born and raised.

And even though she considered herself a patriot—she had to in her line of work—it was much better to live in Centralia. The famed country was the richest in the world when it came to overall wealth and the social comforts provided to its citizens, very much unlike the East.

Centralia had everything. Everything Nadine ever wanted or needed, all the attractions, and if you looked deep enough into its underbelly, Centralia had the worst of everything as well.

Which kept things exciting.

And it wasn't easy working undercover in the Centralian Immigration Office.

Class As from the Eastern Province had practically done surgery on Nadine's brain to prevent any telepathic means of discovering her secret. It had been painful, too, something she wouldn't wish upon anyone.

Because of the procedures, her memories were often cloudy, hard to interpret unless she really focused. Even her mother's and father's faces were now blurred when she thought of them, but that never stopped her from remembering.

Sometimes, she longed to visit her home again, to see her mother and father again.

But she also knew this wasn't in her future.

Nadine had signed a contract, *the contract,* and she would follow that contract to its very end, which was why she reluctantly left the office two hours after she was supposed to get off only to be stopped by Coco, one of the supers that ran security.

"Ah, it's you," Coco said, relaxing her guard. She smiled at Nadine and stepped aside so she could pass.

"Thanks."

Nadine made her way outside, and from there to the station on the other side of the pond that sat next to the immigration offices. She took a seat at the platform, noticing how much more relaxed the station was now that rush hour had ended.

As she waited for the trolley to arrive, Nadine pressed her thumb into the bottom of the ring on her pointer finger—the *Zero Ring*.

As she waited, she thought about her new asset, Lisa Painstake. The Type IV, Class C & F user of Soul Speed was a powerful asset indeed, and Nadine couldn't wait to write a report of how she'd netted her.

It would keep her handler off her ass for at least a couple weeks.

The trolley eventually came, and Nadine was able to find a seat at the back.

She glanced around her and had a sneaking suspicion that the man sitting in front of her was an exemplar. It was hard to tell, but it was no secret this world had just as many supers as half-powereds like herself.

A smile stretched across Nadine's face as she again thumbed her ring; supers were exemplars, half-powereds were non-exemplars. She didn't usually think of the term "half-powered," as it was somewhat frowned upon in the East, but there it was, at the edge of her mind as she took in the man.

No matter—her Zero Ring was her protection, even though she wasn't superpowered.

Nadine let her dirty-blond hair fall, removing the clips she had used to hold it in a bun. It was part of her disguise, like her jewelry, which she unclipped and placed in a pocket inside her purse.

She had learned in training how easy it was to blend in, and how the smallest personal items could make you stand out.

Eliminate one item, and people didn't recognize you the same way as before.

This was why she always wore similar clothing to work. She'd even run into some coworkers after work before, when she was wearing clothing more similar to what she would have worn back in the Eastern Province.

They hadn't recognized her.

Some commotion at the front of the trolley pulled Nadine's attention away from her musings.

Her thumb slipped to the bottom of her Zero Ring, but the explosion came too quickly.

The trolley tore off the track, tossing Nadine sideways into the window.

Chapter Eleven: Late for Work

Roman was wide awake the next morning, oblivious to the fact that Nadine had been in an accident. He'd been pacing most of the night, looking at the Hero Ticket and checking the numbers against the digits provided by a telepath.

"Eight, sixty-seven, five, thirty, nine," he whispered, at just about the same time Harper came out of his bedroom wearing her panties and no top.

He stopped for a moment to admire her breasts, which swept in opposite directions.

"I thought you'd come back to bed," she said, yawning. "After last night…"

"Normally? Yes," he told the tall beauty. "But something work-related came up."

"What happened?" she asked, true concern growing across her face.

"There was, um, an issue with some paperwork filed yesterday."

"Can't that be fixed today? Why the morning rush?"

"It's a bit more complicated than that," Roman said as he approached her. The ticket was in his jacket pocket; he'd already sent a tele-message to Selena telling her he'd be late.

She hadn't replied, which likely meant she was pissed.

"How so?"

"It has to deal with issuing reinstatement through re-entry documents to a Type I, Class A & B," he lied. "A person they now think may be responsible for a recent terrorist attack in southern Centralia."

Harper gasped.

"I know, it's bad, believe me. And you won't, um, read about this stuff in the news. I shouldn't be telling you."

She took a step closer to him and placed a hand on his chest.

"You trust me?" she asked, her eyes softening.

"I do."

Her hand dropped below his waist, where she lightly moved it over the front of his pants.

Yep, a keeper, he thought as he watched her walk back to his bedroom. A good view, too. One of his favorites.

It was almost a relief when she left; the sexual tension between them was thick as smog and it took every ounce of willpower he had not to go for it.

Roman finished getting dressed, combed his white hair, and mentally arranged for a teleport.

I need to go to the Centralian Lottery Commission, he thought aloud, and it was only a few seconds later when he got the reply.

A teleporter will arrive at your location shortly. Please make sure there is a four-foot-radius circle around your body.

Roman did as instructed, and he was adjusting the front of his jacket when a male teleporter wearing Centralian government clothing appeared, touched his arm, and whisked him away to the Centralian Lottery Commission.

They arrived in a flash and the teleporter disappeared again, leaving Roman standing there with a thin smile on his face.

It was a cool day, with a slight breeze that carried over the smell of baked goods from the bakery across the street. Roman's stomach grumbled; he was hungry, but he could grab a snack later.

More commotion turned his attention back to the Lottery Commission.

The front was heavily guarded, not because of what lay inside as much as people trying to see who'd won the Hero Ticket.

This kind of crowd scared the hell out of Roman, but there were telepaths outside the main entrance next to the Type I security guards, and all he had to do was think, *I have the winning ticket.*

A female telepath in Centralian government clothing sensed him and immediately replied, *Thank you, Mr. Martin. I have verified that you indeed have the winning ticket. Please step away from the crowd and walk toward the trolley stop one block away. A teleporter will escort you inside, where you'll be able to claim your prize. Next time, please tell the teleservice that you have a winning ticket so that you may port directly into the winner's chamber.*

You mean I can win this thing twice? Roman thought back, not trying to be snarky but coming off that way.

Please move to the agreed-upon location, Mr. Martin.

"So that's how it works," he whispered as he moved away from the crowd.

A teleporter appeared and grabbed Roman, and a second later he was standing in front of a large pair of doors framed by Centralia's golden flags.

The doors opened and a short woman stepped out, clipboard in hand. She wore her government-issued clothing in a way that accented her cleavage—clearly her best feature—and as she approached Roman, she lifted her nose into the air.

"The Hero Ticket, please, and your identification," she said, her nose held high.

Roman provided both the items and she held each individually, light pouring out of her eyes as she scanned them.

Type IV, Class E, Roman thought as she handed the documents back to him.

"Congratulations," she said, then turned away. "Follow me."

Chapter Twelve: Paris Pretzel

"Roman Martin is *my* asset," Paris told Nadine, whom she'd strung upside down in the back room of a warehouse off 19th Street.

Nadine had heard her the first time, but feigned as if she hadn't, her eyes still clenched shut as she mentally focused on her Zero Ring, her thumb slowly pressing onto a groove on its bottom.

"I will tell you once more: we have plans for Roman, and this is your only warning. If you get in the way, not only will I see to it that you're exposed, but I will personally make sure your family is well taken care of back in the East. And by taken care of, I mean I will kill them. Your father and your mother."

Nadine's throat quivered. She was acquainted with Paris Renara and had encountered the spy who doubled as a super (or super who doubled as a spy) several times before.

"Nod if you understand what I'm telling you," said Paris. "Roman is ours."

Nadine opened her eyes and settled them on the upside-down image of Paris—dark bangs framing her eyes, slim figure, bitchy look on her face. She squinted one eye and looked at Paris with the other.

"You're really fucking stupid, aren't you?" she asked.

Paris licked her lips, her elastic tongue falling out of her mouth as she sneered at Nadine.

"If you want to lick me, then lick me," Nadine said. "And fuck your Type IV shit power anyway."

That did it.

Paris's tongue came flying out of her mouth and wrapped around Nadine's throat. It started to squeeze, and just as Paris's lips curved into the wicked grin of someone who had overpowered another, Nadine activated her ring.

Paris's tongue loosened up, and Nadine grabbed onto the limp appendage as Paris stumbled backward.

A desperate look on her face, Paris tried desperately to use some of her abilities, *any* of her abilities, all to no avail. Nothing happened, and as panic came over her, Nadine pulled Paris closer.

And Nadine was strong.

That was something her physique betrayed; she'd purposely not muscled up just to keep her appearance. But while she wasn't quite an exemplar, Nadine had the strength of two men, a gift passed down to her by her grandfather, an actual super, a famous one in the East.

It only took a few seconds for Nadine to yank Paris over to her, pull her fist back, and knock Paris the hell out, still holding the woman's elastic tongue with her free hand.

Rocking back and forth, Nadine used her strong core to bring herself up to her feet, where she could work getting free.

She undid the knot and thrust her upper body forward as she fell. Rather than land on her head or the back of her neck, Nadine landed on her knees, her fall partially cushioned by Paris's body.

Her right knee aching, Nadine got to her feet and blinked a few times to adjust to standing on solid ground again.

She felt sick to her stomach, but her training had prepared her for situations like this, especially the six-month-long proactive hostage training.

Taking a breath in and focusing on a single stationary object, in this case a pipe jutting out of the wall, Nadine regained her equilibrium.

The Eastern government had spent a lot on Nadine's training, and their limited tax dollars were paying off as Nadine got her bearings and began contemplating how to deal with Paris. She could kill her, but there'd be paperwork for that and oddly enough, spies usually didn't kill other spies if they could help it.

Her training had even gone over this code with her, a code in place namely because everyone was spying on the same authority—the Centralian Government.

But making Paris's life difficult was definitely something Nadine could do, and she knew exactly how to do it.

"Let's see how you like dealing with this when you recover," she said as she spread Paris's right leg wide, scoffing at the fact that the dumb bitch was still wearing a skirt.

Holding Paris's heeled boot with her left hand, Nadine punched her right hand into the outside of her knee, the flesh responding and moving inward.

Paris let out a whimper as she opened her eyes, and Nadine stretched her leg well past its breaking point.

Paris tried to speak to her, making a series of grunting sounds due to air blockage from her tongue. Nadine simply lifted her other leg, pulled her fist back, and cracked it against the outside of her knee, bringing the elastic knee backwards so it matched the first leg.

Both legs splayed, Nadine used Paris's arms to wrap around her ankles, Paris's entire body giving way and showcasing her elastic capabilities. While Nadine knew she couldn't actually break one of Paris's bones, she could tie her up in a knot, making it difficult as hell for her to free herself.

She continued wrapping Paris's arms around her legs until the Western Province spy resembled an oddly shaped pretzel. To make it even harder, she knotted the ends of her arms, tucking the woman's wrists back into one of the folds on her shins.

Paris's eyes were now bloodshot with rage, snot dripping out of her nose as she seethed at Nadine.

"See you next time." Nadine turned to the exit and lifted a single middle finger over her shoulder as she slowly walked away.

Chapter Thirteen: With Great Power

"Roman Martin, the council is confused by your lack of response."

"I apologize." Roman swallowed hard.

The Lottery Council sat like judges behind a high, circular desk, all wearing white robes, and all Type Vs, which was the classification used for supers with god-like powers.

Roman had only ever encountered a handful of Type Vs, or if he'd encountered more, he'd been fooled by them. Most had false papers and identification cards that listed them as the other types.

And the reason he knew they were Type Vs was also strange to him. It was this gut instinct, something he intuited, a whisper at the back of his skull.

"What do you say to the power that has been granted to you?"

Roman bit his lip for a second. He felt no different than he'd felt an hour ago, and even though the council had told him of the power he'd been rewarded, he was completely skeptical of it. "Thanks?"

The council laughed. A white-haired man at the right continued to chuckle as he said, "That is possibly the best response this council has received this year."

"Don't people normally thank you?" Roman asked.

"Not in the skeptical way in which you have just thanked us," the man replied. "Rest assured, while the power we've given you may be random, it is a good one, one that would clearly put you in the Type II, Class A & C range. Possibly even a Type I." He smirked. "I don't know, you're the expert. How would you classify yourself?"

"Type IV."

The man's white eyebrows furrowed. "You have doubts in the ability we've given you?"

Roman bowed his head. "No, and I thank the council for bestowing it upon me."

The lead councilwoman, a rail-thin brunette in a white diamond tiara that matched her robes, narrowed her eyes at Roman. "Most are grateful, and most actually purchased their tickets themselves."

"Consider it gifted to me."

Her lips curled. "It would be very hard for me, or the council, to consider the way you acquired your Hero Ticket as gifted."

"Kevin is dead, isn't he? Poor guy died, didn't deserve it, but that's why I have all his cases now. That's why I had his ticket in the first place."

The council exchanged glances, but only the lead councilwoman spoke. "Regardless of the ticket purchaser's life, you are the one who has turned it in, a controversial rule that the council has debated before. Ultimately, we have found allowing users to gift the Hero Ticket allows for older half-powereds to grant abilities to their children, and we're looking at your case in the same light. So the ability is yours."

"I appreciate it."

"We can tell," the man on the left said, an amused grin on his face.

"Enough, Gary," said the lead councilwoman. "Mr. Martin, there will be much to learn about your power, and to get you started, you will attend your first class on using your new ability this morning."

"But I have work."

The councilman known as Gary snorted.

"Enough, Gary," said the lead councilwoman in a way that reminded Roman of how his manager, Selena, talked to him from time to time. "You have a power now, Mr. Martin. As in, *right now*. And you can't leave here without knowing the basics of it. After today's briefing, you will visit our gymnasium for training on a daily basis. Once you are trained, your new role will be assigned. Until that time, you must keep your new power a secret, or it will be stripped away from you."

I hope the instructor is hot, Roman thought as he offered the councilwoman a tight grin.

"Yes, she is hot," the lead councilwoman said.

"Shit, you weren't supposed to hear that."

"I didn't hear it."

"Please don't read my mind."

The man known as Gary laughed. "Trust us, we've already seen enough there!"

"*Enough, Gary.* Now, Mr. Martin, your instructor will be my younger sister, Ava," said the lead councilwoman. "Until you have been cleared by Ava, you will need to continue the things you'd do normally, including taking part in the mandatory Heroes Anonymous program and going to work. Once you are cleared, you will be able to put in for a position more related to your new abilities. Good luck, Roman Martin, and remember, with great power comes great power."

The other councilmembers chuckled, all aside from Gary, who was giving the lead councilwoman a salty look for having put him in his place.

Chapter Fourteen:
Interrogation

"Wake up, Kevin," Turquoise hissed.

The two cat girls had tied Kevin's wrists and feet to the bed posts. He was nude, his chest and large stomach covered in bloody scratches. The former immigration advisor was delirious, his peripheral vision tinted in soft orange hues.

Obsidian, the cat girl with black hair and pigtails, sighed. "He's sleeping."

"I'm... not sleeping," Kevin said, suddenly more awake than he'd been in the last two hours.

Has it really been two hours? He had no way of knowing how long the two had played with him, clawing up his body while rubbing their tails and mounds all over him, occasionally using their sandpaper tongues to grind into his new wounds.

The clawing was fucked, but the fact that they seemed to be getting off on doing it was straight-up disturbing.

Kevin had the feeling they were poisoning him in some way, but he didn't know why, because they could just as easily kill him. They were at least Type IIIs, maybe even Type IIs, and that they believed he was someone other than himself was beyond Kevin.

He was a goddamn immigration advisor, a glorified administrator, a government employee who had tried to commit suicide and failed miserably.

He was a fucking nobody.

"I really wish you would say something we could use," said Turquoise as she scraped a finger along the inside of his thigh. Her counterpart straddled his other thigh, rubbing her wet mound against the fresh wounds on his leg.

What was happening to the middle-of-the-road salaryman made absolutely no sense to him.

And Kevin was an honest guy, the type of guy who never lied, who actually cared about the clients he worked with and tried his best to not really disturb anybody.

He wasn't a bad dude, and the fact that he had tried to commit suicide didn't make him a bad guy either, just misguided.

He didn't deserve any of this.

So with a deep breath in, which got both their attentions, Kevin decided to do something he never thought he'd do.

"Okay, okay," he mumbled, not quite certain of where this was going to go. "I'll talk…"

Turquoise stopped scratching at the inside of his leg and looked up at him, one of her ears twitching. "You ready, dear?"

"Ready," he barely managed to say.

Obsidian purred. "We're tired of hurting you. We want to pleasure you, but you're going to have to speak to us first."

"I will tell you everything I know, just…" Kevin gulped. "Loosen up the ropes on my wrists—it really hurts."

"That's all you want?" Turquoise exchanged glances with Obsidian.

A laugh formed at the back of Kevin's mind, but it didn't reach the front of his lips. "Of course I want more than that, but just do that and I'll talk, I promise."

"No problem," said Obsidian as she loosened the ropes. She sat behind him and laid his head across her knees. "There, there, just relax."

"What do you want to know?" he asked, not able to fully focus on her.

"First, there has recently been a decrease in exemplars admitted from the Western Province," said Turquoise. "Why is this? And are the Centralian authorities planning to make another move on the West?"

The thought came to Kevin and he felt stupid for not realizing it earlier: These two were actually after his better-looking brother, who just so happened to also share the same name as him.

It was a cruel joke played on them by their father, because Kevin, the one tied up, nude, with a semi-erection from being tortured by topless cat girls, was older and had always been somewhat of a failure.

The younger Kevin Blackbook was about half his weight, handsome, and had risen pretty high in the Centralian government.

Just go with it, whispered a voice at the back of his head, and Kevin obliged. "Okay, the truth is… there has been a decrease in supers admitted from the Western Province because… there aren't any, um, healers there, and Centralia wants to have more healers immigrating than other classes. So you see? It's basically about healers."

Kevin was lying out of his ass, and since the floodgate of bullshit had opened up, he figured he might as well continue. Watercooler gossip wasn't really his thing. He didn't have many friends at the office, but he'd heard people ask questions in meetings and whatnot.

So he went with it.

"All this is about healers, then?" Obsidian asked, looking down at him.

"Yep, it's all about healers."

Kevin smiled at Turquoise, hoping they couldn't see through his lie; the curious look on her face told him she was buying it.

"And to answer your second question, yes, we are planning to make a move on the West, but not in the way you may think. We are recruiting certain classes, and to do so, we have to, um, work out some agreements." Kevin sucked back snot.

He could get through this, but the only way to do it would be to keep his responses incredibly vague.

Chapter Fifteen: Talk to Me, Scissors

Roman stood in a large gymnasium, easily four stories high. There were mats in the far corner, mirrors on one of the walls, a rock climbing wall and sparring equipment.

The woman leading him, the same who had accompanied him into the council room, told him to wait there.

"Just stand here?" he asked.

"Yes, that's what 'wait' means. Ava will be here shortly, and until she arrives, you need to wait for her."

Roman started to say something, but then realized it was pretty much pointless. He too worked for the Centralian government, and he knew what it felt like as a government employee to be asked a dumb question.

So he waited, his hands in his pockets as he paced back and forth.

He still wasn't entirely convinced of the power that had been bestowed upon him. It seemed completely useless, and as he paced, he raised his hand and tried to do something to one of the mats on the floor.

"Useless power," he mumbled when nothing happened.

He was in his work clothes, an off-white overcoat with matching pants and a crisply pressed shirt. Otherwise, he would have lain down on one of the mats. Thing was, Roman was incredibly tired, his previous night filled with sex—and then with the hope that he would be granted a power that was actually useful.

Sure, he could have his house clean itself now, or make a glass of wine go fill itself, but how useful was that really?

A mental message came in, this one from Harper, the waitress who was responsible for the soreness in his thighs.

Hi! Just want to say I had fun. I know we aren't supposed to contact each other like right after these

109

things happen, or that's how this usually goes, but I figured I would just give you a little morning message. And that message is this: Whenever you're free, I'll try to be free. Just let me know.

She's sweet, Roman thought, and in a way, he'd dreaded this.

He wasn't one to get close to people anymore, not after what had happened, and it always pulled at his heartstrings when he met someone who was genuine, who was good, and he knew that at some point he would have to push them away.

And as he had done before, Roman didn't reply to her message.

Oh sure, he would see her again, but he knew from past experiences that putting a little tension there, especially at the beginning, always made things shift in his direction.

In fact, in a way, Harper had just played her card, and Roman always kept his hand as close to his chest as possible.

"Sweet girl, though."

"I'm glad you think so," said the woman standing behind Roman.

He turned to find a hot redhead in a slick white bodysuit. Her hair was in a ponytail, one that reached all the way to the top of her ass, which he noticed because she stood turned to her side, looking at him over her shoulder.

A smile crept across Roman's face.

Even if he didn't like his newfound powers, at least he had a hot teacher.

And this fact became even more evident when a spark of flame appeared in her palm.

"A Type II, Class C," said Roman.

"Close. Type I."

"A Type I? Makes sense, especially with fire. Congratulations. Also, are you posing right now?"

She still stood with her back to Roman, looking over her shoulder at him.

"It's always important to make an entrance. Every true exemplar knows this."

"I'm aware."

"I'm glad."

"I met your sister. The one on the council."

"She's a ballbuster."

"Your words, not mine." Roman had seen some pretty diva-like behaviors from supers. Even if there was supposed equality in Centralia, and in the greater provinces and authorities, this didn't mean exemplars *didn't* know how much stronger they were than half-powereds.

"Anyway, enough about my sister. I'm the one who will sign off on the paperwork that allows you to become one of us. I have seen this take as short as a couple of weeks up to as long as two years—it is really up to you, and how carefully you listen to my training. Also, as I'm sure my sister said, your powers are a secret until you've been fully approved."

She walked away, and Roman zoomed in on her rear and the way her red ponytail bounced between her ass cheeks.

"Well?" she asked. "Are you coming?"

He quickly caught up with her, and he wondered then how she had appeared in the room in the first place. When she had arrived, he had been facing the door, and she had appeared behind him.

Strange, he thought as Ava stopped in front of the table with a few items resting on it. The table was against the wall, and if it had been there earlier, Roman hadn't noticed it.

"A rock, a sheet of paper, and a pair of scissors," Roman said as he took in the contents of the table.

There was also something that looked like a watch, although the face was black onyx and it didn't have a dial.

"Put this on," Ava said, retrieving the watch. The exemplar stopped before him, dangling it from her thin fingers. "Once you do so, your powers will be activated from here on out. We do this so people aren't immediately given their powers, as that can be quite jarring. For a power like yours, the power dial is doubly useful."

"And the watch activates it?"

"Yes, but after that, the *power dial* is always active. And it isn't a watch. It's a power dial, in case you didn't pick up on that."

Roman placed the power dial on his wrist and the screen turned on.

He'd never seen anything like it before. He'd heard rumors that the Centralian government had tech the citizens didn't know about, and this looked to be one of those items.

The face of the power dial flashed.

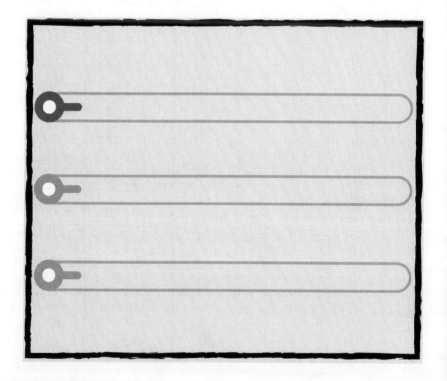

Roman noticed a red, a green, and a blue indicator, and each appeared to be at their lowest levels.

"We're going to get into what the indicators mean in a moment. For now, though, I want you to remember the phrase: *Red is dead. Green is mean. Blue is cool.* Say it for me now?"

"Red is dead. Green is mean. Blue is cool." Roman glanced from the power dial to Ava, not certain if he was supposed to be feeling something different or not. "Should I be feeling something different?"

"It really depends on your power," she told him as she turned away again. "Rock, paper, scissors," Ava said as she examined the table. "Which one of these do you think would be the easiest to bring to life?"

"I don't know."

"You were granted the ability to animate inanimate objects, a Type II and sometimes Type I ability, not a Type III or IV, as I'd bet you're thinking. It is an amazing power."

"Is it really that high up on the listing?" he asked.

"I don't want to say, 'Stick with me and I'll make you a type I,' but that is a possibility if you really drill down to the nitty gritty of your new power."

Roman sighed. "I am grateful for this power, but I just thought it would be something else. It doesn't sound like such a great power, considering that I've done immigration work for supers who could lift trains with their pinky fingers, and that just yesterday I was assaulted by an exemplar who had the ability to manipulate shadows. He was a dick, too."

"Sounds like it."

"You get my point, though. I mean, it's cool to be able to make things that aren't alive come alive. But I don't know, I just don't see how this is such an amazing power. Helpful? Yes. Amazing? No."

"You don't?"

"If anything, I would list it as a Type III."

Ava smirked. "You know, I actually appreciate the skeptic in you. I have dealt with some people who think that they are god's gift to Centralia after they've been given the power to see through walls. Type IVs, you know how they are."

Roman nodded, impressed that she knew as much about the various types as he did.

It made sense, sure, but it was still impressive. He almost felt like he was talking shop with one of his coworkers at their yearly retreat in northern Centralia. He'd been to two, and while it was a great time to try to bang an intern, it was also a time to bond.

Thinking of last year's retreat reminded him of Kevin.

He couldn't quite say that he and Kevin were close, but last year's retreat had brought them closer than before, mostly because they'd been roomed together.

At first, Roman hadn't really liked the fact that he'd been forced to room with Kevin, but the often shy, pudgy man grew on him. And he'd felt bad for him anyways, because Kevin's wife had sounded like a total bitch.

Ava continued, "I'll say this one last time: Your power is unique, one of the more unique abilities I've come across. And I had to scramble to do some research on how to train you to use it better. Well, I didn't personally scramble; I had one of our Type IV Class E researchers check it out, transfer the information to a telepath, and forward that along."

"Ah, Class E, intelligence-based."

"Exactly, and this guy's ability is to consume gross amounts of data in the time it takes you to take a piss. He can read four or five books at once and has a photographic memory of all the things that he has already researched. But enough about him. It's time to get started. Take a look at your power dial."

Roman did so, noticing the red, green, and blue strips again.

"When you animate small objects, it will increase the size of the blue indicator. Medium-sized objects increase the green indicator, and large objects—or other objects that require a boost of intelligence—the red indicator. This is actually why you are considered a Class A, a telepath, *and* a Class C, someone who can utilize organic and inorganic objects and power."

"And what happens if the bars fill all the way up?"

"Good question." She turned back then and placed both hands behind her back, which jutted her chest forward in a way that caused Roman to glance quickly from her bosom and back to her face. "Shall I continue?" she asked.

"Sorry."

"If the red indicator fills up, just like I told you in the little rhyme, you die. *Red is dead.* And the red bar goes up when you animate something that is rather large and needs intelligence to operate. Also, from what our researcher could tell, you can improve over time by animating more objects. So it is a trainable skill."

"Why would I die?"

"Because to animate these objects, you are giving them a small part of your life. Give too much of your life, and you'll die. I believe there is a more scientific explanation than that, but let's just stick with that for now." She cleared her throat. "The rock. Let's start there."

Roman focused on the rock. He didn't know how he was supposed to use his ability, so after cursing for a moment, he mentally told the rock to move.

The rock scooted forward a little bit.

"You can do better than that. Your ability isn't to move objects; rather, it is for you to animate them. Turn the rock into something that you would like, or make it do something interesting."

Roman raised an eyebrow at Ava.

"Go on, give it a shot."

Roman begin to imagine what Ava's breasts must look like, and as he did, the rock started to reform like it was made of clay, until it had become a half mound with an areola and a nipple on top.

"Is that supposed to be some type of joke?" she asked.

"Sorry, it was the first thing that came to mind. But I did animate it."

"Yes, but you don't have control over it. Look at your power indicator."

Roman glanced down to his power dial to see that none of the bars had moved.

"The bars move when you officially have the item under control. With the boob rock that you have just created here like a fucking high-school kid, you don't have it under control, you just briefly took control of it and morphed it."

"Okay, then what should I do to take control?" Roman asked, eying the boob rock.

"Let's try the sheet of paper this time; maybe that will give you a better sense of what you can do with this power. Turn this flat sheet of paper into an assistant."

"An assistant?"

"Do you see that rope over there?" Ava nodded to the other side of the room where a rope hung from the ceiling, clearly used for some type of endurance training.

"Turn this sheet of paper into an assistant who can go over there and climb that rope. Pretend that climbing the rope would save your life. Just follow me here. Give it a shot."

"Turn it into an assistant—got it," Roman told her.

The sheet of paper trembled at its corners as Roman tried to fold it with his mind.

Once he realized this wasn't going to work, an idea came to him as to how he could communicate with this object.

Become human, Roman thought to it, and sure enough, the paper folded in half and jumped up onto its wedge. From there, it crumbled and reformed into something resembling a stick figure.

"That's good!" said Ava.

The paper figure stood at the edge of the table for a moment, looking over at Roman.

With the flick of Roman's hand, and while he mentally thought the figure needed to go to the rope, the paper person leapt off the table. It ran towards the rope, and once it got there, it careened its makeshift head back and looked to Roman for guidance.

"Climb it," Roman whispered, and sure enough, the paper figure uncrumpled itself into a long string of thin paper, and like a cobra enchanted by music, it lifted to the bottom of the rope and latched on.

"Perfect," said Ava. "Now look at your power dial. Notice anything different?"

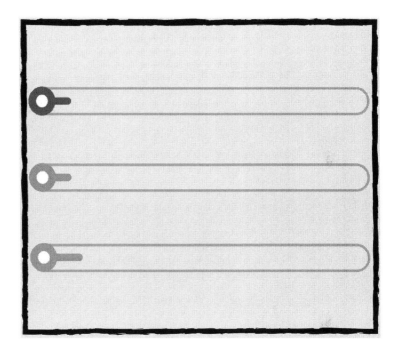

"The blue indicator is longer. Not by much, though."

"Yes, it is, but the other two haven't moved. Now, on to the scissors, and keep the paper figure active."

"Got it," Roman said as he focused on the pair of scissors.

The pair of scissors righted itself and opened, the sharp ends forming two legs to hold its weight up.

Still balanced on the two pointy ends, the curved handle began to gyrate, moving back and forth.

"Okay," Ava said. "Use the scissors as a weapon."

"As a weapon?"

Roman instructed the scissors to fly into the wall, which they did. He also noticed that his power dial flashed, the blue line longer than before.

"Great! Do it again—attack your paper creation."

Using his mind, he zipped the scissors across the room, where they sliced the paper man in half. He was getting the hang of it, and a few more minutes of sending the scissors around the room had him feeling confident.

Ava placed her hands on her hips and cocked her head to the right. "Now animate the table and have it battle the scissors."

"Are you sure?"

She laughed. "Yes, I'm sure. That's why we have these items today. I want you to see what it is like to use the various tiers of your abilities. And another thing, I don't want you to just use the telepathic part of your power as a handicap. Instruct the objects to fight for themselves. Give them life. What I'm saying is don't just manipulate them telepathically."

Roman ran his hand through his white hair. He grinned at Ava, offering her the same grin he'd used to win over countless women in Centralia.

"Stop smiling—start fighting," she said. "I don't think you're cute."

Roman gulped. "Got it."

She winked at him and stepped aside, again offering Roman the view of her backside.

"Fuck it," he said, and mentally instructed the table to right itself. To his surprise, it started bucking like a horse, its surface rippling and the wood holding strong as the boob rock flew off it.

"Sorry, little guy," he said to the scissors as he instructed them to attack the table.

The pair of scissors kept low as it stalked the bucking table, which caused quite a bit of commotion as its metal feet slapped against the ground. Ava's hand was covered in flame, just in case things got out of hand.

"Kill the table," Roman whispered to the scissors.

Without any hesitation, the scissors flew up into the air and straight into the back of the table.

The table's legs scraped against the gymnasium floor as it tried to buck the scissors off its back. With one shear stuck in the table, the scissors pulled the other shear back, curled it a bit, and stabbed into the table's surface again, nagging the damn table to death.

"That's it!" Ava said. "How do you feel?"

"I… I feel fine." Roman glanced down at his power dial to see the blue line had moved up considerably, and the red line had moved by just a hair.

"Now it's time to animate something even larger. Actually, I want you to do something else."

"What's that?" I asked.

"I want you to make the scissors smarter. I want you to make them talk to us."

Chapter Sixteen: Skipping Lunch

~⌒⌐

Nadine stepped out of the shower, and even though she'd just bathed, she still felt dirty. There were bruises along her side from where she'd struck a seat in the trolley, and her ankles were sore from being strung upside down.

Who had strung her up anyway? She had this itching feeling that it hadn't been Paris.

There'd be an investigation regarding the trolley explosion, and she wondered why she hadn't been contacted yet. The Centralian authorities were pretty good at sniffing out terrorists, which was why there weren't many in the famed country.

Nadine smirked as she wrapped a towel around her body. She knew damn well the attack would be covered up, that all such attacks were covered up, and that there was little she or anyone else could do about it.

Obfuscation was a way of life when it came to dealing with Centralian authorities.

Standing in her living room now, directly in front of an old mirror she'd purchased from a market on the outskirts of the city, she let the towel drop so she could admire her nude body for a moment.

Nadine looked good and she knew it.

She'd trained hard to maintain her body weight, and while her breasts could have been a little bigger, that was about the only thing she'd change about her form. That and the scar on her side, which stretched from the bottom of her armpit down to her hip bone.

Nadine dressed quickly, placed her blond hair in a bun, put on a small amount of makeup, mostly eyeliner, and mentally arranged for a teleporter to arrive in a few minutes.

The teleporter appeared, a woman in Centralian government clothing, and their forms took shape in front of the immigration office seconds later. Dark clouds overhead signaled that a rainstorm was coming, but that wasn't what got Nadine's attention.

"Roman?" she asked, taking a step back as the mysterious white-haired man came to a stop. Maybe "mysterious" was a bit much, but there was something unique about him, something that made him different from the others.

Which was why she'd wanted to use him as an asset.

"I'm sorry about last night," she said, remembering she'd stood him up. "Just, things came up. That's all. No excuse."

Roman wore a collarless shirt under a jacket with a stiff collar, the lining of which was a light golden color. He looked good. A little shaken up—Nadine didn't know what that was about—but good nonetheless. She didn't always like the people she planned to use as assets, but Roman would be different.

"Looks like we're both late today," he said.

"Ha, I didn't think of that."

Even as they shook hands—a handshake that Roman initiated—Nadine was reminded of Lisa Painstake, the super she'd dealt with earlier who could travel via Soul Speed.

Her newest assets, while limited in number, were beginning to shape up. And if Paris wanted Roman, he must have something hidden that she could exploit.

"I really owe you," she told him. "I mean, that was just vile to not show up."

"It's fine, really," Roman said, for the second time since they'd greeted each other. "Things happen."

"No, I insist on making it up to you. What about dinner?"

"I can't tonight."

"Not tonight, and I'm not talking about dinner at any old restaurant. Let's do something interesting." She smiled at him, her green eyes darting up and down as she took in his form. "Tomorrow night."

Roman looked up and to the right. "Yeah, that should work."

A light drizzle picked up, and rather than stand outside and chat, the two entered the immigration office together.

"You okay?" Nadine said as he turned toward his office.

There was something different about him, something off. It was times like these Nadine wished the Eastern Province tech designers could crack a way to create artificial telepathy.

"Fine. Just a long night."

"Want to meet at lunch and talk about it?" she offered.

"Lunch?" Roman cracked a grin at her. "I'm three hours late. It's practically already lunch time."

"Good point."

"Why are you late, anyway?" he asked her.

Nadine shrugged. "I got tied up. See you tomorrow night."

With that, she turned toward her office, making sure his focus would be on her moving hips. This was part of her plan, and even if Roman knew what her plan was, he wouldn't have protested this part.

Roman didn't mind being seduced, for better or for worse.

Chapter Seventeen: Reinstatement

Roman sat at his desk for a moment, just getting used to being back in his office. It was hardly noon, but a half day off was a half day off, and it had been a hell of a day thus far.

He glanced at his power dial and saw that the red bar had some activity.

"Please, I can't breathe," the pair of scissors said as Roman took it out of his pocket. He placed it on his desk and examined it for a moment.

The scissors, which had taken on a woman's personality, now stood with the shears wide enough to hold the weight of the handles. The handles were metal, the pivot point polished silver.

"I'm going to put you away now," Roman started to tell the pair of scissors. "I have work to do."

"This stack of paper? Please, honey, if you want me to work on that paper for you, it'd be my pleasure."

Roman didn't know why it spoke in such a sultry way. He hadn't told it to do that, but the point remained: he was wasting power by animating a pair of scissors.

"Sorry," he said, and with that, the scissors fell onto his desk, lifeless as ever. He checked his power dial and saw it had returned to its baseline.

From there, his eyes darted to the things he had posted on his cubicle wall, including the power classification cheat sheet created by Kevin, of all people.

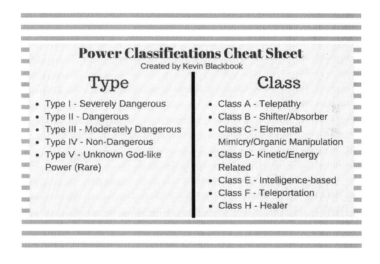

Power Classifications Cheat Sheet
Created by Kevin Blackbook

Type	Class
• Type I - Severely Dangerous • Type II - Dangerous • Type III - Moderately Dangerous • Type IV - Non-Dangerous • Type V - Unknown God-like Power (Rare)	• Class A - Telepathy • Class B - Shifter/Absorber • Class C - Elemental Mimicry/Organic Manipulation • Class D- Kinetic/Energy Related • Class E - Intelligence-based • Class F - Teleportation • Class H - Healer

He had already missed his first meeting, another one of Kevin's leftovers, and the next was scheduled for just a few minutes later. After pushing everything else aside, he briefly went over this particular exemplar's case.

Catherine was a Type III Class C from the Northern Alliance who specialized in air manipulation. He briefly went over her bio and then moved to her known skills, which each contained a brief explanation:

Aero-telekinesis: The ability to use air as the user sees fit, from floating, to flying, to building structures to advance to higher levels of altitude.

Electrical Immunity: User is able to insulate self from electrical attacks.

Pressure Manipulation: By controlling air molecules, user can generate, put pressure on, and otherwise modify most structures.

Enhanced Sensing: User is able to sense and feel things nearby through fluctuations in the local atmosphere.

Atmospheric Adaptation: User is able to adjust to various atmospheres and control the atmosphere around them.

From there, he moved on to her immigration issue.

Apparently, Catherine Blaine had let her Student Visa expire, and she currently needed to go through reinstatement. She would have to provide a reason for why she'd let her S Visa expire and hadn't maintained minimum enrollment at...

Roman looked at her records again.

Centralian Southern.

He was familiar with the university. Even though he was pushing thirty, Roman had recently hooked up with a co-ed from there, something he was both ashamed and proud about.

After skimming through a few notes Kevin had left, most of them semi-legible, he moved to Catherine's pictures and examined those as well.

He saw her passport photo with the various markings they put on the passports in the Northern Alliance, and he also saw her visa, and the fact that it was expired.

"Hi."

Roman looked up to see Catherine. She was a shy girl, a bit mousy, petite with broad shoulders and a windblown look to her. Her hair was white like

Roman's, aside from a braided red strand behind her right ear.

"Did you take a tornado over here?" he asked with a cheesy grin.

Roman couldn't help it. If a woman was beautiful, or if he could find even just a small part of her that was cute, his flirting game always made itself known.

It was a coping mechanism, a part of him that hadn't been there two years ago, before the incident. He swallowed hard to forget his past just as Catherine responded to his cheeky joke.

"Nope, took a teleporter. Sorry, I've just been so busy, and then I got the message that I need to come here because my visa had expired, and it's really stressful, and my parents are concerned."

"They should be," Roman said as he closed her case file. "Reinstatement isn't an easy process, and before we can begin, I need to know how you fell out of status. It seems that you were enrolled full-time at a university, correct?"

"No," she said, looking down at her hands. She still hadn't sat down yet, which was making him feel a little uncomfortable.

"Please, sit," he said, a smile still on his face.

"Sorry."

"No need to apologize, just sit and relax a moment so we can work through this."

After she was seated, Catherine crossed her arms over her chest and leaned back. "Confession: I didn't enroll full-time this last semester. I know I was supposed to because of my visa situation, but… some things came up in my personal life. I don't want to go into too many details here, but my ex-boyfriend was dealing with some mental issues. He's a non-exemplar, and there were some jealousy issues, and then he tried to do some heroic act. The fucker. Sorry."

"No need to apologize."

"And then he got arrested, so I was in and out of jail to see him, and then I helped him register for Heroes Anonymous, and he hasn't been able to work, so I had to ask for money from my parents in the Northern Alliance, and then we broke up, and here I am."

Roman knew the people who administered reinstatements would not accept these types of personal excuses. And normally, regardless of the fact she was cute, he would have been firm in telling her this and he would have denied her reinstatement.

But something was urging him to go ahead and do it, to figure out an angle she could use. After all, it wouldn't be long until he was done with his lowly immigration advisor job.

"Look," Catherine said, "I know I screwed up here. I know there's nothing I can do. I just wanted to come in, and be honest, and find out the next step. To see if there's any hope for my case."

"Well, I think you may be in luck." Roman cleared his throat. "I'll see to it that your reinstatement is approved on the grounds that you fell ill. I want you to go back to class and finish your degree. You need to be enrolled full-time next semester. No exceptions. And just in case you're thinking otherwise, dump your loser boyfriend—and yes, I know you said you already did that, but seriously, he doesn't sound like a great guy."

Her eyes softened. "You'll do that for me?"

"Yep. Us supers have to stick together."

She smirked. "You're an exemplar? I thought all the advisors were half-powered."

"It's a job."

"Okay. Well, thanks. And…"

Roman gave her the smile he'd perfected over the last several years. "Yes?"

"I would love to know more about this job, and what it's like working with so many different supers. I mean, I'll work in a similar field when I go back to the Northern Alliance, so if you ever want to grab coffee…"

He appreciated her sudden transformation. She had gone from distraught to cute, her brow unfurrowing and the stress leaving her body as if it had been a blanket draped over her shoulders. Still, that wasn't the reason he'd granted her reinstatement, and he didn't want her to think she could just flirt her way out of most situations.

Even if she could.

"So, coffee?"

"We'll see. Thank you, Ms. Blaine."

The next person to show up at his office was the last person he wanted to see. Roman was finishing up Catherine's paperwork when the woman barged in, her hands on her hips and a furious look on her face.

"Your little stunt this morning left us without coverage," Selena told him, practically snorting fire. "With Kevin gone, we're short-staffed, and you have to just disappear some morning without any reasoning. Short-staffed! What part about that word do you not understand?"

"Hey Selena," Roman said, noticing she wore a frumpy dress demarcated by a belt that was partially covered by her belly fat.

"You know, I keep hoping you'll improve as an employee, but you never do. You're practically useless; you're the slowest at processing paperwork in our department, and you kind of make your own schedule. How is that okay? You knew Kevin died—you knew we'd have more work to do, especially because you've taken on his caseload, but here you are, coming in three hours late!"

"Sorry about that," Roman said, focusing on her belt.

Selena continued to bitch him out, and as she did, her face grew red.

His hand under his desk, Roman rubbed his fingers together, *tightening* his manager's belt.

She didn't notice it at first, but once it started to squeeze her belly fat, sending the blood rushing the other way, pushing her breasts up like she was wearing a corset, her bulging eyes filled with embarrassment. Selena stormed out of his cubicle, letting him know this wasn't over.

"See you," Roman said, the blue bar on his power dial flashing.

Chapter Eighteen: Kevin's Reward

"I told you we would reward you," Turquoise said as Obsidian sucked Kevin off. Somehow, lying out of his ass had rewarded Kevin with a blow job.

The last few hours had gotten progressively better with each lie he told, each scenario he made up.

The cat girls let Kevin go to the restroom, they let him eat, and as he continued to fabricate reasons as to why Centralia was set on invading the Western Province, he found himself in the position he was in now: relaxing on a white fur carpet, his head on Turquoise's lap while her counterpart went to town on his only claim to fame.

"Thanks…" he said, not sure what else to say. "Thank you!"

He was still scared shitless, and he was pretty sure the two cat girls were definitely unstable, as evidenced by the scratch marks covering his body. But they'd believed his lies, and there was no way he'd turn down what Obsidian was doing now.

Turquoise continued speaking over the slurping noises.

"We talked about it, just a little bit, and we thought you would never come clean," she confessed. "But since you have, we think you would be an asset to have on our side."

He heard her prayer beads clinking against the ground as she cycled through them. That was another thing he'd noticed, especially about Turquoise—she practiced some type of religion that had her cycling through mantras every hour or so. She kept her prayer beads wrapped around her left wrist to make it easier to utilize them.

"An asset?"

Turquoise's tail dropped onto Kevin's face, tickling his nostrils. He sneezed, which caused him to lunge forward a little bit and nearly knock Obsidian off his knob. She recovered and kept going, using her soft hand—no claws!—to jerk him off as she focused on the tip.

All of this was unpredictable, and Kevin was a man that liked predictability. He was a creature of comfort who did everything by the books, and now he was not only selling out his brother of the same name, he was selling out his government.

He'd said a lot of things in the delirium he'd been in earlier, a delirium he believed had been caused by some excretion from the sadist sisters, and while much of what he'd said was false, some was true—or at the very least, speculation.

"Are you going to finish soon?" Obsidian asked. "It's hurting my jaw."

"I'll show you how to do it." Turquoise set Kevin's head on the ground, relaxed her prayer beads, and joined the other cat girl just below Kevin's waist.

Not that Obsidian was bad, but when Turquoise took over, Kevin moaned in response.

He glanced down at her as she went at it, watching her perky ears move up and down. His belly was too large to see all the action, but he got the picture.

And a picture was worth a thousand words, or possibly, a single orgasm.

There was a lot to his impending orgasm, considering that he hadn't been with his wife in quite a while, and that he was too prude to jerk off.

"So much!" Obsidian said in astonishment as he finished. Turquoise stood with her hand over her mouth and then moved towards the restroom.

After a moment to come down, Kevin tried to send a mental message. For some reason, this wasn't working, and he couldn't understand why.

It should work. He'd only been in a few situations where a mental message hadn't worked. But here he was, lying on a fur carpet in someone's large bedroom, at a loss for words.

The strange part about all this was that aside from the fear, Kevin felt good. It felt good being wicked, good going against his perfect brother and their overreaching government, good getting his body covered in scratches and then sucked off.

Kevin was afraid, sure, but he was also afraid of the thought that kept flickering at the back of his skull: *Join them.*

And he knew it wasn't some telepath hiding in the shadows—this was all Kevin.

While he didn't show it, Kevin knew more about superpowers than most people at the immigration office. He was an expert. And no, he didn't have some fancy Exemplar Studies degree or anything; his expertise came from constantly dealing with supers, from actual experience.

And he knew what a telepath in the area would feel like, even a Type I.

No, this thought at the back of Kevin's mind was his own; there really was only one option in this scenario, and luckily for Kevin, he liked it.

Turquoise returned and cuddled up next to him.

He placed his hand on the bottom of her ass, his fingers probing at her tail a little bit, the place where it met her skin. Obsidian came on the other side and got in an equally comfortable position.

"I want to join you," he said, still a bit breathless from his orgasm, "but I don't have a super power."

Turquoise laughed. "I think that's something we can take care of. What do you think, Obsidian?"

"Sounds like fun."

"Even without a superpower?" Kevin asked.

"Your power is information," Turquoise said, purring softly now. "And there are ways for us to give you some type of power, but we'll need to talk to our handler. She would have to approve it."

"Your handler?" Kevin hadn't considered this aspect. "Who's that?"

"Paris," said Obsidian. "Her name is Paris, and she's the one who told us to take you from the hospital."

"Paris, huh?" Kevin searched his mind, hoping to remember meeting someone with that name. When it was clear he wouldn't find anything, he returned his attention to the two cat girls. Obsidian had pressed her head next to his, her ear lightly touching his cheek.

Kevin was in a good place, a damn fine place, and considering how ordinarily shitty his former life had been, it was a place he planned to stay.

Chapter Nineteen: Worth a Shot

Roman slipped out of work ten minutes before five, figuring he'd catch the early trolley towards 30th Street, where he'd attend Heroes Anonymous in an hour.

He'd been going to H-Anon for over two years now, and if it hadn't been for the fact that'd he'd started using it to pick up women, Roman would have hated every minute he spent there.

While the last woman he'd met there, Paris, had tried to kill him and was now using him for information, this didn't change the fact that his attendance was court ordered, another reason he was inclined to go.

So that was how Roman found himself walking towards the exit doors at the bottom of the Centralian Immigration Offices, a trash bag in his hand.

Roman would have normally placed the files Paris requested in his briefcase, but his briefcase was at home, and rather than transport there and transport back, he'd figured a trash bag would do.

Besides, the info wasn't even classified, which was odd in itself.

The papers she'd requested all seemed to center around healers and any immigration numbers related to the rare Type Hs. He'd skimmed through it twice, looking for anything of importance, and he'd uncovered absolutely nothing.

There would be more to Paris's requests in the future, and he figured this was just the tip of the iceberg, but there wasn't much he could do now aside from continue to commit treason.

Had Roman thought more about what he'd gotten himself into, he would have contacted the authorities as soon as Paris had left his flat. But he hadn't, and now it was too late to turn back.

Coco, the security officer on duty, gave him a funny look as he passed with his trash bag in hand. Roman played it off, offering the Type I Class D a charming smile.

"See you tomorrow," he said with an overly friendly wave.

Coco didn't wave back, but she did smirk at him.

"That would be interesting," Roman said under his breath as he continued towards the trolley station. He'd thought once or twice about hitting on Coco, but figured she'd break him if it ever came down to it.

Hooking up with exemplars, while incredibly exhilarating, always had a chance of backfiring.

Once Roman reached 30th Street, he grabbed a sandwich, scarfed it down, and had the notion to animate the paper the sandwich had come in.

Sitting on a bench, Roman focused on the folded paper until it stood upright, formed arms and legs, and looked up at him as if to say, "What would you like me to do?"

"Dance," Roman whispered.

The piece of paper cocked its head sideways at its creator.

"You heard me."

With a shrug, it started dancing, and Roman noticed that this barely twitched the indicators on his power dial.

Watching the paper dance reminded him of…

Roman swallowed this thought; now wasn't the time or place to revisit the past. He stopped the dancing paper when an older woman passed him, a non-exemplar by his guess.

The paper folded back to its original form in a flash. The woman passed, and once she was gone, Roman entered the Heroes Anonymous meeting space.

"You speaking today?" Bill stood at the front of the room preparing the podium.

Roman stopped in front of the trashcan and dropped the sandwich wrapper in. "I was hoping not to."

Bill laughed. It was pretty clear why he'd been put in charge of these meetings in the first place. The man was a monster, easily twice Roman's size, yet he was a non-exemplar. *Just like the rest of us,* Roman thought, which was absolutely not the truth.

Roman wasn't like everyone in the room any longer. *Nor was the woman he'd taken a seat next to.*

Paris had an indecipherable look on her face, hardly acknowledging Roman's presence. She still wore her pencil skirt, but her outfit seemed more rushed today, and she'd forgotten to put on makeup.

"It's in the trash bag," Roman said out of the corner of his mouth.

"Is this some sort of joke?" she asked, her eyes narrowing on him.

"Long day."

Paris swept her black bangs out of her face and turned to Roman. "Long day? Do you even know the meaning of that?"

"Yeah, it's what I had today. You okay?"

She took a deep breath. "Sorry, it's been…"

"A long day?"

"Yes."

"What happened?"

"I got tied up with some things."

"Yeah, I get that."

"I don't think you do. But anyway, good work. Or maybe I should save the compliments for after I've gone through the docs you procured."

"Well, the trash bag is all yours. Glad to be of service. And it's not like any of this stuff was classified."

"Attention," Bill said. "It looks like everyone is here. Let's begin." He cleared his throat. "Everyone bow their heads."

Roman did as instructed and everyone began speaking.

"I am not a superpowered individual. I am not an exemplar. I have never had a superpower. I am not a hero, nor will I ever be a hero," everyone said at the same time. "I am not a superhero. I am half-powered. I will always be half-powered. I am a non-exemplar. There is nothing about me that is extraordinary. I am not a hero. I am not a superhero. I am half-powered. I will always be half-powered. I am a non-exemplar."

"Great," Bill said as he clapped his big hands together. "Who's up first? How about you, Sam? Everyone welcome Sam, our new guy."

Sam, a thin man with dark hair and a five-o'clock shadow, walked to the podium. He cleared his throat, placed his hand on the outer edge of the podium and began.

"My name is Sam and I am not a hero. It all started with my brother, good guy. He's not a hero either but he's a good guy, just a little misguided. He always goes off on tangents, never can keep to a subject."

"Ahem," said Bill, a muscle twitching in his neck, "let's get to what you told me earlier."

"Sorry. Anyway, so I tried it. I tried to save someone, and I lied about my powers. That's why I'm here. It started with very small hero crimes, like telling someone I could make food out of thin air."

A Type IV, Class C, Roman thought as he listened to the man's explanation.

"And then it moved to larger things. I liked it. People believed me. I mean, okay, well, a few children I know believed me. Adults, other non-exemps, knew the truth. But that was to be expected. Whatever. I'm not ashamed I was lying to children."

"Sam…"

"Sorry, Bill, I'll continue. Anyone ever tell you you're large for a non-exemp?"

"Yes. Continue."

"I even started to believe I was one, that I wasn't just a non-exemp, that there was some unlocked power in me. So to prove it, I bought a sex doll."

Roman's ears perked up and he exchanged a quick glance with Paris, who clearly had better things to do than listen to the losers that attended H-Anon meetings. She wasn't quite dozing off, but she was staring at the corner, contemplating something.

"And I bought the sex doll because I wanted to rescue something," said Sam. "It kind of became my thing; it even felt like she was alive sometimes. I'd go to northern Centralia—family has some land up there—and I'd set up a scenario in which I'd have to rescue her."

Sam struck a pose. "I'd take out all the North Alliance forces. *Pew! Pew!* And I'd save her, my Dolly, and then we'd have sex right then and there. Right in the middle of my family's vineyard! Grapes all around us, squirting their juices, broad daylight—"

"Please, Sam," Bill said.

157

"It's part of why I'm here," Sam said, suddenly ashamed. "I got caught having sex with my sex doll, Dolly, on a sunny Monday that just so happened to be the day a local school was touring the vineyard. Now I'm here at H-Anon. Because they ruled that my delusion was tied to the fact that I thought I was a hero—because I was, dammit!"

"No, you weren't," Bill gently reminded him.

But all Roman heard in all of Sam's nonsense was the word "sex doll."

He'd seen the lifelike dolls they sold in the various red-light districts around Centralia. *How much power would it take to animate one?* he thought. *And how many could I animate without killing myself?*

Roman's plans after the meeting had originally been to go home and get some rest, and possibly see what Harper was doing. But after Sam's confession, he figured it would be worth it to take a detour.

Worst-case scenario, Roman could chalk it up to practicing his new power.

Chapter Twenty: Lisa Painstake

Nadine took a teleporter home instead of the trolley. She hadn't gotten a lot of sleep last night, and part of her was still amazed she was alive. Not that she'd actually expected Paris to kill her—but the superpowered woman from the West was definitely pissed at how their meeting had ended, and she would likely strike back at some point.

Nadine was fine with that.

The Eastern Province was nothing like the West. Sure, it wasn't war torn, but it was exceedingly poor. Nadine would have spent most of her life destitute had it not been for the chance to join an elite group who worked for the governors of Eastern Province.

The sacrifice, what she'd had to do to become one of these Elite members, the people she was never allowed to see again—these were the things that haunted Nadine's nightmares.

There was hope in Centralia, but there was also a lot of red tape, a lot of politics, a lot of people looking to get in.

And it wasn't like Nadine hadn't entertained the idea before. She knew a few people, enough to disappear, but there was a catch-22 with that. Sure, she may never be seen again, but this would also apply to her family back East, her mother and father.

If she disappeared, so did they.

"It's me," she said when a slit opened in the door. A pair of oddly-colored eyes looked out at her. The door opened and she entered a dark cellar, where she took a flight of stairs down to the basement.

It was colder here, the air thick with wax from a candle burning in the corner.

"Your disappearing act is getting better," she told Oscar, the East's information mule. Oscar had been at this job for years, and Nadine liked to tease him about it. It kept things light, took away their shared longing for home.

"And you're still as loud and clumsy as ever," said Oscar, who now stood in the shadows, his bright eyes the only thing visible, one yellow and the other blue. She knew what Oscar looked like: a long face, sagging skin, a sharp haircut, short hair parted on the right.

Nice clothes, too. Whenever she saw him, he was in a vest that matched his slacks, a pressed shirt, a cravat, and a pair of perfectly shined shoes.

Your typical rich older Centralian non-exemplar, at least on the surface.

Aside from missing their shared homeland, Oscar had the life Nadine eventually wanted. He had been trained as a spy, became a handler for a while, and was now simply the person that transferred information.

The necklace he wore granted him a special telepathic ability, the ability to communicate with the other wearer in the East—these communications completely secret, unable to be intercepted.

It was almost a confessional. Oscar sat in a chair against the wall and Nadine sat next to him in another chair, both of them enshrouded by darkness as she relayed the information. Nadine had a handler, but this was the quickest way to get information back to the

Eastern Province, where it could be registered, interpreted, and strategized upon.

In the end, there wasn't a lot of information to relate, aside from the fact that she'd been attacked last night, and that the West was also looking to use Roman as an asset.

"And have you contacted the other asset you are working on, the female exemplar with a special teleportation ability?" asked Oscar, a hand on his necklace as they continued to sit in the dark.

"Not yet, but I was planning to tonight."

"I see. Well, you'd better get started then."

"Nice to see you again, Lisa," Nadine said as the young super approached.

Nadine had chosen a bar not too far from her information drop-off point. She liked the bar, especially since the owner was from back East, and he knew the importance of private booths and dimly-lit spaces.

Lisa Painstake wore a different outfit than she'd worn the previous day. It was still tight, but the fabric at her hips was baggy, allowing for deep pockets. Her pink hair and blond bangs were slicked back, pressed to her head with two hair clips.

"I know you are trying to help me—or you, um, helped me already," Lisa said after the waitress left. Nadine had ordered waters and left a tip already, letting the waitress know to leave them alone.

"I did help you, that's true."

"But I don't want to take part in anything that's against the law," she started to say.

"That's not why I called you here," Nadine said, trying to stifle a yawn.

"Then why did you call me here? I thought this was how it worked?"

"You've experienced something like this before?"

Lisa sighed. "Actually, yes. It kind of comes with the territory, considering my power. You aren't the first to want to exploit my abilities, and I don't believe you'll be the last."

Soul Speed, thought Nadine. *The ability to move at an extreme speed by detaching one's soul.* It allowed for the type of spying the East couldn't currently

163

perform. As Nadine removed her earrings—she'd meant to do that earlier, before seeing Oscar—she considered what Lisa had just said. She didn't doubt for a minute that people had tried to exploit Lisa's abilities, which meant she would need to come at this a different way.

"Let's not use the word 'exploit,' because that really doesn't describe what I'm interested in."

"Then what are you interested in?"

"Are you familiar with the plight of the Eastern Province?" Nadine asked as the waitress brought over two glasses of water. This wasn't the first time the owner of the small bar had seen Nadine here, always meeting with peculiar people.

Lisa took a sip from her water. "The poorest province."

"Yes, the poorest, but also the most beautiful. Have you been to the East?"

Lisa shook her head. "I don't know anyone who has."

"It's the views that get you. The magnificent coastline, the mountains, the natural hot springs, the abundance, and the poverty. And it's not just that the Eastern Province is the poorest; it also has some of the richest people in our world. The separation of rich and poor is something you've never seen before. The exemplars, and a few powerful non-exemplars, are at the top with the rest on the bottom, which has created a lopsided situation in which the poor outweigh the rich, and the rich are at the point where they can do nothing to stop it."

"Can't they just give their money away?"

Nadine laughed. She could tell by the look in Lisa's eyes that her words were reaching the young woman. To really deliver her message, she needed to change the topic from the poor to her family. Lisa was from the Southern Alliance, which meant that she likely came from money. Better to change the focus to something she could relate to.

"I guess I should just come out and say it: all this is for my family. Everything I do is for my family." Nadine took a sip from her water to let that message settle.

"Are they poor, too?"

"Extremely, and it is why I signed up to be what I am now. There are only two ways out of poverty in the Eastern Province: government service, or simply being born rich. At least for a non-exemplar. Exemplars have other options, but not many."

"So you spy for your family?"

"I wouldn't say I spy." Nadine cleared her throat. "I consider myself an information gatherer; I let the others do the real spying, as I don't have a superpower, so I'm not as useful as someone who could, say, fly, or take over someone's mind. Everything I am, everything I've accomplished from my training forward has been through sheer willpower."

Lisa took a sip from her water, nodding as Nadine continued.

"But to cut to the chase: there's information about my parents that I need your help to uncover. For one, they've been taken by Centralian forces in the East. So we can start there."

"You mean they're prisoners here?"

"They sure are," Nadine lied, maintaining the sad look on her face without making it feel forced. "And I need your help to get information about them. That's

166

all. I don't want you to think I'm trying to exploit your power here; I really want you to be the one who wants to help. Just like the way I helped you with your immigration issue. So, what do you say? Can you help me?"

"Yes," Lisa said, a stoic look coming across her face. "If it's for your family, I'll help."

Chapter Twenty-One: The First Doll

"I'm here to buy one of the dolls," Roman told the man behind the counter. He was an older man, half bald, with a bulbous nose and a pair of round spectacles.

It hadn't taken Roman very long to find this place. Centralia's various red-light districts made it easy to find anything depraved a person might desire. Drugs were legal, but they could only be purchased in this part of the city and only after their purchase was registered by a telepath.

Weapons were illegal, but there was a certain type of Class A that could force a controlled hallucination or a dream state, which allowed a person to go on as many killing sprees as they wanted—popular with office workers.

Then there were the sex workers.

This too was legal, and the sex workers ranged from supers, who could use their powers to get you off, to your more traditional sex workers in the form of non-exemplars.

There was also gambling, illegal fight rings, some trafficking, and probably some stuff even Roman had never heard of—or desired to be part of.

"It really depends on what you want," the older man finally told him.

He was picking at something in his teeth, giving Roman the fuzzy eye. Many people in Centralia looked unique, and Roman was one of these people. With his longer white hair, his orange eyes, and his professional manner of dress, he seemed a bit out of place in the sex doll shop, not that the man behind the counter hadn't seen a wide variety of clients.

"I want something beautiful," Roman said, "and life-sized."

"Follow me." The man beckoned Roman into a back room, and once Roman joined him, he gasped to see dolls everywhere, of every shape and size, wearing different outfits and posed in different ways. The room was cluttered, too, likely because it doubled as both a showroom and a storage area.

"I'll show you my favorite." The man coughed for a moment, apologized, and then began searching through the stack. "She just came in, which is probably why she's my favorite. I always like the new ones. These ones are designed in the Southern Alliance. It's cold down there; those people don't get out much, so you can expect some true quality with their workmanship."

The man entered a dark room and flicked the lantern on.

"Her?"

Standing before them was a female doll about five feet tall, wearing a maid outfit and a silk mask. Her hair was jet black, her eyes a striking shade of red.

"She's the newest," said the shop owner. "The most realistic, too. I swear she watches me walk across the room. It's weird."

Roman approached the doll and reached his hand out to it, touching her arm. He couldn't tell what material she was made out of. She was soft like cloth, her skin almost like Roman's but much colder.

"Couldn't tell you what she's made from," the man said, holding back a coughing fit by beating his hand across his chest. "It's some polymer they invented down South, I know that much. Feels real." The man smiled. "Insides, too."

Roman raised his hand to the doll's face and traced his finger along her chin. He reached out and touched her lips, and had to stop himself from animating her right then and there.

"I'll take her," he said, without looking away from the doll.

Chapter Twenty-Two: We Have Plans for Kevin Blackbook

Paris was sitting in the top room of her warehouse when she got the message from Turquoise, letting her know the cat girl was on her way. She took a sip from a glass of wine, her second for the night, still brooding over the bullshit she'd dealt with earlier that morning.

The damn non-exemplar known as Nadine would get hers, but Paris had time. When she did make her move, she'd call on Ian Turlock, her go-to muscle, to do it.

And it wouldn't be pleasant for Nadine.

At least she had the information she wanted from Roman. Just as she had expected, and just as her handler had predicted, Centralia hadn't had any healers immigrate since this time last year.

And even though her wine was sweet, having this proof in front of her put a bitter taste in her mouth. Most people did not know suffering like those who called the Western Province home. It was the most war torn of the provinces, and it seemed to always be a battleground for the other countries, even if the Western Province wasn't involved.

Why did they always go to the Western Province to wage war? It was maddening. And now, just as she had suspected, Centralia was up to something—and whatever that something was, it had to do with healers.

Centralia managed the world's healers based on its central location. If they hadn't taken any in for a year, it meant they were hoarding them, and while the other countries may have had healers, they generally sent them to Centralia for schooling, as Centralia had the only school for healers.

Something wasn't right.

And this in itself wasn't of concern to her—no, Paris had seen her fair share of tragedy over the years, enough that she wasn't foolish enough to think war wouldn't take place, or that Centralia would just cough up healers to send to the Western Province.

But the suffering. The abject suffering. This was what drove her to do her job, and this was why she needed to know more about what they were planning. If there was a way to alleviate it in some way, she'd give anything to see it done.

A teleporter appeared, along with Turquoise, the petite exemplar who had worked with Paris for some time now.

Paris didn't care for her or her cousin, Obsidian, but they were more powerful than they let on. The fact that Turquoise stood before her in a skimpy bathing suit barely concealing her lady parts and prayer beads wrapped around her left wrist betrayed just how dangerous she was.

"The poison has taken effect," she told Paris as soon as the teleporter was gone.

"Has it?"

"Yes, and we have been keeping him entertained all day, for it to set in better," she said, wiping her mouth with her arm. "We have noticed that it takes a little longer for the poison we secrete to actually work. It comes on strong at first, but then it seems to waver a bit. No matter."

174

"Kevin Blackbook has joined us, then?"

"Yes, and it was his choice to join. We didn't have to persuade him as much as we thought we would. He actually doesn't seem…"

"I don't care how he seems. He should be useful in the future, and that's all that matters. Do you think he's ready?"

"I believe he will be ready as soon as tomorrow."

Paris took another sip from her glass of wine. "Good, but I'll need more than a day, so keep him busy. I've come across some useful information, and I would like to come across a little more before we make our first move. Keep him entertained."

"With pleasure," Turquoise said.

"And don't get too attached to him."

Turquoise's ears flattened, her look darkening. "We'll try not to."

"I'm serious; tell Obsidian the same thing. Remember, we have plans for Kevin Blackbook."

Chapter Twenty-Three:

Animated

Roman appeared back in his apartment minutes before the teleporter arrived. He hardly had time to go to the restroom before she showed up.

"Your delivery," a woman wearing the official clothing of the Centralian government said. She sat on a coffin-like box, her legs crossed over one another.

Cute, he thought as she smiled at him. The teleporter had midnight-blue hair and she wore a bandanna around her neck. Stylish.

The woman was gone before he could say anything else.

"Oh well," Roman mumbled as he moved over to the wooden coffin. He placed his hand on a strip of metal that had been hammered into the top of the box and his abilities activated, the metal bending and then falling to the floor.

He removed the top of the box and stared at the woman's face. Her ruffled maid outfit had shifted in the transportation process, and the tops of her breasts were more exposed than they should have been.

Roman suddenly felt uneasy, nervous for what he was about to do.

He lifted a single hand over her body, and with a deep breath in, *he activated his power*. Roman felt something move through him, a heavy vibration as he gave the sex doll life.

And it was when she gasped, when she blinked her red eyes, that he realized the extent of his ability.

A quick glance to his power dial and he saw that he had really moved the indicators.

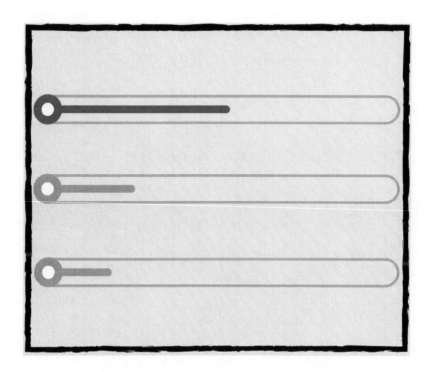

This explained the feeling in his chest, the pounding of his heart. He still had power left, clearly, but he would need to be careful, because *red is dead*, as Ava had said.

"Hello?" the woman asked without getting out of the coffin.

"Hi," Roman started to say.

A mental message came in from Harper: *Getting off work soon, if you're interested...*

Even in the midst of all this, Roman knew not to pass up an opportunity like Harper. But from what he could tell, tonight of all nights would be the wrong night to invite her over. So he decided to get back at *Nadine* instead:

Let's meet at my place tomorrow night, and if you have to work, I'll come and drink there until you get off work. How does that sound? I'm busy tonight.

Her response came seconds later: *That's fine. And I do have work, but I get off early, so come when you can.*

"Hello?"

"Hi," Roman said, looking at the doll.

"How long have I been in a coma?"

This question tore at Roman's heartstrings—it was the *one word* he hadn't expected her to use.

"You weren't in a coma; I just animated you," he said, looking down at his hands. Suddenly feeling the guilt wash over him.

"Animated me?"

She started to sit up, her red eyes flaring as she took in Roman's form.

She was undeniably beautiful, with a hint of mystery due to the mask she wore. There was a softness to her skin that Roman had never seen in a woman before, a unique enchantment, something that almost reminded him of a statue or a magnificent work of art.

No blemishes, only perfection.

Roman felt his heart quiver. He lowered to one knee, no longer able to stand.

"Are you okay?" the doll asked as she stepped over to him.

Roman lay on his back, breathing in deeply as he tried to catch his breath. The doll he'd given life to crouched next to him, resting on her knees now.

She looked down at his face—her own soft, his in pain—and she slowly reached her hand out to touch his cheek.

"Who are you?"

"Roman," he told her.

"And who am I?"

"Coma."

The single word came out not in a response to her question, but in response to the part of Roman's life that continued to haunt him.

The woman smiled. "Coma. That's an interesting name."

"Not… a name," he told her, the lights dimming all around him.

"Are you tired?"

"I can't tell."

Coma placed her eyes over Roman's face. "Please rest. I'll take care of everything."

Chapter Twenty-Four:

Coma

Roman awoke the next morning to find all his clothes removed. He'd been sleeping in a sitting-up position, his back against the couch.

His vision was a bit blurry, and when he rubbed his eyes, he found Coma standing before a stack of his things.

His nightstand, his clothing, a few personal items, some toiletries—she had moved everything into a single spot in the living room and arranged it in a strange way, trying to stack as much as she could.

The nightstand made the base of whatever sculpture she was going for, followed by a lamp he had in his bedroom, some of his collarless suit jackets on top of that, his toothbrush and other assorted sundries jutting out of various places.

Whatever it was, it had taken some time.

"Why did you do this?" he asked.

"I want to rearrange this place. So I started by getting as much out as I could and finding different things to move around. I'll work on it for the rest of the day, if you don't mind."

"I mind."

She crouched in front of him, so that he could now see the front of her panties. If Coma was embarrassed to be giving him full view of her undergarments, she didn't show it.

The life-sized, animated doll merely looked at him, her head cocked to the side as she continued to stare.

She still wore the same black mask she'd worn back in the sex shop, but her hair was now in a ponytail, tied up with one of his handkerchiefs.

"Do you know where we are?" he asked, figuring he would begin there.

"We're in your home."

"Okay, so you know that much. Do you know what you are?"

"I am your creation. I am a portion of you, and according to the dial on your wrist, I am a good portion of you. I am this red line, correct?" She turned his wrist over and checked out his power dial.

"How do you know all this?"

"You made me smart. You want a smart woman, don't you?"

"Smart? Yes, sure, that's true. Among other things."

"I've had a lot of time to think, you know. You've been sleeping forever."

"How long was I out?"

Judging by the light coming through the window, Roman assumed it must be at least six in the morning.

"Why did you create me?" She was still crouched down, and she no longer wore her high heels; Roman could see them next to the door, against the wall.

"To be honest with you, I don't know how much about all this you know…"

"About your life? I'm not really a psychic. I am just an extension of you. And while you have given me life and intelligence, you didn't download your history into

184

me or anything, which is why I'm asking you that question. I know some things, but what I really want to know is simple: *Why did you create me?*"

Coma fell back and sat on her ass, her thighs spread, her feet pressed into the couch as she got comfortable sitting on Roman's legs.

"To be honest with you, I don't really know why I created you. I just wanted to prove myself right, that I could give life to something larger than a pair of scissors. But I haven't decided what to do with you."

"I'll make that easy. I'm going to stay here and clean up your place and rearrange things. You're going to go out, or go to work, or whatever it is you do. You're going to come back here, and we can figure it out from there."

Roman raised an eyebrow at her.

"You asked, and I gave you my answer."

He smiled at her. There was something about Coma that he liked, something that gave her this aura of being hard around the edges but soft at the core. Similar to Roman.

Exactly like me, he thought, remembering how others had described him.

"Well?"

"I'm supposed to have a guest tonight."

"Man or woman?"

"Woman, same as you."

"Sounds fun. We can discuss that later." She tried to tickle him with her toes, which were pressed up under his armpits.

"What are you doing?"

"Trying to see if you are ticklish. I guess not."

He looked at her curiously for a moment. Even with the mask over her eyes, he could tell she was raising an eyebrow at him.

"Interesting…" he mumbled.

"Well? Do I pass the test? Are you going to keep me around?"

"I think," he said as she continued to try to tickle him with her toes.

"Good. I laid your clothes out on your bed."

"How did you know what I want to wear?"

"I'm here to help you. And besides, most of your clothes are dirty anyway. I need to wash everything."

"I don't want a maid—even if, um, you're dressed as one."

She rolled her red eyes. "This isn't a maid costume; it's a gothic Lolita outfit."

"How do you know?"

"I came with other clothes in my box, and it said gothic Lolita on the tag."

"I don't want a maid."

"You may not want one, but you definitely need one. I'll clean up for now, but after that, I expect you to keep things my way."

"Do you, now?" he asked, still not sure what to make of all this.

Aside from the fact that a sex doll was alive and real, and sitting on his legs, he also didn't like other people doing his dirty work. Roman didn't have many codes, but one of them was that he liked taking care of himself.

"Are you doubting me?"

"No, I just would rather help if I can. I can afford a maid; I don't have one for a reason."

"Because you'd flirt with her?"

"Okay, two reasons."

"Because you don't want people to know you're a slob?"

"Three reasons."

She laughed—a light, musical laugh that he immediately enjoyed. "Just this time, then. After that, you have to help out. Now hurry, you're going to be late."

"How do you know what time I have to go to work?"

"What part about 'I'm a piece of you but I don't know *everything*' do you not comprehend? That means I know some things."

"I have things to do before work," Roman said, thinking of the hospital. He'd missed going yesterday, something he allowed himself once per week.

"Then do your things. When should I expect you?"

188

"After eight. And I'll have a guest."

"I'll be on my best behavior then."

"We'll see about that part."

Coma pressed away from him. She stood and offered Roman a hand. The doll was surprisingly strong, which was at odds with her dainty form.

"Go get ready."

As soon as Roman turned away from her, Coma slapped him on the ass.

Chapter Twenty-Five:
Paperclip War

Roman exited the hospital. There were no tears to wipe from his eyes, but the back of his palm went to his face anyway, a natural reaction by this point.

He was running late, so he mentally ordered a teleporter.

It was a warm day outside, and a small part of him wished he could just run away, not go back to work, find the nearest park and rest there, eat some ice cream—do whatever the hell he wanted.

But the middle-class non-exemplars of Centralia were rarely allowed to do whatever they pleased. Sure, they had freedom, but the majority of their freedom was tied to their bondage. Roman had figured long ago that for him to gain more freedom, he would have to work harder, which was exhausting, and which meant his free time would revolve around recuperation. And that sounded absolutely terrible.

At least he had a good salary, with benefits too, and while he had been a non-exemplar up until yesterday, he hadn't been treated like a non-exemplar most places he went.

Segregation was banned in Centralia and all the countries around it, but that didn't mean people weren't segregated.

Exemplars had their place in society, the neighborhoods and buildings in which they lived, the places they frequented, the jobs offered to them. Non-exemplars were the same—well, more or less.

Non-exemplars didn't have a lot of options when it came to protesting the rules given to them by a lopsided society.

This was another reason why so many non-exemplars worked in government. It was the one option available to them to give them some sort of power, or to get closer to exemplars, who had all the power.

Literally.

A teleporter appeared, a man with a crew cut, and he placed his hand on Roman's shoulder. They reappeared in front of the tall immigration building, sparkling bits of light settling everywhere, and once the teleporter was gone, Roman strolled in.

He said hello to Coco, who was at the station at the entrance to his floor. The Type I Class D with short hair and a smoking body simply offered him a nod.

I wonder if I should tell her when I officially become an exemplar, he thought as he made his way up the stairs and to his desk.

This was something he would need to ponder. It wasn't often that one became part of the class that had previously oppressed them, even if "oppressed" wasn't quite the word that best described the social stratification of exemplars and non-exemplars.

Roman leaned back in his chair and sighed.

A stack of papers stared back at him, and he started going through them, doing his morning approval rituals to the sound of...

Nope, Kevin was no longer there, which meant Roman didn't have to sit through the guy's bouts of morning indigestion.

And it would have been about this time that Kevin came around to offer extra help, or just to tell Roman whatever past glory story he had on hand that day.

Kevin had a damn good memory; he could recall situations he'd dealt with years ago, down to the supers' types and classes. Some were pretty crazy, others just glorified ramblings.

Without Kevin, the morning seemed duller, even more mundane than it already was.

So he dove in head first to the stack of paper on his desk, hoping to get things sorted out.

Once he had cleared most of the paperwork, he decided to do a little experiment.

Roman got a handful of paper clips and placed them in a pile in front of him.

With a single breath in, he animated four of the paper clips, which unfolded and joined together to make a stick-figure-like amalgamation, twisting at the middle.

Happy with the way they'd turned out, Roman made several more until he had ten of these figures.

He checked his power dial. Just as Ava had said, all his power indicators were tied to one another, but it wasn't taking too much to animate the paper clips. He did notice, however, that the red indicator was still at about the halfway point due to the fact Coma was alive and well at his home.

Red is dead, green is mean, blue is cool.

He instructed five of the paper clips to get on one side of his desk across from the other five. Figuring he would make this even cooler, he took two from each group, four in total, and placed them off-center, intending to bring them in after the fight had started.

"Now, fight for my appreciation," he said, realizing just how stupid he sounded, yet still feeling cool saying it.

The three paper clips on the left charged toward their opponents.

Their little metal arms met, and they began bashing each other and wrapping around each other's forms.

Since they had no heads, just two Vs twisted together in the center, it was easier for them to try to strip their opponents of their arms than it was for them to beat their opponents to death.

The two paper clips to the north and the two to the south waited for their opening.

The northern front moved first.

These two paper clips were ruthless, and rather than attack individually, they twisted together to form an anthropomorphized paper clip with six arms on top, each flailing as they charged into battle.

"Fuck yes," Roman whispered as the paperclip battle royale continued to heat up. The southerners had joined; their strategy was to take down the six-armed behemoth, which they did by straightening out and forming a trap to ensnare its two legs.

No longer paying attention to his surroundings, Roman glanced at the box of paper clips on the far side of his desk.

The box spilled open and the paper clips poured out, forming various structures as they made their way to the melee.

Roman smiled as the paperclip war waged on.

Lunch was also entertaining.

Roman purchased a sandwich from the canteen on the bottom floor, and he'd taken his lunch late purposefully so there wouldn't be very many people at the canteen.

With less people around, Roman was able to do something his mother had always told him *not* to do.

He started by animating the bread, splitting away two strips from the top half to form two arms on the hoagie.

The piece of bread hopped around waving its two stub arms, much to Roman's amusement. Like an old man rising from bed in the morning, the exposed slice of lettuce pushed off the rest of the sandwich and hobbled into existence.

The meat came next, which Roman mentally folded and rolled off its sandwich bread. He then animated a fork, which bowed at the waist and leapt into the air, coming down onto the rolled piece of meat.

The fork righted itself, and, after checking to make sure no one was looking, Roman bent down and bit the meat off of it.

He laughed at this. His power to do stupid things made him feel like a kid again, and the fact that he could pretty much animate anything around him only added to the fun.

He saw one of the chefs exit the kitchen and focused on the swinging door.

Wanting to try something new, something experimental, Roman stopped the door from swinging shut.

He then mentally removed the hinges, the bits of metal wiggling themselves out of their clasps.

The door tipped forward, and Roman stopped it just before it hit the ground, so that it now looked as if the top portion of it was levitating. Concentrating further, Roman lifted the door back to its correct position and leaned it against the wall.

The chef came back into the canteen, looked at the door, looked at Roman, and tried to put the pieces together.

Roman simply returned to his food, trying his best to hide the smile that was moving across his face. While he had been disappointed before regarding the powers he'd been given, he was now truly starting to see just how unique they were.

As if waking up with an animated sex doll sitting before him hadn't done the trick already.

This reminded Roman that he needed to get the evening's plans in order. He would wait a little bit longer to cancel on Nadine, though, figuring the best place for that situation right now would be on the backburner.

There were other, more pressing matters.

Chapter Twenty-Six: Spy Problems

There was both danger and adventure in being a spy, especially one that was embedded in the field. There were also spells of extreme boredom, which was what Nadine was experiencing that day in the Fast Travel Department.

She tried not to let this boredom get to her, but every now and then, she would find herself sitting at her desk wishing she could be taking part in some sort of mission, even though she was already taking part in an operation.

Though she longed to be doing something else, Nadine was good at her job, and as soon as a stack of paperwork came to her desk regarding a group of S Visas for a squad of teleporter trainees from the Southern Alliance, she got to work.

It was hard to see all these innocent faces, to know that they, like most other exemplars with teleportation powers, Class Bs, would find government jobs spending eight hours a day handling teleportation needs, from goods to people.

Lisa Painstake, Nadine's newest asset, was nothing like the teleporters.

It was a wonder that the Southern Alliance hadn't picked up on the numerous ways they could exploit her power. Notorious for their exclusiveness and their vast wealth, the Southern Alliance's actions were always unpredictable. They weren't isolationists like the Northern Alliance, but if Centralia's immigration process was hard to navigate through, the Southern Alliance was a maze with no end.

Always one to work her hardest, Nadine powered through lunch, deciding she would just eat at her desk.

Since Sarah wasn't in the cubicle next to her, she decided to go all out and order something. Normally, this would have been a drawn-out process she would have somehow had to loop Sarah into, or Sarah would have made her feel guilty for not asking her if she wanted anything. That sort of thing.

But Nadine was solo today, and since she was solo, she mentally ordered a delivery of Eastern Province homestyle food. Thirty minutes later, a teleporter appeared with a bag of Nadine's favorite: a large baked potato with stewed meat inside that had been covered in cheese and fermented spinach.

It was an hour or so later when she received the mental message from Roman, who was only a floor away but had decided to send a message instead.

Hey. Something came up and I need to cancel for tonight. I figured I'd let you know before you showed up and I wasn't there. Kidding, I'm not bitter about it. Anyway, you owed me and now I owe you, so let's settle this tomorrow evening. What do you say? It's getting closer to the end of the week, so if there wasn't something to celebrate before, there is now.

"Asshole," she whispered, knowing exactly what it was he was trying to do. If Roman was busy tonight, then she could go ahead and move forward with her plans regarding Lisa Painstake.

We need to quit canceling on each other, she finally thought to him. *So sure, tomorrow night. Let's both try not to cancel this one.*

Roman's message came about a minute later. *I promise. And believe me, I'm looking forward to it.*

"I'll bet you are," Nadine said as she returned her focus to her work.

Chapter Twenty-Seven:
Lost and Found

Ava Montague paced back and forth in front of Roman, not yet sure how she should respond to her pupil's latest action.

"Let me recap: you animated a sex doll, who is now at your home, re-arranging and cleaning the place. Is this what you're telling me?"

"I figured I should just go ahead and come out with it," said Roman. " I mean, you would see the red bar on my power dial at some point, and I didn't want it to conflict with whatever training you had in store."

"And why didn't you cancel your creation?"

"It just didn't feel right. Sorry, I know that's not a great answer. I thought she was…" Roman searched his brain for a word to describe Coma. "Interesting. I don't know. I'm not a lonely guy or anything, not that it matters. I have friends, girlfriends, that sort of thing."

He winced at what he'd just said—it really sounded stupid.

"I'm sure you do." Ava raised an eyebrow at him. She looked as hot as the first time he'd met her, in tight exemplar clothing with her red hair pulled into a tight ponytail. "I just find it strange that your first inclination was to animate a sex doll."

"She's life-sized."

Ava snorted. "Not the response I thought you'd give me. My point remains: she's a doll."

"Agreed, but she's alive now, and I'd like to keep her that way."

"I'll definitely have to meet her at some point, because this is something I'd like to see for myself. And I don't think it would be wise for you to pursue an actual relationship with her."

"I don't know if all her parts are, um, working or not, if you get my drift. I didn't check."

She squinted at him with one eye. "I suppose that's another thing that would be interesting to know. As I have mentioned to you before, there aren't many like you—exemplars who can animate inanimate objects.

It's too bad we don't rate powers on their rarity, because if we did, this would definitely be up at the top. So part of me wants to see just what you are capable of—for science!—but I also want you to be extremely careful in what you animate."

"Got it."

"So with that said, and keeping an eye on your power dial, I want you to animate my clothing. I want you to make it come alive."

"Are you serious?"

"I'm dead serious, and I thought you'd like this task. Of course, there is something else that might make it more difficult."

"What's that?"

"I'm going to be attacking you in the process." A thin smile cut across Ava's face.

"Yesterday, you had me animating a rock, a piece of paper, and a pair of scissors. Today you want me to attack you? Seems like a bit of a jump, no?"

"That's right. Seeing as how you are already becoming an expert, I figured we might as well step it up to the next level. And besides, do you just want to animate small inanimate objects, or do you want to see what you're truly capable of?"

Roman cracked his knuckles. He'd been in a good many fights before, in the various fighting bars of Centralia. He'd even fought a super, but not one with elemental powers. He had no idea what he would do if she actually burnt him.

Of all people, Roman knew healers weren't easy to come by.

"Well?" Ava dropped her hands to her side, flames boiling up her wrists and flickering off her forearms.

She looked sexy as hell in that moment, and even though he was seconds away from becoming Centralian barbecue, Roman figured he would give it his best shot.

A ring of fire appeared around him, and his skin instantly started to feel as if it were boiling.

The fire was far enough away that he wasn't actually being burnt, but the proximity of the heat definitely had him sweating, and it would start to affect his skin if he didn't do something soon.

"My clothes," Ava called from outside the fire. "Animate them!" But Roman was no longer paying attention to her clothing. He needed to get this fire to stop, and for a second, he thought about trying to control the actual fire.

It is an inanimate object, isn't it?

Figuring this idea was stupid, Roman animated the floor around him, lifting himself above the flames and forming a small plateau to stand on.

Sweating now, his heart slamming against the inside of his rib cage, Roman tried to get a grip on what was happening. Even as the flames spread higher, he steeled himself, glanced down at his power dial and seeing...

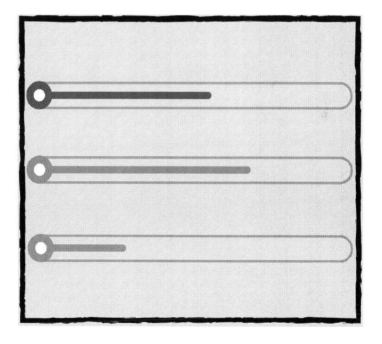

Shit.

The floor was clearly considered a mid-sized object, likely because he was only animating a portion of it.

Another thought came to him:

My power usage responds to my level of anxiety.

He responded by trying to take control of his breath, focusing on what he was creating yet protecting himself from the flames as they rose higher and higher. Ava, who stood a good thirty feet away, was staring at him intently, her brow furrowed and the control evident on her face as she made sure...

She's not actually trying to hurt me.

This was good news for Roman, because he really did not want to be hospitalized with third-degree burns.

She could have already done it by now, he concluded, and rather than continue to fight off the flames, he figured he would take this little exercise to its very limit.

One more glance at his power dial and he saw that relieving his anxiety had helped. Fear really did play a larger part than he'd originally thought.

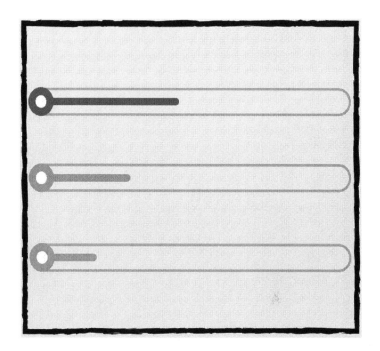

Roman didn't have superhuman strength, but like most half-powereds, he did have *enhanced* strength, which was further enhanced through the time he'd put in at various gyms in his youth.

Focusing on the ceiling now, he forced bars to form out of the paneling.

Without looking at his power dial, Roman jumped into the air and latched on to one of the bars he'd created, glad to see that it held his weight. He swung to the next bar and then the next, his muscles pulsing as he held on for dear fucking life.

Roman mentally banished all the other structures he'd created and used the bar to lower himself to the ground. Ava was just about to create a new ring of fire around him when he pulled the floor from beneath her.

He used the floor to pin her arms and legs, and even though she sparked with flames, he kept doubling down on his structure until he could no longer breathe.

Roman fell to the side, striking his head on the floor of the gymnasium.

"Goddamn that hurt."

He didn't know how long he'd been out for. All Roman knew was that when he woke up, Ava was crouched before him, his head resting on her lap. He looked up at her flowing red hair, her black eyes, her incredible rack.

It wasn't a bad place to be.

"It seems you have a bit to learn," she said with a chuckle.

"I didn't know my second lesson would be a full-on brawl."

"You call that a brawl? I was going easy on you."

It felt good to be in his teacher's hands—he wasn't going deny that—and rather than get up immediately, he feigned that he was still injured, which he technically was since his head was still spinning and he felt queasy.

Ava's hands ran down either side of his head, her fingers massaging his temples.

"So you're a healer as well?"

"No, nothing like that. You hit your head, but it didn't seem like it was very hard, mostly because the floor rose up to meet you."

"It did?"

"It sure did, which tells me that your power is truly stitched to your instincts. This isn't always the case with non-exemplars who take on a power. Sometimes they have to always tell their power to activate, or think it awake. I don't know how to describe it other than that, but you get what I'm saying, right?"

"I think I do."

"So that's the good news; and there isn't really any bad news here, but you are going to have to be careful as you level up your ability. You overpowered yourself back there, and if you let that red bar get to the end of your dial, you're as good as dead. *Red is dead.*"

Roman squinted up at her.

"Yes?"

"Are there actual healers here?"

"It's a training facility, so yes, we do have someone available to us who has some healing ability, a Type IV Class H, to use your phrase. Although there is a small waiting period if you get hurt... So, don't get hurt? Yeah, don't get hurt."

"Wait a minute, are you telling me that because I'm now an exemplar, I have access to healers?"

"You aren't part of a combat unit, so no—that's your short answer. But the long answer is you have better access than non-exemplars, meaning that you can and will be healed before they are. Also, you aren't an exemplar. I thought we went over this."

Roman gritted his teeth. "That's so fucked up," he said as he pushed away from her.

"Fucked up?" Ava looked at him curiously for a moment. "You do realize what you are now, right? And that your life is more valuable to our country than their lives, right?"

Roman stood, his fists at his side as he considered the way she'd phrased that last sentence.

"Relax, it's simply a fact of the matter, nothing to get worked up about. Once we get you trained, your new ability will be useful to the Centralian government and its mission. Maybe I'm exaggerating, but I can think just off the top of my head of a number of different tasks you could undertake."

"What if I just disappeared?"

Ava laughed. "If you just disappear, we'll find you. There are Type IVs for that, and you'd know this better than I."

"Yeah," he said, turning away from her, his fists still clenched at his sides.

Chapter Twenty-Eight:
One of Us

Kevin had gone from a guy who had just been cheated on by his wife to a man doted upon and banged by two sexy cat girls, their tails bouncing in the air as they led him to a table.

"Just wait here, honey," Obsidian said as she turned away, heading towards what Kevin believed was the kitchen. He watched her go, her perky little ass wiggling as she moved toward the revolving door, her black tail bobbing up and down.

Turquoise, the cleverer of the two, sat across from Kevin fumbling with her prayer beads. She glanced up at him and as she smiled, her ears lifted ever so slightly.

"What are you thinking about?" she asked him.

"Just the choices I've made over the last couple days."

While it had dawned on Kevin that he had seriously given up on ever living a normal life after what had transpired here, and while it was starting to dawn on him that he would never be able to see his old friends again, his brother, or anyone else that he'd known in his previous life, there was still some part of him that was excited by the change he had enacted.

There was also something fuzzy to everything he looked at, including Turquoise, who had hopped onto the table and was crawling over to him. She lifted a clawed finger and scraped it across his cheek.

"Shhh," Turquoise said as she drew blood. "We were a little rough with you, and this is the only way we've kept you from dying from shock."

She licked his wound, her sandpaper tongue rough against his skin. As soon as she did, he felt a sense of euphoria wash over him.

Kevin was in his happy place again, no longer worried about Centralia, the future effects of his supposed death, or the fact that he had no idea where he was. For all he knew, he was in the Southern Alliance, well past the border, smuggled out and being held hostage.

But was he being held hostage?

If you had asked him two minutes ago, he would've said yes.

Now he wasn't so certain.

"You're keeping me alive?" he finally asked.

Turquoise cocked her head at him. "Yeah, that's one way to look at it. You were going to die, but we used our power to keep you alive."

"And your power comes from...?"

"Yes, our power comes from our secretions. You could say it like that. Or you could call it our blood. Or anything else that is liquid from our body. Including our urine."

"That is one of the strangest powers I've ever encountered. So you're a Type I Class C? Or a Type II? Do you know?"

"You Centralians always like to rank and list things. It's something I've noticed. It's different where we're from. The West has things that Centralia has never heard of or classified."

Kevin nodded his head as a single drop of blood dripped down his cheek. "I can see that."

"Don't worry, Kevin, you're one of us now."

Turquoise scooted forward and brought her petite body into Kevin's lap. She wrapped one arm behind his head and smiled at him, her little slit eyes enlarging as she dragged her claw against the back of Kevin's neck.

"I'm not worried," he said, dizziness coming over him. He could still sense Turquoise, her soft hairless skin, the way she moved in his arms, her light flowery scent, but he could no longer understand what she was saying.

And he was fine with that.

Kevin was in his happy place, or at the very least, *a* happy place.

Chapter Twenty-Nine:

Dessert

Roman sat at the same table he'd been sitting at when he'd first met Harper.

She was busy with another customer, the only other customer in the joint, and he'd already had a shot while waiting for her to get off work, some tropical number the bartender had concocted on the fly.

It was nice watching Harper move around in her apron—the curve of her back as she came to a stop to greet the customer, the way she arched forward ever so slightly, just showing the tops of her breasts, and aside from the sexual part, the fact that she was actually happy to see him.

He didn't know what was going to happen with her in the long run, but for now, she was a dominating, beautiful woman who actually was interested in Roman Martin.

Nothing to shake a stick at.

"Are you just going to watch me walk around all night, or are you going to order another drink?" Harper asked.

"Is 'both' an option?"

"I suggest the Ocean Blue. It's tart, has a smooth finish, and the bartender here is pretty good at making it. I mean, I've seen the way other people make it, but they usually mix the liquids when they pour the top ingredient. He manages to keep them separated. I swear sometimes the guy has a superpower."

"He could be an exemplar. Type IV, Class..."

"No, he's a non-exemplar. I'm sure of it. He just knows how to make a good cocktail."

"Is it always this slow?"

Roman especially liked Harper's eyes, which were further apart than most women he'd met. With her long neck and her short brown hair, she looked almost alien—this coming from a guy who had white hair and orange eyes. Still, it was visually appealing to say the least.

"Yeah, midweek is usually like this."

"Any chance you'll get off early?"

Harper sighed audibly, blowing the hair out of her face. "Probably not. I'm here until the next person gets here, which should be thirty minutes from now. Maybe, and that's a big *maybe*, she'll let me go early, but we'll have to see. Why? You getting bored?"

"Well, you told me I couldn't watch you, so what else am I supposed to do?"

"You would like to watch me, wouldn't you?" she said in a low voice.

Roman raised an eyebrow at her. He absolutely loved her energy, and if it weren't for the fact that he knew she was a non-exemplar, he would've thought she was at least a Type III Class E.

"We can figure that out later. For now, I'll have that ocean drink you were raving about. And I'll behave. It can't be much longer till you're off work."

Roman had experienced aggressive women before, but he'd never had one slam him against the wall outside his apartment building and start kissing him.

They were both lucky he had the wherewithal to keep his powers from activating. As Ava had said, his powers played off his instincts, and he'd actually felt a surge in his chest as she'd pushed him forward.

Harper was ready to go then and there.

There were enough shadows around that they could make it happen, and Roman's stairwell wasn't usually that busy anyway, as most people took the elevator.

Maybe a few years back, a different Roman would have gone for it, but there were laws and he had powers now; he didn't want these things to mix.

Besides, he was only a few floors up.

"Let's take the elevator," he said between her kisses.

"Quickly," was her only reply.

She hopped into his arms, and, carrying her, Roman made his way over to the elevator. He slammed her back into the elevator button and she cried out in pleasure and pain, that strange mixture.

When the elevator door opened, she hopped down and they both entered. She immediately grabbed his cock and continued kissing him passionately. As they kissed, he pulled at the back of her hair, extending her neck so he could kiss her throat and her chest.

"I like it," she whispered as his hands went into her shirt and came up to her bra.

"You really are something," Roman told her as he kissed her again.

They got to his floor and she hopped into his arms again, her legs wrapping around his body. He had the notion to blow his door off its hinges, so he didn't have to fumble for his keys, but a small voice at the back of his mind reminded him that his power was secret.

He got his key out between Harper's increasingly powerful kisses, and he opened the door as she bit at his lips.

His entire home had been rearranged and it was clean, cleaner than he'd seen it since the incident.

But that wasn't the strangest or the most pressing matter.

Coma the love doll sat on the couch, on her knees, in a short skirt that barely covered her thighs. She had her hands over her breasts and before Roman could de-animate her, Harper turned to see the strange young woman with the jet black hair and striking red eyes.

"Who's she?" asked Coma.

"Who the fuck is she?" Harper asked as she hopped out of his arms.

Coma played with a single strand of her hair. Her mask was removed, and Roman couldn't decipher the look on her face.

"Is this your new lady friend?" Coma asked.

"I can explain," Roman said hurriedly to Harper.

"No, it's fine…" A grin spread across the waitress's face. "I didn't know this was the type of thing you were into."

"What you mean?"

Harper took a step closer to Coma.

"Come closer," Coma said.

Harper did as instructed, sitting on the couch next to Coma. She reached her hand to Coma's face and cupped it, her thumb stroking against the skin on her cheek.

"Are you a super?" Harper asked.

Coma smiled. "Do you want to kiss me?"

"Sure," said Harper.

Their lips met, and Roman just barely saw the red bar on his power dial spike up. He wasn't breathing—this he was sure of—and as they kissed some more, he took a deep breath, noticing that the power dial responded, the red bar diminishing some.

"I've always wanted to try this," Harper said, as she pulled away from Coma.

"Then let's try it," Roman said. He'd been in this kind of situation twice before, and knew better than to try to stop the momentum. "You two just kiss for a moment," he told them as he started unbuttoning his shirt.

"Yeah," said Harper, "kiss me."

Coma did much more than that.

She moved onto Harper, pulling off the loose blouse she was wearing in the process. Coma let her breasts spill out and Harper responded, taking her nipple into her mouth and sucking on it for a moment.

Roman, who had practically ripped all his clothes off by this point, was on the periphery now, waiting for his opening.

At that moment, everything in his life that he hated, everything that was troubling him and causing him extreme anguish, vanished.

All he could do now was focus on the immediate pleasure presenting itself to him, the carnal offering. And that was the entire point of pleasure—it was a rewarding distraction, but a distraction nonetheless.

His animal instincts had taken over, and he watched hungrily as Harper continued to kiss Coma's breasts.

Hell, he hadn't even kissed Coma's breasts; he had no idea what they would be like, the texture, the softness.

No idea.

He was almost jealous of the fact that Harper was the first to try, but he was also completely fascinated by the way they were moving, their female forms, their curves and their secrets.

Coma had her legs around Harper's waist now, and she was bent over her, kissing her, both of them feeling each other, Coma's hand behind her back and pressed firmly into Harper's mound.

Roman dropped to his knees, stroking himself as he watched them go at it.

He was consumed by their sexual energy; he had to remind himself to breathe every now and then when his power dial flashed, the red bar creeping up.

He didn't have time to process it at the moment, but he was starting to notice just how stitched he was to his creations.

This was something Ava hadn't told him, that his powers could fluctuate based on his emotions.

Of course, this likely wasn't her fault. How could she have known? His power was something entirely new to her.

"Aren't you going to join us?" Harper asked through quick breaths.

"Join us, Roman. Try me," Coma hissed. She wrapped her fingers around Harper's neck, and, keeping her hand there, she began to pull at Harper's shirt.

Roman stopped jerking.

Something about the way Coma was moving reminded him of himself, as if he were looking in a mirror.

She was a part of him, and it dawned on him in that moment that if he animated something else and gave it artificial intelligence, whatever he animated would also exhibit some part of him.

But which part?

Seeing Coma in control as she went down on Harper reminded Roman that there were other parts of him, darker places he had visited in the past, and they might arise if he wasn't careful in what he animated.

He would have to be careful. But for now, he'd have his cake and eat it too.

Chapter Thirty: Ghost in the Administrative Building

"How much do you need to know about the location to travel there?" Nadine asked Lisa Painstake.

"Not much, really. If you can tell me what part of the city it's in, that will narrow it down a little for me, and if I've ever seen the building before, then I'd definitely know how to find it."

The two were in Nadine's apartment, both sitting at her dining room table. Nadine had some plans laid out on the table, some instructions from her handler, something she would file after she got the information she was looking for.

"And all I have to do is touch you to travel with you, correct?"

Lisa nodded, the tips on her pink bouffant hopping up and down as she maintained eye contact with Nadine.

"Then we should do this from a more comfortable place. And to be clear, what happens if my real body somehow lets go of yours?"

"Then your shadow form will come back here. It can be a little painful, but I've had it happen before and you won't die or anything."

"I didn't figure I'd die," said Nadine, "but I want to make sure our bodies don't somehow separate. Let's do this from my bed."

"Okay."

A small part of Nadine was actually jealous of Lisa, her looks, the fact that she was from the Southern Alliance and clearly well off, and that wasn't to mention her incredible power. She swallowed this little feeling of jealousy as they moved to her bedroom.

"Get on the bed."

Lisa did as instructed, Nadine retrieving a thin scarf from her closet. She sat next to Lisa and used the scarf to tie their wrists together before lying back.

"I'm sure there's an easier way of doing this," Nadine started to say.

"There is, but I don't know you well enough for us to cuddle."

Nadine smirked. "Got it. Well, I'm ready when you are." She lay down and positioned her arm so it was under Lisa's, their hands clasped.

And before she could even get comfortable, she was standing in her bedroom with Lisa at her side, both of them looking down at their bodies.

They were translucent, Lisa's head encompassed by a golden halo.

"This is what it's like? This is Soul Speed…" Nadine looked down at her hand and saw that she could see through it now, her Zero Ring missing. She also saw a thin stretch of energy akin to an umbilical cord connecting her phantom body to the body that lay on the bed.

Lisa nodded as she approached Nadine.

It had been a long time since Nadine had felt fear, even with the fact that she'd woken up just a few days ago strung up from the ceiling of a warehouse. Those things were typical for her line of work—she'd trained for most scenarios.

But seeing translucent Lisa pluck at Nadine's light-filled umbilical cord bothered the hell out of her, made her feel small and insignificant, like she really was just a sack of flesh lying on a bed with her spirit gone from her body.

"This is what tethers us to our bodies," Lisa said, pointing out the obvious.

She spun around once, and Nadine saw that the cord of light never left the front of her body.

"It doesn't matter which way we move or how far we go."

"And it can't be cut?"

"Not that I know of."

"Okay, so how do we go there from here? Don't tell me we walk," Nadine said, a half-assed attempt at a joke.

Lisa was clearly in her element, evident in the way she moved towards Nadine, comfortable with her second skin. She didn't seem cocky at all, just comfortable, as she should have been. Lisa had been soul traveling since she was five; in many ways, she was more comfortable in this form than in her real body.

She reached her hand out for Nadine and after a moment of hesitation, Nadine took it, noticing that their fingers didn't pass through one another. They were solid.

The two appeared in front of the building in question, a government building used solely for record-keeping. The building wasn't as tall as the immigration offices, but like most buildings in Centralia, it was higher than anything in the Eastern Province.

That had been one of the things that had taken Nadine time to get used to after arriving in Centralia.

The country was so successful, so populated, and so rich, its buildings seemed to touch the bottom of the clouds. Sure, there were parks and other public works, but Centralia didn't have any of the pristine nature that the Eastern Province had, which was something that took getting used to.

Especially the oxygen.

Nadine noticed there was still an umbilical cord of light attached to her waist. It seemed to stretch into the distance, eastward, towards her apartment and in a way, towards her birthplace.

"Are you getting used to it yet?" Lisa asked, the nineteen-year-old's face rimmed with light.

"It's something else," Nadine managed to say.

"It's fun, but it does take some getting used to. Come on, let's get inside and then you can tell me what we're looking for."

"And you said you can actually interact with stationary objects, right?" Nadine asked.

"That's right, but I don't think you'll be able to. Try."

There was a trashcan not far from them, and someone had missed the bin.

Nadine bent over to pick up the discarded waste; her hand passed right through it.

It even passed through the concrete beneath the trash, which made her wonder how she was standing in the first place. It was only when she looked down at her feet that she noticed she was actually floating, just two inches or so off the ground. She wasn't standing on anything.

Lisa, on the other hand, was able to pick up the trash and deposit it into the bin.

Before doing this, of course, she glanced around to make sure no one was watching. They didn't want to give themselves away—not when they were this close to getting the information Nadine needed.

"Looks like you can't do it."

Nadine shrugged. "I'm fine with that."

The two floated towards the records building and pressed through its entrance. There were systems designed to alert officials and the security apparatus if they were being infiltrated, but the systems weren't designed for someone with Lisa's power, which was why she was such a powerful asset. The two ghost-like women floated past a security guard with steel skin and through another wall, where they found an open directory on a receptionist's desk.

Lisa flipped the pages while Nadine stood behind her, looking over her shoulder.

"Stop there," Nadine said when Lisa came to a particular page that listed the offices on the eleventh floor.

"Want to see something cool?" Lisa asked.

"Sure."

Lisa again took Nadine's hand and the two of them began to rise to the top of building, Lisa whispering as they passed each floor. "Three, four, five…"

They arrived on the eleventh floor in the middle of a circular room, the walls of which were lined with records. There was an apparatus before them that allowed a person to say a command and be granted instant access to a telepath familiar with the files in the room.

Nadine had seen similar tech before; the East was poor, but their technology was better than many of their rival countries, due to a lopsided investment on the government's part. Her Zero Ring was evidence of this.

"This is going to take a while," said Lisa, looking around the room.

The floor-to-ceiling files were arranged in bookshelves that could be swung to the left or right on ball bearings. There were more bookshelves behind these, the second ring visible through the gaps in the first ring of shelves.

"We'll just have to figure out how they've organized them."

Nadine walked to the nearest bookshelf and started reading some of the information on it. This had more to do with prisoner transfers than it had to do with actual data regarding how many from the Eastern Province were being held, so she moved on.

Once she'd skimmed all the labels on this shelf, she asked Lisa to move the shelf to the left so she could start on the next layer. Again and again, Nadine carefully examined each shelf until she found the information she was looking for.

And it wasn't easy.

It took her a good hour and a half to go through all the bookshelves. Some had much more information than others, and for these, she actually needed to open the files to examine what was inside.

Luckily for her, Lisa could interact with the environment around her.

It was on the very last bookshelf she came to, in the final row, that she found the information she was looking for.

Rather than comment on the irony of their discovery, Lisa brought the book of numbers to the center table and opened it, stopping at the last recorded mark.

"It was written last week," the young exemplar said as she looked at the number. "What does it mean?"

Nadine was glad she wasn't in her body.

She was glad there wasn't something for her to punch or kick, or that she couldn't cry out and blow their cover. She had seen these types of documents before, and it wasn't as much an encoded message as it was a way to write information that changed often.

"I just can't believe it's that many…" she finally said through gritted teeth.

Lisa's eyebrows rose. "Wait, this number represents people?"

Chapter Thirty-One: Ian Turlock

It was dark when Roman woke up, Harper on his right and Coma on his left.

He'd had sex with Harper, and while he'd fondled Coma's breasts, that was about all he'd done with her.

For some reason, this was comforting to him; the more he watched Coma in action, the more he saw himself.

It was utterly fascinating.

Roman had focused mostly on Harper, not even kissing Coma. He'd placed his hand on her, running it up her side and moving it to the small of her back. Her skin was incredibly natural—or better, it felt normal. Coma's skin felt just like Harper's skin, slightly warm, soft, real.

And thinking about these things, going over what happened, had made it impossible to sleep. It was too early to go to the hospital; Roman needed to wait at least two more hours before he did that.

Which meant he'd have to either lie between these two and face his demons, or figure something else out.

He chose something else, carefully rolling up to a seated position. Once he was sure he hadn't disturbed either of them—or so he thought—Roman stepped into this house slippers and quietly shuffled into the living room.

It threw him off that everything was reversed, but the couch was still in the center of the room, so the only issue was that it had been flipped around.

Roman sat, now facing the outside windows, the blinds partially shut. Not that it mattered.

Unlike many in Centralia, his apartment actually had a pretty decent view, and even if the three of them had put on their little show with the blinds wide open, no one would have seen.

He stepped to the window and stared outside for a moment, looking at the lights in the distance, the tall buildings of downtown Centralia. He could see the rooftop of the building next to theirs, a man standing there with his hands tucked behind his back as he stared down at the street.

It could've been anyone, from a super to a non-exemplar. Whoever it was, he was awake as well, a restless soul like Roman.

He kept staring at the man, wondering what it must be like to see from his perspective, what this mysterious man was looking at, what had inspired him to be on a rooftop so early in the morning.

"You know I don't sleep, right?"

Coma's voice startled Roman, and it took a full fifteen seconds for his heart to settle.

He turned on his heels to find her standing there, one of his throw blankets draped over her thin shoulders.

"Careful sneaking up on me like that," he finally said.

With his newfound powers, there might be a point when someone did something sudden and he reacted impulsively, causing the ceiling to collapse or a vase to fly across the room.

There really was no telling.

"Did you have fun last night?"

"Sex is always fun."

"Do you really believe that?" Coma sat on the arm rest of the couch. She was wearing her black superhero mask again; he couldn't remember if she'd slept with it on or not.

"Yeah, I believe it. Or, at least I think I do. Look, I came out here to be alone."

"But you created me to keep you company, did you not?"

"I'm still trying to figure out why I created you. It is interesting to be able to test my powers like this, but I think there may be a little more to what I can do. I don't know, just a hunch, so I hate to say you are kind of an experiment, but…"

"You think I'm an experiment?"

"I'm just being honest with you. You are, well, I don't know what to tell you just yet. I felt I needed to get to know you better. Then again, I feel like I know every bit about you. Like I'm looking in a… mirror."

She smirked. "There are things you don't know about me."

"Okay, tell me something I don't know about you."

"You don't know what it was like before you gave me life."

"And you have memories from that time?" Roman asked, as he made his way over to her.

He sat on the floor so he could look up at her, and in that brief moment, he felt as if he were staring up at a goddess, a blanket over her head, her life shrouded in mystery.

"They are fleeting memories—delicate, but I have them. Just flashes, really. I do enjoy being alive, though, and I would appreciate it if you let me stay this way."

"I really don't mind you being around, but there may come a time when I need some of the power I've given to you. Do you understand that?"

"I understand," she said as she continued to stare down at him. "One more thing before I leave you alone. Did you have an episode or something today? I felt like there was a disturbance in your power this afternoon. I

242

could sense it; it nearly made me fall over while I was rearranging the plates. Did you see that I rearranged the plates?"

"No, I didn't see that. I came back and you were on the couch raring to go, and I haven't even looked around the place since then. And to answer your question, my teacher—I guess I should call her that—was testing my abilities."

"You have a teacher?"

"I sure do, named Ava."

"I would love to meet her someday."

"Yeah, we'll see about that. She's sort of a new addition to my life, and I don't know how long she's going to be part of it. Basically, if I get through her training and she approves of it, I no longer have to be a non-exemplar."

"Okay, here's something I am unfamiliar with. You are a non-exemplar, correct?"

"I was, until I got this ability. But Harper, for example, she's a non-exemplar."

"And is it a problem being a non-exemplar in this world?" she asked, curiosity sparking across her red eyes.

"The non-exemplars, also known as half-powereds, have sort of a separate-but-equal status with exemplars, which is a fancy word for a person with a superpower."

"I see."

"The Centralian government is generally pretty fair about this, considering that it's a parliamentary government that's based upon exemplars and non-exemplars having equal say in the matters of the country. Some would argue this is why our country is the most powerful in this world. Others would say it's why we'll never reach our full potential. Anyway, I don't want to get into it any deeper than that. I really try to keep out of these types of discussions."

"Which type?"

"Political discussions, discussions about a non-exemplar's status versus an exemplar, those sorts of things. I'm not a freedom fighter. I'm in it for myself, and I'm not ashamed to admit that. I think that makes me a better person. I know who I am, I know what I'm capable of, and the fact that I can now do this…"

Roman said, pointing his finger at her, "doesn't change this part of me."

"Okay, we'll see."

"What's that supposed to mean?"

"We'll see."

Coma stood, offering Roman a mischievous smile. He watched the blanket-draped woman walk back toward his bedroom, a ghost if he'd ever seen one.

Roman left the hospital and wiped a few tears away. He went through phases now. Oftentimes, he wouldn't be emotional at all when he left; every now and then, he'd feel like curling up in a ball and sobbing, which usually led to him calling upon the services of a teleporter.

Then there were times like today, when he felt sad and angry at himself for not feeling sadder, hence the few tears rather than a full-on emotional attack.

If only he could animate a person in the way he could bring life to an inanimate object. What a power that would be.

The trolley ride from the hospital to the administration building took fifteen minutes. He was on time, surprisingly, and much to his delight, Selena wasn't around to see him when he shuffled in three minutes early.

The stack of paper on his desk showed no signs of diminishing.

Roman didn't know when they'd hire a replacement for Kevin, but he hoped the replacement would either be a woman or a guy he actually enjoyed being around.

"Kevin wasn't that bad," Roman whispered as he sat at his desk, wincing as the back of his chair gave way. He'd put in for a chair replacement six months ago, and there'd been no word if it had been approved.

A glance down at his power dial showed him he had plenty of juice available. Figuring it was worth a shot, Roman focused on his chair.

The chair came alive with him still sitting in it, the cushions morphing to perfectly hold his back. The seat grew softer, and an indentation formed for his tailbone.

The cushions against his lower back began to rumble as they started to massage him.

"Not bad," Roman said, then got started on the stack of papers on his desk.

For once, he actually focused on his work, adding notes to the various files that needed to be reworked. He would have continued working all the way to lunch had there not been an interruption from Phil, a lanky guy who worked two cubicles down.

"Selena's calling a meeting," Phil said, his voice high and scratchy in a way that perfectly meshed with his overall demeanor.

Phil was the youngest guy on their floor, a recent grad from northern Centralia who had an uncle higher up the administrative ladder. Nepotism wasn't as frowned upon as it should have been in Centralia, and Phil, with little qualifications, had been given a job as a senior immigration advisor.

Which meant he was actually a step up from Roman—not that Roman cared. Phil was a pretty cool guy, and he never treated Roman like he was his boss, which he should have been considering his experience in the Centralian government.

"I'll be there in a moment," he said to Phil, the entirety of his work experience flashing before him, creating a sinking feeling in his chest and making him regret coming in today.

"Something wrong?" Phil asked. "Your face just went white."

"I just remembered something. Anyway, I'm coming."

After a bitter exhale, Roman grabbed the leather binder he used to take notes.

It took a lot of willpower to go to their weekly meetings, mostly because they were a platform for Selena to pretend like everyone gave a fuck, as well as a chance for her to stand atop her soapbox and explain new directives from her higher-ups.

Everyone on his floor was in the meeting, and rather than make eye contact with any of them, Roman took a seat as far away as he could from Selena, who sat at the end of the table wearing a frown and a dark-blue frock.

Her eyes fell upon Roman, the last employee to join them. "Glad you could join us," she said, offering a fake smile. "Now, I want to begin this meeting by talking about metrics. Is everyone following the metrics protocols issued by the Center for Diversity and Inclusion? Remember, these metrics go a long way in deciding our budget for next year, which directly relates to your salaries and whatever retreat we plan to take."

What Roman wouldn't give to be anywhere else right now.

It was a strange prison that a full-time administrator lived in. Kept in a cubicle forty hours a week, Roman felt like a caged animal at work, content enough not to protest but never satisfied with his life, an ouroboros of semi-comfort and disappointment.

There were parts he liked about his job. Meeting exemplars was always interesting, but the overall work environment had completely soured his opinion of the position, and the thing souring it most was the woman speaking before him.

"Some of you seem to be incapable of doing a good job. I can't understand how hard it is to track your appointments and any issues that may arise. If you have a meeting with an exemplar, you note it. When did the meeting start? When did it end? When is the next one scheduled? Did you hit the five points we're supposed to hit in every meeting? Hmmm?"

She glanced around the room, most of the people in it averting eye contact with her aside from Phil, who gave her a toothy grin.

"Everything needs to be tracked. Let's go back to my example of tracking the time spent for each of your appointments. This data can later be used to get an average processing time. Then I would be able to average out all your processing times and present this information to my higher-ups, rather than cobble together the numbers I'm currently given. Class and type approvals should be tracked."

"We are tracking those; they were all turned in to you at the end of last week." Roman knew he shouldn't have spoken up. He usually didn't, but the fact that he was a non-exemplar going on exemplar had emboldened him.

"Those numbers weren't accurate enough," she said, her frown lifting into a visage of fury.

"Not accurate enough? I didn't lie on my metrics— did any of you?" Everyone shook their heads. "Works for me. What do you want from us? We gave you class and type approvals. That was your direct request."

"You could have done more, Roman. You could have also included trends, trend forecasting, graphs, charts."

"But you didn't ask for any of that. And you *have* before, and then still told us it wasn't right," Roman said, his fists now shaking.

"I've never asked for that before."

"You're wrong. I sat in this same chair a year ago when you berated us for giving you charts, but not the right kind of charts."

"That never happened."

"Never happened?" Roman's throat quivered. "And how are we supposed to do trend forecasting anyway if all of our meetings are random?"

He wanted very much in that moment to tell her he was done, animate the table and have it attack Selena. A glance down at his power dial and he saw that he was close to peaking.

"Do you need a moment?" she asked, cocking her head to the left and biting her lip as she squinted at him. "Would you like to step outside, Roman? There are resources available for employees who are struggling with grief. I know you've already had a morning off this week, but if you are feeling like you need more time, you'll have to get that approved by HR because I can clearly see that you are able to work, just not in the mindset to be productive."

Roman considered his options.

He could animate Selena's frock, causing it to squeeze until she burst like a grape. There were quite a few things he could also do with her chair, the floor beneath her, the wall behind her, or the ceiling above her.

Roman would go to jail for these things, but after all the shit she'd given him, and just as importantly, the shit she'd given everyone else, there was a small part of him that thought it would be worth it.

He glanced to some of his colleagues, eventually stopping at Phil.

Phil had a look of utter panic on his face. Roman could tell in that instant that Phil actually cared about him, that he didn't want him to get fired—and that had he known Roman possessed the powers he did, Phil wouldn't want him to kill anybody.

So Roman backed down.

He cleared his throat, looked down at his writing pad, and didn't say anything else.

His day would come—he knew that. And even though he may look weak now, there would be a time when everyone in the office would realize just how powerful he'd become.

Lunch was uneventful, but as he was finishing his sandwich, Roman received a message from Paris Renara.

You have an appointment in thirty minutes with a man named Ian Turlock. Judging by his paperwork, and the fact that he is here illegally, you would normally call your security apparatus and have him detained. But I need Ian here in Centralia, so things are going to work out a little differently this time.

Differently? Roman thought back to her. He was suspicious of how Paris could have figured out his appointment schedule. These things weren't publicly known, but then again, she could have gotten the information from the man named Ian himself.

Which made sense, considering Roman hadn't gone through all the papers on his desk yet, and he usually got new appointments during lunch time.

Roman had processed visa denial appeals before, and it was almost a sham that the Centralian government had people "come in to see an immigration advisor to sort out their paperwork with them," when it really was a not-so-cleverly disguised sting operation designed to snare them.

And the sad part was that people usually fell for it; when an illegal got an official letter from the government offering amnesty, they generally sprung for it. Especially since people trusted the Centralian government more than they trusted the other governments in the world, which for many turned out to be a mistake.

A voice came to Roman. *I need you to modify his paperwork and grant him amnesty.*

You know that's not what I do, right? I really don't have that kind of power, he thought back to Paris. He was pretty sure she was using a secure telepath, likely in her employ. It would be stupid as hell to use a Centralian-government-sanctioned telepath.

I need Ian here. So you will need to figure out how to make this work.

Or else what? Roman grinned as he thought this.

Now that he had some powers, Paris didn't have the same sway over him. Whereas before, she could've choked him to death with her weird tongue, he could now fight back.

Need I remind you that I had evidence of you working with a Western Province spy? You've already done work for me, which means you have committed treason. It would only take me a matter of seconds to port out of this country and back to my own, where I could then expose you for what you've done. Is that what you would like?

I don't know how you got the idea that I have any sort of power here, but to be honest with you, I pretty much sign papers and deliver both good and unwelcome news. That's it. I'm a nobody around here.

I'm sure you'll figure out a way, and you should probably figure it out pretty soon because your meeting with Ian is coming up. I won't normally put pressure on you like this, but this is a situation that needs to be addressed.

Why didn't you just have this guy stay hidden? Any time they call you to the immigration office to offer you amnesty, it's usually a trap. Anyone would know that, especially a person that's a spy.

I would prefer for him to be here legally, as it makes some of the work I need to do easier. So figure it out. And I hope to hear some good news from you soon.

Roman tossed the rest of his lunch away, cursing the day he hit on Paris at the H-Anon meeting. He got back to his desk and immediately started going through Ian's file.

Ian Turlock was a muscular man, with red skin. According to the file, he had outward sharp bones jutting from his forearms that he could grow upon command. Roman discovered what this actually looked like on the next page, where there was a picture of both his arms.

"Gross."

This was one of the things Roman didn't like about his job. Some of the exemplars he encountered had strange abilities and otherworldly appearances that made it distracting when dealing with them, like the

Type IV family he'd dealt with that all had fish eyes and ocular powers.

And one thing Roman had noticed about all these exemplars was that they originated from the same location, the Western Province.

"Great," he mumbled as he scanned through Ian's paperwork. The guy actually had a criminal record, which made it all but impossible for the immigration office to grant him some sort of amnesty.

There was literally nothing he could do.

This wasn't like other countries, where you could pay a fee to have some paperwork modified, or you could call on a well-connected relative.

Say what you want about Centralia, but when it came to paperwork, people generally followed the rules, since the repercussions for disobeying them weren't pretty.

An idea came to Roman as he shuffled through the papers.

Roman stared intently at one of the documents, focusing on the letterhead. It was a common stamp from the Western Province, A geometric figure inside a half circle. As he focused on it, the ink started to blotch, and he was eventually able to move the half circle to the other side, rotating the geometric figure.

The next thing he focused on was the red DENIAL stamp on the Visitor Visa renewal document. By focusing on the word, Roman was able to shift the red ink to the margins.

He pulled the ink together at the bottom left corner of the document, watching as it moved from the paper to his desk, almost as if it were a puddle of blood.

All that was going through his mind at the time was the phrase: *I can alter documents. I can alter documents.*

Taking a napkin from his desk drawer, he wiped the red ink away and reached for his approval stamp.

Now this was something he did have.

Roman stamped the green APPROVAL notice where the red DENIAL notice had once been.

With that document looking good, he went about rearranging some of the others. Roman lowered the level of severity on Ian's criminal record. He knew a little bit about the criminal code, mostly because of the training he'd had a year ago, and he was able to put something from a Class B to a simple misdemeanor.

So the criminal record was good to go, as was the extension request.

There still needs to be a reason that the Overstay Committee fucked up, Roman thought as he looked through the papers, making sure there weren't any other marks that showed Ian had overstayed his visa.

His plan was simple: He would advise Ian to return to the Overstay Committee, housed a floor above him, and tell them there had been an error, that his renewal had been approved and that they had called him into the office under false pretenses.

Roman had seen this happen before, and a letter from him would clarify that this was indeed the case.

Every now and then, someone was mistakenly told they'd overstayed their visa, and they came into the meeting only to have the immigration advisor figure out there had been a clerical error.

Up to the Overstay Committee they went, where the advisor's letter and discrepancies in the paperwork would prove that the error needed to be fixed. No attorney necessary, they would fix the problem within the day and the person would be on their way.

This meant that the last thing Roman needed to change was the supposed date that Ian had overstayed.

Focusing on the black ink this time, he adjusted the dates, giving Ian an extra six months to get his paperwork in for his extension. From there, Roman went to his typewriter, where he quickly pecked out an official note to go with Ian's paperwork.

He was just finishing up when Ian Turlock trudged into his cubicle and dropped into the chair.

"Any problems?" Ian said, instead of hello.

It took a lot of willpower—almost the same amount of willpower he'd used when Selena had berated him—to smile at Ian. The man was a monster, his rippling muscles visible under the loose, collared shirt he wore. His silver necklace was pulled a little too tightly across his chest. His sleeves were rolled up, and his forearms were exposed.

They looked even crazier than Roman had imagined them.

The sharp claws jutting out of his forearms fit somewhere between bone and nail, rigid, his knuckles covered in smaller versions of these same protrusions. Ian noticed that Roman was looking at him, and the red-faced man offered him a smarmy grin.

Roman cleared his throat. "Your paperwork is in order. The Overstay Committee made a mistake, and as you can see here, you are due for renewal in six months. Also, it seems your criminal record might've been part of the decision in denying your last extension request, but this can't be true, because you just had a misdemeanor."

"Nice, a misdemeanor," Ian growled.

"So you're good to go then. I've written a letter here that will exonerate you from any penalties resulting in overstay. Also, I've looked over your documents, and I see you have filed everything in a timely manner, which should make it so your case breezes through the Overstay Committee's checks. Speaking of which, you should get your renewal application in three months before the end date of your paperwork, if you so choose to extend your stay here in Centralia. Any other questions, Mr. Turlock?"

"No," Ian said as he scooped up his paperwork, his movements vibrating Roman's desk. "I'll be sure to go upstairs and handle this now. Wait, I do have a question."

"Okay."

"Do I need to do anything with my visa?" He tossed a leatherbound passport onto the table.

Roman opened it to see that his actual visa was still valid. His criminal violation had triggered the inquiry, which resulted in the Overstay Committee reaching out to him.

"This is fine," said Roman.

"Okay then." Ian dropped his big hand onto Roman's desk, took his passport, and stuffed it into his front pocket. "In that case, I'll head upstairs."

"Have a great day," Roman said as he returned his gaze to his desk and the paper stacked on top.

He wanted to look busy; he didn't want to give Ian a reason to linger any longer.

Once Ian was gone, Roman leaned back in his chair, smiling as the massaging cushion pressed against his lower back started up. It had already been an interesting day, and he still had to train with Ava and then meet with Nadine.

He was actually looking forward to seeing Ava.

She was going to be very surprised when she found out he could modify documents.

Chapter Thirty-Two: Rice Centralia and the Leather Dummy

I have to be honest, Roman, I don't know if I should be annoyed by you, or intrigued with the mysteriousness that surrounds your life. And what's with Coma, exactly? She looks like one of those sex dolls I've seen in some of the red-light districts. But she's human. Is she a super?

Roman sat on the trolley aimed at the Lottery Commission. The training facility was accessed through a different street, so he could bypass the mayhem at the front completely, and this allowed him to focus on Harper's message.

He wasn't really sure of the best way to respond, or where their relationship would go from here.

It had been a fun night, that was for sure, but his life was about to seriously change, and he didn't know how long it would take him to get full approval to be an exemplar. But just by the fact that he could now modify documents, he was becoming more and more of an asset to the state.

He needed a little time to process all this, to sort it all out and figure out what his next step would be. And while Roman was never one to turn away from carnal desires, now just didn't seem like the time.

He also didn't know how long Ava's training would take. The fiery Type II had never indicated an end date to him, and after she approved him, there would still be a whole other round of paperwork.

Paperwork that I can modify, he thought as a wicked grin spread across his face.

He needed to go to the hospital. Now that he knew he had this ability, maybe there was something else he could do, some document he could modify to speed things up.

Maybe it was best if he kept this ability close to his chest—maybe he shouldn't tell Ava about it as he'd originally planned.

"Yeah," he whispered, as a middle-aged man got on the trolley and sat across from him. Roman looked him up and down, noticing that they both shared orange eyes. Roman's weren't as orange as this man's, but there was an orange tint to them that was striking with his white hair.

White hair wasn't a sign of age in Centralia, and years ago, when the non-exemplars had been more divided by class, those with white hair had usually held better positions. They'd migrated long ago from the wealthy Southern Alliance, and because of this, they'd been considered privileged.

In the end, and no matter what era, it seemed that every group had its hierarchy, just like in the animal kingdom, and a person's place on this hierarchy dictated their future. At least in Centralia—or so they led immigrants and non-exemplars to believe—there was always a way to move up to the next rung. But the truth of the matter was a little more sobering: the ladder to the top was booby trapped.

Once Roman got to the facility, he changed into gym clothing that had been provided to him the previous day. He checked the time on the wall and stretched for a moment, then made his way to the gym, where he found Ava waiting for him.

Hit teacher actually looked excited to see him, which threw him off a little bit.

He still didn't know what to make of the rail-thin yet busty woman with red hair and black eyes. He'd already sensed there was something more that could happen between them; other times, he felt like this was just another day at the office for her, which it very well may have been.

"You ready to get started?" she asked him.

"Born ready."

"I figured it would be easier if we brought her here."

"Her?"

A teleporter wearing Centralian-government-issued clothing appeared, causing Roman to gasp.

"Coma?"

The teleporter disappeared in a flash and a fizzle of green energy.

Coma was in her gothic Lolita outfit and mask, a shocked look on her face. "Where are we?"

"You should've asked me before you brought her here—before you went into my home."

Ava laughed. "You, of all people, should know we don't ask questions as much as we give answers. Besides, would you have said no?"

"I may have."

"I was rearranging the living room when the teleporter appeared," said Coma. "She told me that you called me here. And I went with her. Was I not supposed to go with her?" Worry spread across the animated doll's face.

"No, it's fine. You were supposed to go with her." Roman looked intensely at Ava. "So what are we supposed to do now?"

"Test her out."

"He already kind of did," said Coma.

The color drained from Roman's face.

"Sorry if that came out wrong."

Roman looked away from Ava, not able to mask the shame of something that hadn't fully occurred—*yet.*

"It's important for you to test the limits of your abilities, I'll give you that." Ava started to chuckle. "I advise against *those* kind of experiments, but you are the sailor of your own ship."

"It's not what it seems, and duly noted."

Ava stopped in front of Coma and reached for her arm. "It really is remarkable," she said as she pinched Coma's shoulder.

"Hey!" Roman shouted as Coma's body caught fire, the flames licking off her form. He raced over to her and tore his shirt off. The heat practically singed his eyebrows as he began beating the flames off her body.

"What's happening?" Coma asked as the flames continued to spread.

"Fucking put it out!" Roman shouted to Ava, and for a moment—a very brief moment—the floor beneath her feet rippled.

"Just a test." Ava lifted her hands and the flames jumped from Coma's body back to her palm, where they quickly dissipated.

The floor directly beneath her also settled.

Coma was burnt pretty badly, and as Roman cradled her in his arms, he noticed that her flesh *was just like his*. He wasn't met with charred plastic—this was actual skin, burnt skin yet with little to no scent. As he held her and as she looked up at him curiously, her body began to reform.

It began with her skin and was followed by the side of her head, where her hair grew back despite the fact that her mask was gone. She was whole again in a matter of moments, partially nude, but whole.

And Roman was seething.

"So you can heal your creations," Ava said, oblivious to his anger. "Good to know."

"You lit her on fire!"

"Please relax, and notice your power dial while you're at it."

Roman took one look at his dial and saw that the red and green indicators had increased. He started breathing deeply, mentally trying to relax himself, and they eventually went back to their normal levels.

"I'm okay, Roman," Coma said as she ran her hand through his white hair.

He sat her down on her feet.

"This is part of the process," Ava told him. "I'm sorry if that threw you off, but the researcher working with me indicated that people with your ability in the past were able to heal their creations—but only if they had given their creations cognizance. Meaning you couldn't animate a bat, send it off to blindly fight, and keep reanimating it. Although you could animate the shards."

"I can think of a million better ways to test this out aside from lighting her on fire."

"I'm fine, Roman."

"I know you're okay," he told Coma, "but that was just very... abrupt."

"Are you ready for today's lesson?" Ava asked.

"You mean that wasn't it?"

Ava stepped aside and Roman could see there was a bowl of rice on the table behind her. There was also a human-sized doll made of leather, something resembling an artist's mannequin.

The faceless doll was held erect by two metal stands at its feet.

"There are going to be two components to your training today. The first component will be this bowl of rice."

Ava took the bowl of rice and emptied it onto the ground, the white grains spilling out on the gymnasium floor.

"The task you are going to give the rice is relatively simple. You are going to have them construct a small city that mirrors Centralia. Pick any district you like, or that you're most familiar with."

She set a small saucer of water in the middle of the scattered grains.

"Your rice minions can use the water any way they see fit. You see, that's another thing, I want the city to still be standing when you relinquish control of the rice. So it has to be structurally sound for you to do this, and as you may know, you can use powdered rice as a binding agent."

Roman considered this for a moment. He would have to give at least a few of the grains intelligence for them to instruct the others to build.

"But there is more to today's exercise than just a little construction. While this is taking place, you are going to animate the leather dummy." Ava threw her thumb over her shoulder, directing it at the dummy. "And you are going to have Coma battle the dummy."

"Fight?" Coma asked.

"That's right. Since you are part of Roman, you have his normal, non-exemplar fighting instincts and experiences, and from our records, Roman has an extensive background in fighting."

"Thanks," Roman grumbled, not loving being called out as a non-exemplar. "And I stopped fighting years ago."

"We've seen this before with strongmen. The fighter may be out of the ring, but some part of the dance is always with them. Let's get started, and don't make the dummy too weak. This is supposed to be a challenge."

Roman sat down on the floor so he didn't have to focus on standing. Even though it didn't take much power to stand, he knew it was going to take a lot of energy to have a fight going on one side of the gymnasium while building a rice city on the other.

He also decided *not* to look at his power dial this time; he wanted to feel when he was getting to his breaking point, rather than being prompted.

Roman first animated the rice, giving more of his power to a few of the grains on the outer rim. He had to close his eyes to do this at first, but once he opened them, the rice had already started to form several lines, a few of them stretching to the saucer of water while the others waited for instructions.

Next up was the dummy. He focused on the dummy and the leather creation came to life, prying its legs free from the metal that held it upright.

The dummy lifted its fists, and Roman purposefully did not give it a lot of intelligence. This was for two reasons: One, he obviously wanted Coma to win. Two, his power dial wasn't looking so great.

(Of course he'd ended up looking.)

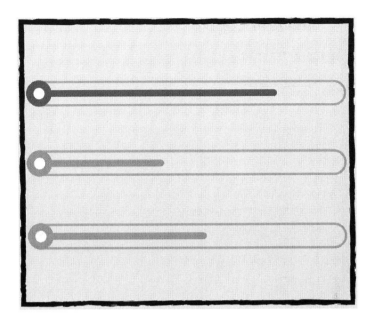

He could feel his heart thumping in his chest and the veins pulsing in his body. He was glad he'd sat down, because until he got better at this, controlling so many things would take a lot of willpower.

As the rice went to work constructing the model city, he focused on Coma.

The petite woman lifted her fists as she approached the leather dummy.

"You can do it," he whispered, his hands clenching up as the leather dummy took its first swipe.

Coma ducked under the punch and gracefully slipped around the dummy's body, bringing her fist into

275

the small of its back. She was much faster than Roman thought she would be, evident in the fact that she was now standing on the other side of the dummy, avoiding another swipe, and then knocking the leather creation to the ground with a kick that swept its legs from beneath it.

Fury in her red eyes, she dropped onto the dummy, her knees suppressing the movement of its shoulders. She began brutally punching the dummy in the face, left and right, the sounds of her striking fists ricocheting into the far corners of the gymnasium.

"Destroy," Roman mouthed, as Coma tore the dummy apart, ripping its limbs from its body, its fluffy white innards floating to the floor.

The fight was over in a matter of moments, and sure, Roman could have animated the stuffing or worked to reform the leather dummy. But his point had been made, his power proven, and Ava saw this.

Had Roman been paying better attention to his teacher, he would have noticed the light flickering of flames at the tips of her fingers, a precautionary gesture, just in case Coma or Roman turned on her.

But he didn't notice, after all, so focused was he on overseeing the construction of Rice Centralia.

Chapter Thirty-Three: A Terrible Ending to a Good Date

Roman's next assignment was one that he could figure out tomorrow afternoon. After changing back into his work clothing, he met Coma in the gymnasium, where she sat with her legs crossed on one of the tumbling mats.

The partially nude woman stood, her hands clasped behind her back. He would need to get her new clothing now, considering parts of her clothes were burnt off, including her mask.

He recalled the flame that had encompassed her body, remembering how terrible it felt to watch someone he knew suffer. He understood Ava's lesson, but that didn't mean he cared for the way she'd taught it.

"What are your plans for tonight?" Coma asked.

"I will try *not* to bring someone home tonight. But if I do, I really need you to behave yourself."

If Coma was ashamed of her performance last night, there was no indication of it on her face. It was odd seeing her without her mask, though, and the fact that her eyes were red only made her look that much stranger: curly black hair, soft porcelain skin, a singed sexy maid's costume, a pair of ballet slippers.

She remained otherworldly.

He placed a hand on her shoulder and mentally ordered a teleporter. The teleporter arrived in a matter of seconds, this one wearing a pair of sleek, wraparound sunglasses.

The woman lightly touched Roman and Coma; they reappeared in his apartment in a matter of seconds, the female teleporter gone in a flash.

"I have to get dressed," he told her as he went to his bedroom.

"Can I help you?"

"No, but I appreciate it. You need to get dressed yourself."

Roman changed into a new collarless shirt and overcoat. He checked himself in the mirror, felt like his face looked a little dirty, and carefully washed it. Once he was in a recently polished pair of shoes, he mentally messaged Nadine.

Where are we meeting?

The message came back a few minutes later. *Good, glad this is actually happening. There is an Eastern Province restaurant I want to try on 21st Street, in the Goa District. The name is Blue Lagoon.*

I'm ready now, if you are.

I'm ready.

Roman ordered another teleporter. "I'll be back later," he told Coma, who leaned against the couch, staring at him in a strange way.

"Do you mind if I go out?" she asked, turning to the window.

"You don't have any, um, clothing."

She smirked at him. While he had washed his face, she'd changed into the second set of clothing that'd come with her package. She even wore a black mask, which matched the heels that'd also come with her getup.

"I look good in it, don't I?"

"I'm not contesting that. It's just that, well, you are dressed somewhat like a super—at least a super tasked with group duties."

"Group duties?"

"Some supers are put into teams by our government, and these teams are used to stop vigilantes, as well as go to war."

She nodded. "Supers war?"

"Yes, and it isn't pretty. Just ask the Western Province."

"How can I ask them if I can't leave?"

The teleporter appeared, a male with long hair that was braided at one side. "Ready?"

"You're right," Roman said to Coma, "and we'll figure all that out soon. Just sit tight for now."

Nadine stood outside the restaurant wearing a tight green dress that matched her eyes. Her dirty-blond hair was in a bun and she had a shawl over her shoulders, the ends of it braided. On her finger was a silver ring with a single gemstone that Roman hadn't noticed before.

"Glad you could make it," she said, as she turned to the entrance.

"This the place, huh?"

"Yep. Blue Lagoon. Hard to find?"

"Not with a teleporter, no. Taking the trolley may have been an issue."

"There's a stop on 20th and 35th just a block away."

"Good to know," Roman said, as a man at the entrance took his jacket and her shawl. The man told them to take a seat, that their waitress would be with them shortly.

"How was work today?" Roman asked, not quite sure what it was they were supposed to be discussing.

"Work was work. You?"

"Learned something new," he said, recalling how he'd been able to modify a document's ink.

"Oh yeah? What did you learn?" Nadine took her seat and the busboy quickly brought two glasses of water.

"I learned something new about, um, document processing."

"Care to share?"

He smiled. "Nothing important, just something new about how I should arrange the pages. Anyway, you? Any teleporter drama?"

"Not really. We had an unauthorized arrival in southern Centralia, from an Alliance school for teleporters, but it was an honest mistake. Still, we had to issue them paperwork. You know how Centralia can be."

"I do."

The menus came, and Nadine placed her hand on Roman's, preventing him from opening it. "Just trust me on this."

"Fine by me."

Roman lifted his hands away from the menu and held them in the air.

"I'm not robbing you," she said with a flirty smile, "I'm feeding you."

"Well, I hope."

"I grew up in eastern Centralia," she said. "There were tons of ethnic restaurants from the Eastern Province. I'm not an expert on Eastern food, but I'm a fan."

"You're in charge. Order whatever you think I'd like."

Their booth was cozy, dimly lit, and the restaurant was done up to pay homage to the East. Looking Nadine over, Roman noticed that her outfit too paid homage; the dress that nicely framed her figure was the same green as the Eastern Province flag.

The waiter set a wicker basket of blackened bread on the table. He poured oil into a small saucer and ground baked garlic on top of the oil.

"Tell the chef we would like a set meal for two."

"Spice level?" the waiter asked Nadine.

"Medium with a tang. Also, a bottle of wine. Do you have apple wine from the border?"

"I believe we got a fresh shipment today."

"We'll take a bottle of that."

"Wonderful."

The waiter bowed his head and was gone.

"So…" Nadine said.

"So…"

They both started laughing.

"You know, I've been looking forward to meeting you for a while, and when it happens, I have nothing to say."

"So you knew it would happen?" Nadine asked.

"No, but I hoped it would happen, and these hopes led me to assume it would take place."

"Well, I'm glad I met your expectations. I have to be honest with you: I've been trying to figure you out."

Roman raised an eyebrow at her. "What's there to figure out?"

"Well, we really hadn't talked much until we met on the roof."

"Kevin."

"Yeah, that guy, poor man, and to think he was saved by the super who was having sex with his wife."

Roman shrugged. "In the end, he really was a loser—a poor loser."

"I thought he was your friend."

"Are you friends with your cubicle mate?"

Nadine thought of Sarah and the fact that she'd taken over all her work this week. "She's okay. A bit annoying, to be honest."

"Kevin was the same way. There was nothing bad about him, but he was just kind of sad."

"Clearly."

"And how it played out in the end…"

"Insult to injury."

"Definitely. Thanks," Roman told the waiter as he poured his glass of apple wine.

Nadine took her first sip and sighed. "Tell me more about you, Roman."

"More about me?"

"That's a cool watch you have, by the way," she said, nodding her chin at his power dial.

"Oh this?" He cleared his throat. "It's nothing. Not a watch. Just a device a friend of mine gave me. He's a Type IV, Class E. Sorry, I shouldn't talk like that in public."

Nadine laughed. "It sounds better than saying he's a non-dangerous exemplar who has heightened intelligence."

"Anyway, it tracks my vitals," Roman said. "He's testing it out on me, so if you see it turn on or anything, ignore it."

"Will do."

Roman took a sip of the apple wine. "Wow, this stuff is really good! I've had apple wine before, but never of this caliber."

"And it's cheaper here than the stuff you'd get at a market in the city center. The stuff from the East is great."

"Clearly."

"How much do you know about the East?" Nadine asked.

"What we learned in school." Roman swirled his apple wine, watching it spiral around the inside of his wine glass. "I know, that's a terrible answer, but not many of the exemplars I've dealt with from the Eastern Province open up about their lives. I've heard of its beauty, and of its poverty. Others have told me it is much nicer than Centralia, or at least the nature is. The cities, not so much. Not like the West and its destroyed cities, but definitely run down."

Nadine bit her lip for a moment.

She'd been in Centralia long enough to know that stereotypes existed, and many of them had a ring of truth to them. That didn't diminish the fact that what Roman had said had been offensive to her—no one liked hearing their country was a shithole. But she knew where he was coming from, and she'd been in Centralia long enough to accept it.

"Do you feel bad for the other countries?"

"I don't feel anything for them, and I don't mean that in a cold way. I feel the same way about Centralia.

It's where I was born. I have an affinity for it because of this reason. I'm not a patriot," he said, honestly. "A person can't help where they're from, just like how we can't help that we're non-exemplars. It's the way things are."

Nadine set her wine glass down. "Don't you feel for your countrymen? If they're injured, or you see one of them being exploited in some way, does it bother you?"

"This is a pretty heavy conversation for a first meeting, don't you think?"

Nadine laughed. "Yeah, maybe you're right. I'm sorry. I didn't mean for it to come up like that."

"Not your fault at all. I don't want you to think I don't care for my country; I just realized long ago that all countries are flawed, that I'm flawed, and that all I can do is hope to survive and not get squashed by a Type II." He lifted his wine glass.

"I can toast to that."

The topic of their conversation changed as food came, and the mood lightened. Roman felt guilty for saying the things he had, but if Nadine cared, she wasn't showing it.

The Eastern Province's food was good—lots of meat, sausage, prime rib, bread, potatoes, hardy things. Stuff with substance, and with that famous Eastern Province spice, which had a totally unique aftertaste that lingered on Roman's tongue, sitting somewhere between his tonsils and the bridge of his mouth. He was completely satiated by the end of their dinner.

Their conversation moved on to work-related topics, from the differences in their departments to their supervisors, to how long they had been in the administration building, to what it must be like to work with immigration for non-exemplars.

Both Roman and Nadine only worked with exemplars, and the protocols for those without powers were entirely different. It was also harder to emigrate that way, especially if you didn't have money.

Roman didn't know what was in store for the rest of the night, but he had a feeling things were going well when Nadine ordered another bottle of apple wine. He would have enjoyed it too, had it not been for the pressing message from the hospital.

Mr. Martin, this is a nurse at the intensive care unit...

The message didn't need to finish playing out. Roman had been dreading it for the last year.

He'd known it was coming, that it would only be a matter of time.

"I have to go," he said suddenly.

"What's wrong?" Nadine asked, concern spreading across her face and furrowing her brow.

"It's my..." Roman gulped. The person's name was what made it hard, the noun only half as difficult.

"Please, if there's anything I can do."

"I need to get to the hospital on 43rd and 25th."

"I'll go with you."

His eyes narrowed on her. "No, I'll go alone."

"Trust me, I can help. Whatever it is, I can help."

Roman laughed bitterly as he tossed his cloth napkin onto his plate. "Unless you know a healer..."

"Just trust me on this."

Chapter Thirty-Four:
Kevin's Request

Regardless of the fact that he was currently blindfolded, Kevin was well aware he needed a new outfit.

It wasn't fair that Turquoise and Obsidian were now wearing body-hugging dark-blue getups, their thighs exposed, with swaths of fabric missing at the back showing the bottoms of their ass cheeks. What they wore wasn't practical, but most exemplars didn't wear practical clothing.

As Kevin had seen multiple times at the immigration office, it came with the territory. Supers weren't all vain, but most knew their clothing set them apart from non-exemplars, which had led non-exemplars to dress in similar ways, imitation being the successful casualty of flattery.

Even though Kevin was overweight, and his BMI alone would have forced the doctor to write him any number of prescriptions to combat diabetes and heart disease, Kevin fancied an outfit that made him look stronger.

He didn't have muscles per se, but his arms were rather thick, so if someone designed a custom number for him, he could have some stitching that forced his arm fat into muscles. Regarding his waistline: as long as his pants were below the bottom of his belly, and not a high-waisted horror show that would give him a weird lump of fat just above his proof of Kevinhood, he'd be good to go.

Kevin had seen some supers—even a Type I— whose powers dealt with their girth. It was definitely a viable look.

Anything would have been better than the hospital gown he currently wore, its back open and his pale, dimpled, white ass visible, a cold draft tickling the hairs on his bum. Add to this his inability to see anything due to the black cloth covering his eyes, and Kevin felt exposed, more exposed than in a while, and this was coming from the man who'd been kidnapped and sex-tortured by poisonous cat girls over the last several days.

"Where are we again?" he asked Turquoise.

"You don't need to know where we are; I've already told you that, so don't ask me again, sweetie."

Sweetie. Kevin liked that. His wife, Susan, had never had such cute names for him. She generally referred to him as Tubby, or Fat Dick, because he was fat and he had a large dick, not because he had a chode. Sometimes she "lovingly" called him Tubby Fat Dick.

So "sweetie" was fine by Kevin.

While the cat girls hadn't given him new clothing, at least the two had been nice to him over the afternoon. They'd fooled around quite a bit, and Kevin's balls felt more drained than they'd ever felt before. He didn't know why the two were so horny, or what they saw in the middle-aged former immigration advisor who was presumed dead, but he didn't question it.

Things were better that way.

The three came to a stop, and the blindfolded Kevin was told to wait outside with Obsidian.

Turquoise entered, and he heard her muffled voice behind a thick door. His nostrils flared; the place smelled like cardboard boxes, like a musty attic.

"We're in a warehouse," Obsidian whispered, her black cat ears flickering. "It's where Paris holds these types of meetings."

"It sounded a bit cavernous." Kevin cleared his throat. "And thanks for telling me."

"I don't know why Turquoise wouldn't tell you. I'm more open," Obsidian said, her tail lightly flitting against Kevin's ass.

He started to laugh. "That tickles…"

"Stopping playing around," Turquoise told Obsidian as she stepped back out of the room.

"Just joking with Kevin…"

"Paris and Ian are ready."

"Ian?" Kevin asked as they continued forward. His blindfold was removed by Turquoise, who kept the fabric gripped tightly in the hand that was always fumbling with prayer beads.

It only took a moment for Kevin's eyes to adjust to the light, mainly due to how dark the room was, only lit by a single panel of glass placed high on the wall.

Paris sat at the front of the table, one leg crossed over the other, a bitchy look on her face that reminded him of his former manager, Selena, who'd been especially brutal with him since taking over their department earlier that year.

Kevin took Paris in for a moment, from her dark bangs down to the tight pencil skirt she wore. He had a feeling she was an exemplar, just like the man who sat next to her, a towering goliath with red skin, black clothing, a silver necklace, and thick protrusions jutting out of his forearms.

Definitely a Type II Class C, Kevin thought, *unless he's killed someone. Then he may be a Type I...*

The two continued talking as if Kevin wasn't standing before them partially nude.

"It really was that easy," said the man Kevin assumed was Ian. "I don't know how this guy did it, either. I know you promised you could do something, but I'm not going to lie, I was ready to tear that place down trying to escape. I was damn certain they'd come for me."

"I don't know what he did, but whatever it was, it worked. You're now here legally. And I hope you

296

wouldn't be stupid enough to attack a Centralian government building."

"Like I said, I was ready. But everything worked out okay. The rest went pretty easily because of his letter of appeal. The Overstay Committee realized their error, and that was that. I just need to file the extension in three months, filing early this time."

Paris rolled her eyes. "You've never done anything on time. That's why you were in that predicament in the first place."

"He also had my felony changed to a misdemeanor, the real reason I was getting caught in the system. I don't know who that guy is, but your hookup at the immigration office is worth his weight in gold."

Immigration office? Kevin tried to parse through what they'd just said. Who could they be talking about?

"And I'm not even paying him—can you believe that?" Paris said under her breath as she turned to Kevin. "So this is the famed Kevin Blackbook, huh?"

"Yes, ma'am," Kevin started to sputter.

Ian laughed, long and hard, a laugh the former immigration advisor was all too familiar with. The big man's tone matched that of many of the bullies who had fucked with Kevin over his forty-odd years.

"And how have the girls been to you?" she asked, an eyebrow lifting. "Have they been treating you well?"

"Sure," he said, not wanting to throw them under the bus. He looked left to see Obsidian smiling, her sharp canines on display. Turquoise had a similar look, although one of her ears was bent forward.

"Good, because we wouldn't want an important guest such as yourself inconvenienced. I see they scratched you some."

"Some" was an understatement. Kevin had claw marks everywhere, on every part of his body. Most were small, but a few—especially on the insides of his thighs—were quite thick.

"I'm sorry for that. They can get a little touchy."

"It's fine," Kevin said.

Ian snorted. "Ever heard the phrase, 'Look what the cat dragged home?' Well, that's what's going through my mind right now. This is our fucking asset?"

"Keep your mouth shut, Ian," Paris snapped. "Mr. Blackbook, what can we do to make you comfortable?"

"Clothes."

"Yes, you want clothing. Any type?"

"Your type."

"A skirt?" Ian asked.

"No, I mean their type, like Obsidian and Turquoise."

Ian squinted at Kevin for a moment. "You want to parade around here in what is essentially a bathing suit?"

"No, I mean…"

"…Ah, you want something an exemplar would wear, correct?" asked Paris.

"Yes," Kevin said, his eyes lighting up. "I've given up on my previous life. I want to fit in better, and I don't want, um, everyone to see my ass." He turned to show them what he meant. "It's a little cold, too."

Ian snorted again, and Paris stared at Kevin for an uncomfortably long time. "Okay, okay. We'll get you an outfit. Besides, you'll need it tomorrow."

"What's happening tomorrow?" asked Kevin.

"We're done here," Paris told Turquoise, looking away from the former advisor. "Call one of our teleporters and wait for them in the other room."

Chapter Thirty-Five:
Hospital Doom

It was nobody's business.

Only a few people knew who Roman visited at the hospital almost every morning. Maybe these visits were out of a need to repent, a false sense of hope, a desire to change everything that had happened.

Goddamn was Roman sorry.

And no one was supposed to be there, no one was supposed to see something like this. No one was supposed to know the truth. This was who Roman actually was, why he had to go to Heroes Anonymous, why he'd become the womanizing fool he had become over the last two years.

The truth of his petty existence.

"Mr. Martin, I'm glad you got here so quickly."

"I'm Nadine, Nadine Under," said Nadine as she shook the doctor's hand. Like all doctors at this hospital, Dr. Logan was a non-exemplar, a male of about fifty-years-old with gray hair and a soft, dimpled smile.

"Well, as you can see, things are starting to turn south."

"Turn south?" Roman gulped. He looked to the hospital bed at a needle that was scratching a jagged line onto a sheet of paper.

Roman sucked back tears, noticing his power dial flash in his peripheral vision.

He'd been ready for this moment to come at any time over the last two years. He'd known it was going to come, that they wouldn't get a healer. Non-exemplars never got healers. Non-exemplars were expendable.

"Two years is a long time to fight," the doctor said with sadness in his eyes. "There won't be much more time now. Maybe today, maybe tomorrow."

"Fuck." With that word, a wave of emotion moved over Roman. He was unable to prevent himself from dropping his head into his hands, tears streaming. "I'm sorry, I'm sorry."

"It's okay," Nadine told him, her hand on his shoulder now.

"She doesn't deserve this," Roman finally blurted out. "I'm the one that deserves this, not her. It was me—dammit it was me."

"Please, you're going to disturb her," said Dr. Logan.

Roman shouldered past the doctor and crouched at the bedside, his vision blurring as he took in his wife's face.

"I'm sorry, honey," he whispered. "I'm just so fucking sorry."

"What happened?" Nadine quietly asked the doctor.

"I'll leave that for Mr. Martin to discuss with you. I have to check on another patient, and I'll be back in about fifteen minutes, okay?"

Roman didn't acknowledge them.

He was looking down at his wife's frail form, a breathing apparatus over her mouth, her head shaved. It was entirely his fault she was here. His behavior since she'd been admitted to the hospital only made him feel guiltier.

His cheating had begun in a red-light district, a drunken night a few months after the incident that had put her in a coma. He had hooked up with a prostitute— one like Coma, who'd been dressed as a super.

His next hunting ground had been his Heroes Anonymous class, which he hated going to. His addiction to the pleasure and escape that he derived from sex had only grown from that point forward, until Roman had become the man he was now, the man kneeling at the bedside of the woman who'd been in a coma for two years.

The woman he'd loved, the woman he'd betrayed.

He cried for multiple reasons: the guilt, her pending death, his promiscuity. Everything hit him in that moment, and Roman could not for the life of him hear what Nadine was trying to tell him. His coworker was behind him now, her hand on his shoulder as she said something unintelligible.

"Celia," he whispered, wishing the words would somehow wake her up. The bed began to rattle, her breathing apparatus and the blanket covering her thin body curling at the ends.

Roman caught himself just in time.

A deep breath in, he tried his damnedest to steel himself and suppress his new ability, his power dial lighting up again.

There was nothing Roman could do. He'd accepted this long ago, and he'd been desperate for a healer from any of the provinces to come through his immigration line. But they never came—they really were that rare. And besides, if a Class H had come through, there was still the issue of his wife being a non-exemplar.

Non-exemplars were rarely healed.

"Left to fucking rot," Roman whispered, each word more bitter than the last. "Left to fucking rot."

Nadine's words broke through to him: "Roman, I have a solution for you."

It was then that he stopped sobbing and wiped his tears away, turning to see Nadine, a kind yet borderline sinister smile on her face.

"I'm sorry you have to see this," he said. "I'm sorry I didn't tell you."

"Forget about that part. I'm going to tell you something now that may surprise you. After I tell you, you will know more about me than I would like you, or anyone, to know. At that point, if you don't go along with what I'm offering, I will be forced to take drastic measures."

Roman almost laughed. His eyes dropped to the floor beneath Nadine, realizing that it would only take a second for the floor to collapse, for her to fall to the next level, where he could pulverize her with the ceiling and anything else he wanted to put down that hole.

"That's an odd look to be giving me," she started to say.

Roman sniffed, wiping his nose with his arm. "What are you proposing?"

"Once I tell you this, there's no going back. With that said, I'm actually…" Nadine bit her lip. She usually didn't have this much of a problem with the big reveal, but there was something about Roman's light-orange eyes and disheveled white hair, his puffy red cheeks, the way he looked at her with resting ill intent… It was making her feel nervous. "I'm a spy for the Eastern Province."

Roman swallowed hard. "You're what?"

"I'm a spy for the Eastern Province, and I've been watching you for a couple weeks now, wondering if you could help me somehow."

It was the second time in the last few minutes that Roman felt like laughing, and even with the tragedy before them, the irony that he was now being courted by two spies seemed like something out of trolley-stand paperback fiction.

"You can't be serious."

"I'm deadly serious," she said, not sharing his laughter. "And I believe there is a way for you to see your wife one last time."

"Celia?" Roman looked to the frail thing in the hospital bed—her shaved head, the way she twitched ever so slightly.

"Celia has been out for a long time, hasn't she?"

"Two years," he said on the tail end of a sob. "Just about. A little less, actually."

"We do not have any healers; that's not what I'm offering you. What I am offering you is a Type II Class A."

Roman raised an eyebrow at her. "A telepath?"

"Not any telepath. This one has the ability to unite two people's consciousnesses."

"But she's unconscious."

"She's in a coma, yes, but the telepath that works with us has dealt with similar situations before. Say the word, and I'll make it happen."

"Just like that?" Roman asked, still eying her in a curious way. Nadine still couldn't figure out why he kept looking at her feet and the ceiling above her.

"Just like that. Of course, I'll need a few things from you in the future."

"I figured as much."

Roman was about to protest when he stopped, realizing that he now had some leverage considering his new power. If there was anything he could do to see Celia again, even if it was semi-artificial, he'd do it, and forging whatever paperwork or whatever else Nadine wanted was worth it.

It could be a set up, he thought as he looked her over.

But it didn't feel that way. And if it was a setup, Roman could end everything pretty quickly by bringing the building down.

"Fine," he finally said. "What do we need to do next?"

"Just let me handle everything from here. Do you trust me?"

"I don't know."

Nadine smirked. "That's good enough for me."

Chapter Thirty-Six: Sleep for Us

Roman stumbled into the red-light district a few streets away from the hospital.

He couldn't really focus on anything, and he felt his feet drag with each step he took. Nadine had offered to take him home, to let him sleep at her place, but he'd blown her off. There was really no point.

It was here that he'd first broken his vows to his wife, on a night similar to this one, with a slight breeze and a fog sitting over the city that covered the stars.

With a prostitute dressed as a famous exemplar no less, which had only dug the knife in deeper. It had sparked a hunger in him, a hunger for flesh that was never satiated. Being close to someone was what he'd wanted, but he hadn't wanted to be close to just anyone, so he'd chosen everyone. And Roman had really gone out that first night.

He'd paid for four women, which was two or three more than he could have possibly needed, and it took a little alcohol, but he was eventually able to pry open a side of himself he had never explored.

Fuck had he felt guilty afterward.

The guilt became a sort of propellant fueling his desire. The guilt, the pleasure, the repentance: a trinity for those who would never recover.

And here Roman was again, just an hour after learning of Celia's condition, walking along and looking at the women behind the large glass windows that lined the street.

All the establishments were set up this way, with large windowfronts that had rotating casts of available offerings. Anything and everything anyone could want, from the bizarre to the slightly normal—no stone left unturned.

Roman stopped and admired a dark-skinned woman whose tits were pressed against the glass. She reached her neck forward and kissed the glass, her tongue flitting out of her mouth as she licked it, her nipples expanding as she pushed her body even closer, her breath now hot against the smooth surface.

He could go in for this, and he was even turning to her door when another sex-doll store caught his eye.

The real reason he'd come here. Roman waved goodbye to the woman, ignoring the pouty look on her face.

This place was different than the first sex-doll shop he'd visited, the dolls nonexistent. There was simply a chair in the center of the room, and another chair across from it where a fit woman sat, one thin and slightly muscled leg crossed over the other.

She was a young woman, dressed professionally, a clip in her light-gray hair and something mysterious about her smile.

"Please take a seat."

Roman did as instructed.

He sniffed, a remnant of the fact that he'd been sobbing just twenty or thirty minutes ago.

A century passed before him in the time it took for him to fully sit.

Roman had done everything Nadine had asked of him at the hospital. It had only taken her a moment to whip together some details. He'd signed the paperwork

312

to put his wife in hospice, and she would be transported there within two hours since teleporters who could move large objects were in demand.

Nadine had set everything up through a clinic in the eastern part of the city, a hospice twenty-five miles or so from the center of Centralia. She'd promised that his wife would be stable, that it would take the telepath a couple days to get approval to come here, that things would work out, and that he should be patient until they did.

And Roman had the chance to stay with her and teleport east with her, but he couldn't bear looking at Celia anymore. Seeing her like that, her head shaved, her body nothing more than a sack of bones, her eyes sunken in, her skin soft and white…

It had been too much, which was another reason he felt guilty as he got comfortable in the chair at the mysterious sex doll shop.

"So, are you ready to get started?" the young woman sitting across from him asked, her voice just a hair above a whisper, yet firm. "You may call me Emelia. And what may I call you?"

"Roman, um, Roman Martin. And I'm sorry, where are the dolls exactly?"

"We don't want this to be a place where you just come in, see a bunch of dolls, and pick one, Mr. Martin. We want to be a place for you tell us what you're looking for, so we can see if we have something that fits your expectations. If we don't, we'll have one made for you. All of our dolls are made in the Northern Alliance via telepathic instruction. It's totally customized, and meant to be a customer-service-based experience."

"Okay. You want to know what I'm looking for, got it."

"There are many sizes available, many ages as well," said Emelia. "Are you looking for someone young? Very young? Or would a woman who is a little more mature fit you better? What about a male?"

"I don't know—not anything young. Around my age, maybe just a little bit younger than me. Female."

It was a strange conversation, but Roman had already come this far, so he just went with it.

"And you are twenty-five?"

"A few years older than that, but thanks for the compliment."

"My pleasure," she said, a smile flashing across her face and fading away. "How tall would you like her to be?"

He thought of Celia, and how she was just a head shorter than him. He stood and indicated the height he was looking for, and the woman named Emelia blinked rapidly.

She's a type IV, Class E, he surmised as he watched her go to work.

"Do you want a woman that looks like me?" she asked, something flashing behind her slightly violet eyes.

"Sorry, I was just wondering about your exemplar classification. It's a bad habit. Ignore it."

"Very well. Do you want a doll that resembles an exemplar?"

"I mean, that's not that important to me."

"How progressive of you," she said with a tight smile. "And to answer your question, I am a Type IV, Class E and A."

315

"You have telepathic abilities as well?"

Emelia nodded. "But they are very light. I can only sense moods and things related to a person's moods. An empath."

"Then you know my mood."

"I do, but I don't know what you've gone through today, and it isn't my place to judge you. Nor will I look any deeper than I've already looked. I'm only here to serve you, Mr. Martin. I want to sell the perfect doll to you, and if that doll doesn't already have a template, I want to create one."

"This is a very strange line of work you have found yourself in."

"It helps both non-exemplars and exemplars get exactly what they want. We have male and female dolls, versions of both, and everyone leaves here with something that completes them. Let's continue the questions."

"By all means."

"What color hair would you like her to have?"

Roman thought of Coma, and her almost white-blond hair. It was almost the same color as his, and if he was going to get another one, he wanted her to have something different.

"Red hair."

"Red hair. Long, short, curly, straight? How would you like it?"

"I've never really thought of that," he told her. "To be honest, I thought I would just see some and be able to pick one out."

"Do you prefer chocolate, vanilla, basil, or cinnamon?"

"Cinnamon."

"If you could be any type of exemplar, which type would you be?"

"Type V," he said, without any hesitation.

"God power, huh?"

"Ever met one?"

"I have not. You?"

"The other day."

"Odd. I was under the impression that very few existed."

"I can report back that they are indeed real."

"Moving on," Emelia said, her violet eyes oscillating with color, "would you rather lie on a wooden, metal, or concrete surface?"

"Wooden."

"What color eyes you prefer?"

"Doesn't matter."

"Are you sure?"

"Yours are nice."

"What type of body would you like?" Before he could answer, she took a bound notebook out of the sleeve attached to her sofa chair. "You can choose from here—top first, then bottom. Also, do you have any requirements for hands or feet?"

"I don't know."

Roman flipped through the book for a moment, looking at pages upon pages of breasts. It was weird, but it made sense, and eventually he settled on a pair that he liked with pointed nipples, a bit larger than Coma's. He then moved to the section of the binder with lower halves. He chose one with some serious curvage, then handed the book back to the woman.

"Not a bad selection at all. Would you prefer to look at art, make art, or destroy art?"

"Look at."

"If it were raining, and you didn't have an umbrella, would you find something to cover your head with as you ran through the rain?"

"I would just run. Faster that way."

"White, cream, or beige?"

"Aren't they similar?"

"Please answer the question, Mr. Martin."

"Cream."

"Last question, and I must say, you've done very well so far."

"Thank you, um…"

"Emelia."

"Emelia, that's right."

She paused for a moment to regain control over the conversation. "Are you the type of person that likes masks and other fantasy superhero outfits?"

"I have no preference here."

"Is that true?"

"Who doesn't want to be an exemplar?"

"I am an…" Roman gulped. "I mean, I get what you're saying. That kind of stuff is fine by me."

"Great." Emelia stood and placed her hands behind her back. "I need to check our stock. In the meantime, if you will wait here, I will have tea brought to you."

"That isn't necessary." But by the time he said this, a door had opened at the back of the room and another woman, this one with a veil covering the bottom of her face, stepped out holding a silver platter. Sitting on the platter was a pot of tea and a porcelain glass.

This woman, who wore an outfit similar to Emelia's aside from the veil, poured a cup of tea for him in a precise, practiced way.

"Thank you," Roman said. The woman offered him a slight bow, smiled with her eyes, and began discussing payment options.

Roman stared at the doll Emelia had chosen, feeling a strange affinity for it. It didn't look like Celia, but there was something about the doll that reminded him of her, a softness to its face.

As he had requested, she had long red hair, and she wore a bandanna around her neck that went with the rest of her outfit. It was a skin-tight exemplar outfit, split by a V-neck that revealed large swaths of her skin, with a belt sitting on her hips.

Even though she wasn't animated, she looked entirely real, and Roman had to keep an eye on his power dial to make sure he hadn't actually animated her.

She was in heels, and rather than carry the lifeless doll out, they'd actually sat her in a chair and rolled her out.

"What you think?" Emelia asked.

"It's interesting."

She bit her lip. "Is that all you can say about it?"

"I don't really know how to feel about it, to be honest with you. I've never seen one that looks this real, though. It's uncanny. But, yes, I'm impressed and she's perfect. I'll take it. Was that response better?"

"That is an adequate response. And since you know that I'm an empath, I concur that seeing this doll has lightened your mood. Would you like it to be transported to your dwelling now? Or would you prefer to schedule a delivery?"

"No, it can come now. Actually, give me just a few minutes to get set up at my home."

"And your home address is the same as your billing address?"

"It is," Roman said, mentally ordering a teleporter.

"Don't you want to touch her?"

"No, not at the moment. But I am very satisfied with her."

The teleporter appeared, a cloud of smoke billowing off his body. He was a heavy man with long hair, and after a quick greeting and one more look at Emelia, the two of them ported away to Roman's apartment.

Coma came out of the bedroom with a smile on her face. She had fixed her mask using what looked to be a portion of one of Roman's ties.

For a moment, Roman wondered where she had learned to stitch, but then he remembered it was something he had picked up when he was younger, and it apparently had been imbued into her.

"We have a visitor coming."

"Should I get on the couch?" asked Coma.

"Not all visitors that come here are into that," he told her, quietly chastising himself because it was technically his fault she assumed this. "In fact, that won't be the case most of the time."

"What kind of visitor?"

"Another one of you."

Her eyebrows rose behind her mask. "Another creation?"

"That's the plan; I'm going to create another one of you. I want you to be nice to her, and friendly."

"Sure, I can be nice and friendly."

A purple poof in the center of his living room indicated that a different teleporter had arrived. The female teleporter held the lifelike doll in her arms.

"Where would you like me to set her?" she asked, no judgement whatsoever on her face.

"The couch will do," he told the woman, and as soon as she set the doll on the couch, she disappeared in another purple flash.

"Are you ready for this?" Roman asked Coma.

"I hope she's nice."

After a breath in to steady himself, Roman took one more look at his power dial, then raised his hand over the red-haired doll.

He thought of his wife, her personality, her constant happiness and the way she always smiled, even through turmoil. He thought of how relaxed she was, how open, how engaging she could be, and he thought of the little slivers of him that had been modified because of her kind behavior—the fighter she'd tamed, molded.

Roman pressed this feeling out of the palm of his hand and into the doll, and as he opened his eyes, he saw that she too had opened hers.

"Where am I?" she asked, her violet eyes flitting across the room.

"You are here with us," Coma told her, jumping to the task of greeting his new creation. "I am Coma. What's your name?"

"Celia," Roman said, choking back a sob. Now animated, there was less about the doll that resembled his wife than he had intended, but there was something there, and as she sat up and looked around the room, he saw a very small hint of his soon-to-be-deceased spouse, something that shook him to the very core.

Roman was by her side in a moment, her hand in his. Coma also approached, placing her hand on Roman's shoulder.

"She's pretty, beautiful."

"Thank you." The newly animated doll touched her chest. "And you said my name was Celia, right? It's a nice name."

"No, that's not a good name for you," he started to say.

"I think it is pretty," said Coma.

"I'd like to keep the name Celia," said the newly animated sex doll.

"Right," Roman told her, tears forming. Again with the guilt, but this time it was mixed with the surprised fascination that he could actually do something like this. One glance down at his power dial and he saw that he was using a good amount of power now, but less than he'd thought it would take.

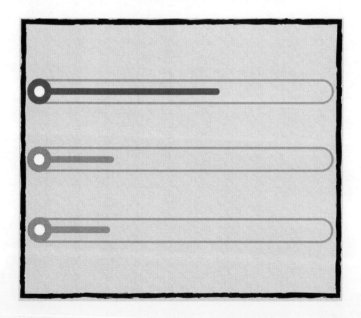

"Welcome to our world," Coma said as she approached Celia.

She stared down at Celia for a moment, an indecipherable look on her face. Finally, she stuck her hand out, helping Celia to her feet. It only took Celia a moment to get stable, even though she was wearing impossibly tall high heels.

Roman's focus again hopped from the doll to his power dial. *Red is dead...*

He didn't feel as drained as he'd felt previously. Even though his red bar was one fourth of the way from maxing out, he didn't feel as much strain as before. Sure, his heart was beating rapidly, but with a few more concentrated breaths, he was able to bring that down a little as well.

He wondered for a moment what Ava would think.

He would tell her about it the next time he saw her, but he still planned to keep his other discovered ability secret. The fact that he could now modify documents was something he didn't want anyone knowing about.

"I'm happy to be here," Celia said in a sweet, singsong voice. Her voice was higher than Coma's, a lithe sound that relaxed Roman with each word she spoke. "Will you give me a tour? Will you explain to me more about this place?" she asked Coma. "I see it has recently been cleaned."

"Sure, and I'm the one who cleaned it. Roman told me not to, but I got bored." Coma took her hand and the two moved around the apartment, Roman's first creation talking about the space and what she'd done to rearrange it.

Sitting down on one of the chairs in his living room, Roman brought his elbows to his knees, cupping his face with his hands. Again, those feelings of guilt and remorse came to him, and he pushed them away, deciding to focus on the present and its strangeness.

"Roman can give anything life," Coma explained to Celia, both of them now in the kitchen. "For most objects, he just gives them enough life to move around, or an instruction for what he wants them to do. With you and me, he has actually given us intellect, and this intellect comes from him, so I understand parts about this world that I never actually experienced. He has also given us some of his emotion. Right, Roman?"

"Yes," he said from the living room.

"Is that how I know that we're in Centralia?" Celia asked.

"That's exactly how you know that. And like me, you probably understand a few things about Roman's life, too. Maybe not everything. Like your name, for example. Do you understand where your name comes from? I learned more about this when cleaning and going through the medical papers."

"His wife."

"I've never met her, but she sounds like she's great. He also has a friend named Harper, who I enjoyed meeting last night."

Roman laughed bitterly. For just a second, he thought about sending a message to Harper and asking her if she was interested in visiting him tonight. But he knew better; he knew he was in a vulnerable state, the cusp of his wife's inevitable passing. And besides that, he had enough entertainment with the two living sex dolls taking a tour of his apartment. No need to add another person to the mix.

"The place seems spacious enough," said Celia. "Do you ever go out and explore? I like to explore."

"No, Roman doesn't let me explore. 'Maybe later,' he said. You like to explore, too? So do I. That is probably part of Roman's personality, then. I don't know. I'm still figuring out which of my preferences and thoughts belong to me and which belong to him."

Roman considered what Coma had just said, amazed that her cognizance and understanding of this world had grown so much since he'd first animated her. It truly was remarkable, and if she evolved this quickly, there was no telling when she would be a semi-autonomous being similar to him.

"Can I try to wear your mask?"

"Only if I can try to wear the bandanna around your neck."

Roman moved to his bedroom to find Coma taking off her mask and Celia removing her bandanna. It was entirely odd to watch: two petite women in sexy cosplay outfits exchanging clothing, one with red eyes and one with purple eyes, one in gothic Lolita clothing and one in a mock exemplar outfit, Coma helping Celia attach the mask she'd made out of Roman's ties to the back of her head.

Seeing this made him question his existence, what his life had become and where it could possibly go from here. Ava would eventually approve his exemplar status, which would create an entirely new series of questions. What type of job would he have then? What would the future hold? Would he animate more dolls?

Could he eventually build an army?

This last thought resonated within him. If he continued to decrease the amount of power it took to make one of these dolls, where would that leave him?

"Are you tired?" Celia turned to Roman and approached him slowly, her hips swaying. She stopped before him and looked up at him, her face partially hidden by Coma's mask. There was a glittery nature to her purple eyes, something he found himself lost in as she looked him over.

As Coma had done earlier, Celia extended her hand towards Roman, and he readily took it. She led him over to the bed and told him to sit at the end of the mattress.

She moved between his legs and smiled down at him. Celia removed his jacket and began unbuttoning his shirt. Coma stood nearby, smiling as it all took place. Oddly enough, it was the type of smile Roman would have on his face if he were to see something like this happening—the exact same slightly crooked smile.

Once he was shirtless and feeling a little exposed, Celia instructed him to stand. She undid his belt, giggled to herself when she realized she had to take off his shoes first, did that, and then removed his pants.

"What are you doing?" Roman asked, a question he should've asked a few minutes earlier.

"I'm getting you ready for bed. You've had a very long and difficult day. I think it's time you rest."

Roman yawned, suddenly feeling tired.

He saw Coma taking her dress off, and he lowered his guard enough for Celia to help him lie down.

Coma unclipped her bra and folded it, then placed it on top of her dress, which sat on a chair pressed against the wall. Her heels off, but still wearing a pair of dainty socks, she walked over to the bed and got in next to Roman.

On the other side, Celia was doing the same, removing her superhero getup, folding it, unzipping the front of her sports bra, then crouching and arranging everything neatly against the wall, nude, her high heels keeping her ass several inches off the ground.

Celia got into the bed and moved closer to Roman, her large breasts brushing against the side of his chest.

One of the things that was strange about the two animated dolls was that they had no real scent. They didn't wear the lotions or perfumes a typical Centralian woman might wear. Nor, from what he had noticed, did they have any scent to their skin.

Their skin was particularly remarkable to Roman. It was so soft and perfect, a fact that he was keenly aware of as he lay between them, one arm around Celia. He moved his hand up and down the side of her body, still surprised that he'd been able to bring life to something entirely dead.

"Sleep, Roman," Celia told him, her voice a shade above a whisper. "Sleep for us."

Chapter Thirty-Seven: Cat-Scratch Fever

Kevin crawled on the ground, Obsidian riding him and smacking his ass with a little whip. He was nude, and she was partially nude, still in a bra but missing her panties.

A feeling of euphoria moved through him. This was exactly what he wanted, what he needed, what he liked. He was panting just like she had asked, and with every whip came the light touch of her tail, smoothing over the spot she'd just hit.

They had moved to a different space, and after noticing a few similarities in their surroundings, Kevin believed they were now in the same warehouse where he had met Paris Renara.

Turquoise had gone out to pick up some better clothing for Kevin, clothes an exemplar would wear, and somehow, a little flirty behavior from Obsidian had led to what was happening now.

"You like when I ride you?" Obsidian purred.

Kevin was also gagged, which was his idea; rather than tell her anything, he just mumbled incoherently, nodding as he did so.

For the entirety of his previous life, Kevin had been a man who'd known three sexual positions: missionary, cowgirl, and doggystyle. Because of the size of his cock, this usually sufficed with the two lovers Kevin had had—his first girlfriend and then Susan, the woman who would later become his wife. The cheating bitch who had hooked up with an exemplar in their living room.

And while Kevin could think these words, *cheating bitch*, he still couldn't verbalize them.

Kevin knew that people were multifaceted creatures, with desires and secrets that could define any number of personas they showed to the outside world. He also knew that while perhaps he was a decent husband, he wasn't adventurous or exciting in any way, nor was he all that good of a listener. A mediocre husband at best.

And even though his mind was spinning at the moment, his nerves firing, his knees hurting from crawling on the hardwood floor, he wondered if any of this would've happened if he had been a better listener.

If the stars *hadn't* aligned, he never would've been on the rooftop; he never would've jumped, only to be saved by the goddamn super who had been fucking his wife; he wouldn't have ended up in the hospital where he'd been kidnapped; he would never have decided to join his kidnappers after they mistook him for his twin brother; and he currently wouldn't be crawling on the floor while a sexy cat girl whipped him.

"Do you want me to whip you harder?"

"Actually," Kevin said, now out of breath, his heart slamming against his chest. He spit out his gag. "I need to relax a second. This is fun, but my knees are starting to hurt."

Without a word, Obsidian stepped off his body and pushed him onto his side.

"Hey!"

She rolled him onto his back and took a seat on the tops of his thighs, showing him an incredible view of her ass. She began massaging his knees, and as she did so, Kevin watched her tail flicker, her puckered asshole twitching ever so slightly, the bottom of her vagina so close to the base of his penis.

With little concentrated effort, mostly due to his girth, Kevin used his hands to aim his penis forward like it was a torpedo, where it brushed against her wet pussy.

Noticing his erection, Obsidian scooted back just a little bit, so the tip could slip inside. Her hands still on his knees, she began moving her hips up and down, Kevin practically crying out in ecstasy.

He didn't know how long he could last like this, especially seeing her ass, and her tail flicking at the air, and with Obsidian now looking over her shoulder at him, her black ears perked, a wicked smile on her face.

This was the life Kevin had been born for.

He knew in that moment, he knew as he orgasmed, and he knew as he gasped out: all the bullshit in his life had led him to this moment. He would do whatever he had to do to stay with the two cat girls. It didn't matter if he had to lie, cheat, steal, or even kill. No one had cared about Kevin before. No one gave a shit about him at all.

And hell, the two cat girls probably didn't give a shit about him either.

Then again, he sensed that they had an affinity for him, that they liked being around him. Would they simply be hanging out in safe houses and getting into weird sexual things forever? Probably not, but if that was his future, Kevin didn't mind.

Obsidian continued massaging his knees with her back to him, his member still inside her slowly losing its girth.

"Want to go again?"

Kevin placed his hands behind his head and lay back. "Let's just see how it plays out."

Chapter Thirty-Eight: Administrative Retreat

The next morning came a little too fast for Roman. After getting dressed, *without* the assistance of Celia and Coma, he would have normally gone to the hospital before work. Since this was no longer a possibility, he got to work earlier than usual.

A definite bad start to a shitty next couple of hours.

Rather than go to the next floor up to help set up today's administrative retreat, because Roman knew better than to put himself in that position, he took a seat at the bench on the side of the building, which offered a nice view of a small pond that had been constructed the year before he'd started there.

He needed to get some paper money. He normally just transferred money out of his bank account via a telepath, like he'd done at the sex-doll shop last night, but that wouldn't work for the plan he was cooking up.

Roman wanted Celia and Coma to find some new clothing, which meant he needed to go to a clothing market, and most only accepted cash. With his ability to modify documents, Roman's plan was self-evident: get low denomination notes and convert them to high.

Easy.

As he sat on the bench watching a pair of ducks land in the pond near his office, their wings slapping against the surface of the pond, the smell of morning dew tinging the air, Roman thought of Celia, the real Celia, whom he hoped to see later today after his Heroes Anonymous meeting.

Maybe he shouldn't have trusted Nadine, but he'd been desperate last night, and the hospital had already had a plan to put her in the hospice.

He'd just sped up the process.

And what would he say if it worked? If he was actually able to meet her, what could he possibly say? Would he ask for forgiveness? What would Celia say? How would this play out?

Memories of their time together flashed across his mind's eye. He recalled her soft features, her reddish hair, how she affected any room she walked into, her kindness, her soft voice.

How she'd tamed him.

He had put a lot of these ideas into Celia the doll, and he was keenly aware that it would never be the same—but there was something there. Something that reminded him of her. And he assumed it was the part of himself he'd put in the doll when he'd animated her.

With a glance down at his power dial, he saw the red bar had retreated just a little bit. Roman was calmer now, used to this type of energy expenditure.

"You ready for today?"

Roman looked up to see Phil Pott, the twenty-two-year-old senior advisor that had gotten the position through contacts. He wore a light-gray suit, a white shirt, and a lime-green cravat—cool, expensive clothing that would only be available to someone who had deep pockets.

Now that he had the ability to manipulate paper money, Roman would probably also get some new clothing, stuff that would rival Phil's.

"I'm as ready as I'll ever be," Roman finally told him. "The retreat we had six months ago was brutal as fuck."

"Yeah, I hate these damn things too."

"If it weren't being run by Selena and her lackeys, I wouldn't worry."

"Agreed. But what can we do?" The young advisor shrugged.

"I guess we can just suck it up and wait for five o'clock to roll around."

"We actually get out a little early today."

"Even better.

"Shall we get in there?"

Roman sighed audibly. "Five more minutes. Let me pass on to you something I learned long ago: The early bird gets the worm, sure, but he's usually exhausted by the time the party starts."

"I want to remind everybody that the importance of our data is paramount. You should be tracking everything you do, from meetings to processing times. If you sneeze, I want you to note it. If you take a bite from a candy bar while sitting at your desk, I want you to note the time. If you meet with a client randomly in the hallway, I want you to note it down to the minute."

Selena stood at the front of the conference room, her administrative assistant behind her, arms crossed over her chest. Everyone in their division was there, including Coco, the lead security for their floor. The shorthaired Type I Class D stood by the door, her hands on her hips as she pivoted from foot to foot.

"Today will be about our development as a team, and your development as individual team players. We will meet with the Immigration Inspection for Fast Travel Powers Department for a group activity, lunch, and then move into breakout spaces so we can practice our collaboration. A few of you lack the performance of your peers. You lack the speed, attention to detail, and one might even argue you lack the ability to do this job. Today, you will be joined by people you can learn from, peer mentors who can help you improve upon yourself. Without further ado, let's begin."

"We're going to start with an icebreaker," Selena's administrative assistant said as she came forward. Her assistant, either named Sally or Sammy (Roman could never get it right), handed out slips of paper. "I want you to write three things about yourself on the sheet of paper. Once you've written these three things, I want you to write a fourth thing that is a lie."

A few of the employees to Roman's right chuckled, fake laughter if he'd ever heard it. The smarter ones groaned, but they did so in a way that was masked by the chuckles.

"We will then read these details aloud, and we will all guess which detail is the lie! Sound like fun? So make your details interesting, don't just write 'I'm a woman, I live in a house, I can play piano, I ate a snorkel for breakfast,' because we'll all know which one is the lie."

A snorkel? Roman gave the administrative assistant a funny look as she handed him his piece of paper. He glanced down at it for a moment, trying to swallow the bitterness he felt as an adult male who had to do these types of things and somehow call it "work."

"Remember," Sally or Sammy said, "three things need to be true, and one thing needs to be a lie. Please don't make it too obvious."

A grin stretched across Roman's face as his pen hit the paper. Once he'd finished, he turned the paper over and waited for the others.

Phil, who sat next to Roman, was the first to go. "As you all know, my name is Phil Pott, and I am a senior immigration advisor. Okay, so here are my four sentences. I like to go hiking on weekends. I was in the Southern Alliance last weekend skiing. I have relatives that live in the Southern Alliance. I once killed a snow tiger that was twice my size with my bare hands."

"Snow tiger," Roman said to the murmur of the others in the room.

"Really? You guys got it that quickly?"

"Thank you, Phil," Sally or Sammy said as Phil sat down. "Remember to make your lie difficult, and don't make your lie the last sentence of your four sentences. Hint: that makes it easier to decipher."

Roman heard a few pens scribbling on paper as people made adjustments and renumbered their sentences.

"Are you ready?"

"Yeah," said Roman, avoiding eye contact with the woman. "Here goes. I am an exemplar, and I have the ability to animate inanimate objects. I can swim. I usually don't eat breakfast. I was born and raised in Centralia."

"What part about 'make this difficult' do you not understand?" Selena asked him. She had the power position at the front of the room, which only made the fact that she was calling him out more uncomfortable.

"I beg your pardon?"

Phil snorted. "It's clearly the first one! You aren't an exemplar."

Even Coco, who was standing in front of the door looking like hired muscle, cracked a grin. The others in the room started to snicker.

"You got me," Roman told them as he quickly sat down. One day, when they all found out the truth, they would remember this moment. "Guilty as charged."

Roman tuned out the rest of the icebreaker, focusing instead on thoughts centering around Celia, and how tragic she'd looked in that hospital bed. He suddenly felt like shit, and rightly so. He'd been a terrible husband; there was no doubt about it.

It was when Selena said there would be another icebreaker that his ears perked up.

Why they needed to have an icebreaker in a room full of people who already knew each other was beyond him, and the second one seemed like it had the potential to actually do some damage.

As she had done before, Selena started with Phil. "Okay, Phil, before I ask you the next icebreaker question, I want to remind everyone this exercise is supposed to bring us closer together. Sometimes sharing in each other's sorrows is one way that we can feel closer. Now, this is a little bit experimental, and something I came up with on the trolley ride over here this morning, so bear with me. That said, I think it will help us all grow closer. And we need to be close, because the closer we are, the better our metrics will be."

"Great," said Phil. "I'm ready."

"What was the worst day of your life thus far?"

Roman looked at her incredulously. *Was there really any point in sharing tragic experiences?*

"The worst day of my life, hmmm, that's one I really need to think deeply about. Okay, I got it," Phil said, and the fact that it had only taken him a second to "think deeply" worried Roman to no end. "The worst day of my life had to be, um, one of my last days in northern Centralia."

"Did something tragic happen?"

Phil snorted. "Yeah, at the time it was tragic. I had my thesis due, and then my buddy told me there was this big sorority party going on, and they were even going to have some exemplars there, if you guys know what I mean, and well, like an idiot, I went. Long story short, I ended up pretty intoxicated and had somehow hooked up with a Type F and ended up in the Western Province—can you imagine that?"

A few in the room exchanged furtive glances.

"How did you get back?" a woman named Tara asked at the back.

"By sheer luck! I sent a mental message to my uncle, who arranged a military pickup. It took about twenty minutes before they came to get me, and let me tell you, I was pretty scared during that time. It's a different world over there."

Roman started to comment on the fact that "sheer luck" and "the benefits of nepotism" weren't quite the same, but he kept his thoughts to himself.

"Moving on," Selena said, a hint of annoyance in her voice. "Roman, you're next." She cocked her head to the side a little, causing her jowls to jiggle. "What was the worst day of your life?"

"Pass."

"There is no passing. You need to take part in this activity so we can strengthen ourselves as a team."

"Pass," Roman said, louder this time.

"Everyone's taking part in this, including you, Coco. Will it help if she goes before you, so you can see that even exemplars have to take part in this as well?"

Coco looked to Selena. "You want me to answer that?"

"Yes, if it will motivate Roman, please answer my question: Coco, what was the worst day of your life?"

Coco stood there for a moment in silence, her fists clenched shut. "I... My family is from the Western Province," she said, her eyes narrowing on Phil. "When

349

I was a girl, we went to visit my grandfather and grandmother, who lived near the border. My sister and I were playing outside when the field around us ignited. A battle had begun not too far from us, a team of Centralian exemplars tasked with bringing Centralian democracy to the Western Province."

"Great story, let's move…"

"I'm not finished yet," Coco told Selena. "My sister has water mimicry abilities, so putting out the fire wasn't very difficult for her. But what we saw next was our grandparents' home had been partially destroyed. The supers had been fighting there, and there was collateral damage." She sniffed, a single tear falling down her cheek. "I saw my grandparents' dead bodies, and that was the worst day of my life."

"Great, um, thank you for sharing, Coco. I feel closer to you now. Okay now, Roman, your turn."

"Pass." Roman said, and for once, Selena paid attention to the stone-cold look on his face. It was a good thing too, because had she pressed them, he may have done something drastic. Luckily, she moved on.

"Maybe we can circle back to Roman." Selena offered the woman sitting next to Roman, Tara, a tight smile. "Tara, what was the worst day of your life?"

The retreat dragged on. A small part of Roman thought about playing with some of the people's note-taking papers, turning them into little military soldiers and having them charge at each other across the tables and fight. But he didn't want to create an issue, especially considering the fact that he wasn't an approved exemplar, which still meant they could take his power away if he did something they deemed a risk or inappropriate.

The retreat continued on, with Selena leading everyone in discussions about their hopes and dreams, and how they related to one another. Of all people to be leading this, Selena seemed like the worst choice, especially since she commented on everything everyone said, from nice little comments such as "That's nice" to mean and unnecessary comments like "Bonnie, you're not going to win the super lottery and get the power to create money out of thin air. That's just stupid."

Lunch was catered, by a Centralian restaurant in the district that had pretty good fare. Their focus was on ingredients that were in season and didn't have to be stored.

Roman placed a piece of the baked squash onto his plate next to a stir fry made of lamb and carrots, which was garnished in scallions. Hoping no one would join him, he took the seat at the back of the room, only to be joined by Phil.

The youthful senior advisor rambled on and on about his family in the Southern Alliance—how they had castles down there, and how Roman should come skiing sometime, but he would have to get his own ticket and visa to visit.

Roman commented occasionally, and rather than engage in conversation, he simply stuffed more food into his mouth.

In the afternoon, it was time for the collaboration with the Immigration Inspection for Fast Travel Department.

It was odd seeing Nadine in this setting, especially after last night, and while everyone was being introduced, Roman couldn't help but give her a sidelong glance, waiting for her to make eye contact with him, to share that sense of recognition.

It never happened. Nadine remained completely neutral.

After Selena rambled off some details about their next teambuilding bullshit exercise and quickly chastised one of the employees for being late back from lunch, they were sectioned off into groups.

As fate had it, Roman was paired with Nadine.

"Hi, how are you?" Nadine asked, as they waited for their other group members to join them. They'd been placed in groups of four and told to go to the smaller breakout rooms.

"Doing better. Is everything still on?" he whispered.

"Is what still on?" Selena asked as she entered the room. "Sorry, Bonnie got sick to her stomach, so I'll be joining your group. Phil should be here any moment; he had to use the restroom."

It took a lot of willpower to smile at Selena. So much that Roman dropped his eyes to his power dial to see if the red bar had gone up any.

It hadn't.

"Who's going to be our writer?" Selena asked on the tail end of a burp. The slightly obese woman had eaten three plates of stir-fried lamb, and there was still a small stain on the front of her blouse.

"I will," Nadine volunteered.

Sheets of paper hung on the wall, each labeled with an empowering word like "engage" or "collaborate" or "together." The hotbody of the group stepped up to the sheet of paper, in her perfect skirt and her blond hair in a bun, looking once over her shoulder at Roman.

"Are you planning to contribute to the group any today, Roman?" Selena asked. "Or are you going to just sit in the back and pretend to participate?"

"I'll be here."

"That's not what I asked you."

"I'll be here," he said again, gritting his teeth.

Phil entered and lightened the mood almost instantly. He was jovial as always, and Roman could sense that he was overcompensating for the fact that Roman despised Selena.

This was why Roman liked Phil—he was a good guy at heart.

"What's a way we can engage?" Selena asked as she walked to the white sheet of paper with a pen in her hand. "Come on, people, think."

"With each other or with exemplars?" asked Roman.

"Exemplars," Nadine whispered.

"Wrong, both of you. You know, I thought the people in the teleportation department had a little more sense. Hmph. I guess not. Phil? Any ideas?"

"One thing we can do to engage is know each other's names and each of our roles in the office. Going to the right person with the right question is better than asking around indefinitely and then later giving up. Also, sending an exemplar to the right person to answer their specific question, to help them engage with the correct coworker, is another aspect of this."

"I'm so glad to have you on our team," Selena said as she wrote this information down. "What about you two? Any answers?"

"We can all go out on dates with each other and get to know each other better," Roman said, casting a grin at Nadine. "Which saves us time to work when we're here at the office."

"Wow, and here I thought you had finally figured out that this isn't some big joke, that this actually serves a purpose. But, like I have been every time I've made an assumption about you in terms of your work ethic and ability, I was wrong. Dead wrong." Selena glared at the piece of paper in front of her as if it were Roman's face.

"We can plan meetings with similar roles in other departments?" Nadine asked, coming to Roman's defense and likely preventing him from cursing under his breath at Selena.

"Good! Write it!"

Nadine wrote down an abbreviated version of what she'd just said.

Roman's fingers twitched. He imagined ripping the paneling from the wall and using it as a projectile to impale Selena. He even noticed one of the panels start to quiver, which reminded him that he really needed to bring his hatred down a notch.

"One way we can collaborate is by asking questions," Roman finally said, practically forcing the words out at knifepoint.

"Great answer, except that we are still working on engagement. Please do not get ahead of the process."

"Okay, one way we can engagement is by asking questions."

Roman glanced up to see Nadine giving him a comical grin, and for a moment, he thought of her as a coworker, rather than a spy who was going to be manipulating him at some point. It was so clear to him. She was standing right there, at the same retreat, trying to "personally develop" herself.

Only it was all a guise, a ruse. Underneath all the bullshit, she was a woman from the Eastern Province, and he hadn't started working with her yet, but Roman was already actively engaged in treason considering his relationship with Paris. Now he was in a similar boat with Nadine.

And this forced an odd, ill-timed grin on Roman's face. He was working with the Eastern and Western Province. How long until the North or the South contacted him?

"What's so funny?" Selena looked from Phil to Nadine, hoping they were supporting her continued belittlement of Roman.

Had she been Class A, she would have seen that Nadine had a great distaste for her, and that the Eastern Province spy had, in that very moment, been contemplating a way to poison her, only discarding the thought once she realized it wasn't worth the risk.

If Selena had somehow been able to skim the surface of Phil's mind, she would have found the young benefactor of nepotism trying to get a peek at her breasts, as he had a thing for bigger girls and had jerked off to Selena's mental image a couple times now.

But she didn't have any special abilities, aside from a little extra stamina, and all she could do was look for support. "One way we can collaborate is by respecting supervisors and being modest," Selena finally said. "Write it, please, Nadine."

Respect supervisors and be modest? Roman didn't shake his head this time, but he wanted to. Damn, did he hate that woman. He thought about rearranging the ink to say something vulgar, but caught himself just in time.

And not a moment too soon. One of the letters Nadine had written started trembling ever so slightly.

Luckily for Roman, no one saw it; they were too busy focusing on ways to engage.

Chapter Thirty-Nine: New Faces

Roman expected a lot of things, but he didn't expect to see Catherine, the Type III Class C from the Northern Alliance, waiting for him after work. He briefly recalled that she was a student at Southern Centralia, that she'd had a visa issue due to failing to enroll full-time that he'd fixed, and that'd she'd asked him out, but he'd declined.

Interesting, he thought as he stopped before her.

Catherine was a bit mousy with white hair, a strand of which was dyed red and braided behind her right ear. She wore the high-end fashion that was common in the North, where it was warmer, less overcast.

"A couple days ago you said something about coffee, to talk about being an immigration advisor. I mean, I could've had a telepath look you up, but I thought that would be inappropriate, so I figured I would come here and just wait for you to get off work. Shit. I hope this isn't awkward. It's definitely awkward, isn't it?"

"It's fine," Roman said as he took in her form. There was a sexual predator in him that was hard to suppress once it showed its ugly head. Staring at the fit, slender rarity from the Northern Alliance was definitely sparking his interest. Not that it mattered, but he had never been with a Northern woman, and he didn't think it would be difficult here.

After all, she'd come to him…

But he had a Heroes Anonymous class to get to, and two animated sex dolls waiting for him at home, on top of the fact that he was supposed to see about his wife tonight—and possibly see her for the last time. Plus there was Harper, who had sent him a flirty message earlier, and Paris, who would likely be at the Heroes Anonymous meeting.

He would have to throw this one back. Roman's real life was a train wreck. He needed to sort some things out before he added another potential casualty.

"Look, you seem like a smart lady, and I would love to talk to you more about this position, and what you

361

may encounter in the North, even with the more—pardon me in saying this—*isolationist viewpoint* the North has on immigration. But I'm absolutely swamped today. And probably will be for the next few days."

She looked down at her feet, which were enshrined in cute ballet flats with buckles shaped like dragonflies. "It's fine, I figured it would be a bad idea to show up like this. What can I say? I have an elemental ability that allows me to utilize the wind, and because of that, I can be sort of impulsive, also like the wind. At least this is what I tell myself."

"It's fine, next week. You and me. What do you say? I need to sort some things out first."

"A meeting with a non-exemplar, huh?" she asked as a smile moved across her face.

"You're the one that came to me," Roman reminded her.

He could tell by the way she was smiling at him that she'd meant this in a funny way, yet at the back of his mind he did think it was odd that she would frame their relationship in this way. This was to be expected of an exemplar, just not in such a verbal manner.

"I'm a little superstitious... Okay, I'm really superstitious, and it feels like what I'm supposed to do," said Catherine. "Does that make sense? My ex was a non-exemplar too. I'm attracted to them, apparently. Oops, I'm saying too much! So, get in touch with me next week; let me know a day ahead of time. I'm giving you permission to contact me now, so do with it what you will."

Roman started to crack a grin, and by the time he could bring his hand up to his chin to consider how odd this incident had been, she was gone. And her disappearing act had been fast, too. The bottom half of her body had vaporized and zipped away in a tornado, the rest of her form dissipating in an instant.

Roman shook his head as he walked to the trolley.

There would be more time to deal with the wind-powered super named Catherine, but that time would be later.

He had more pressing matters.

"There is nothing about me that is extraordinary. I am not a hero. I am not a superhero. I am half-powered. I will always be half-powered. I am a non-exemplar."

The big half-powered named Bill smiled at all the fresh faces in the audience. Roman stood beside him, the first to be called to the podium to tell his sad tale. Since all the people were new aside from the sex-doll guy named Sam, Bill wanted to start off the Heroes Anonymous meeting with something familiar, a fact that bothered Roman because, like most of these meetings, he didn't want to be there.

And his one incentive for coming to these meetings, possibly meeting women, had been nullified by the fact that there weren't any in attendance.

"My name is Roman Martin and I'm not a hero," he said to the group. "I've been coming to these meetings for a while now, and I wish I could say that a few of you have heard my story, but I don't recognize any of your faces, aside from you, sex-doll guy."

"Sam."

"Hi, Sam, great story the other day." Sam waved at some of the others, proud to be called out, which wasn't quite what Roman had been hoping for. "Show of hands, who's new here?"

To confirm what Bill had already told him, six of the seven attendees raised their hands.

"Yeah, so welcome, and I hope this program is as meaningful to you as it has been to me. I want time for each of you to be able to tell your story, so I'll make mine quick." Roman paused for moment, figuring out how he would frame this.

"I, um, was convinced I had the power to seduce women into having sex with me. An increased charm, Type IV, Class C by my estimates."

A few of the men in attendance chuckled. Bill scowled as Roman continued:

"To elaborate, I thought I had this power to adjust pheromone levels and make women want me. So, I walked around like a rooster, my chest out, my white hair slicked back, whistling my own tune, thinking it was my power that was getting me so much tail, not the fact that I'm a relatively handsome guy, fit too, who can be charming given the right type of wine."

"Roman," Bill started to warn him.

"Heroes Anonymous is no joke, and lying to people is a bad thing. And this is how I ended up at an exemplars-only resort in eastern Centralia, near the border to the Eastern Province. I had a friend who worked at the registration office and was able to have my ID modified, so I figured I would pick up some hot supers using my charm power."

Roman shook his head bitterly.

"I guess you could say I was just playing the role, convinced of my own power. I met this one super, a Type III, that had the power to multiply herself. If you're thinking crazy orgy, you'd be thinking correctly."

Bill dropped his head into his hand. "Dammit, Roman."

"That's right," Roman said, ignoring Bill. "Everything was going well with not two but *four* of her clones until her friend showed up, who happened to be a Class A, a telepath, who quickly realized I was just a regular guy, a non-exemplar like all of you. Show me a telepath who isn't clever, and I'll show you someone who isn't a telepath. This telepath was the ultimate cock block. She knew instantly that I was a fake, but she didn't reveal it to her friend, nor did she do anything about it at first."

Concern flitted across a few of the faces in the small audience. Everyone knew what a telepath could do to someone, and an unhappy telepath was even worse.

"The thing about lying is—for me, personally— once I start, I can't stop. It's a weird addiction, to see how far you can go, how close to the truth you can tread. And by that, I mean when you yourself start believing a lie—like how at the time, I actually believed I had some control over women. I had fallen for my own lie. And I didn't have this power, obviously. I wouldn't be here if I had it. If I were an exemplar like the ones at that resort, I wouldn't be standing before you telling my sad tale."

Bill crossed his arms over his chest.

"Almost done, big guy. Anyway, I kept parading around like I was an exemplar, and even though the multiplier never asked me what my power was, which is a little taboo sometimes with other exemplars, I could tell she had wondered what I could do. And the telepath wasn't giving me away, at least not yet, which would've made things a lot easier for me in the long run. She was just watching me make out with and undress the multiplier's clones.

"The law of Centralia states that if you are a non-exemplar, like Bill over here, like you, like me, you cannot misrepresent yourself as an exemplar. There is a clear difference between us, a line that segregates who we are based on our abilities."

A few in the crowd nodded; one man simply looked down at his hands, shaking his head.

"Exemplars lead a different life than us, we all know that. They have different jobs, live in arguably better parts of the city, experience things we will never experience. They're better off, you and I both know that. And what non-exemplar wouldn't want to experience those things? When the 'outside looking in' isn't just a state of mind, what do you do? Who wants to be half-powered?"

Roman sighed. Even though he was making his story up, it was starting to affect him. What he'd just said about non-exemplars being envious of exemplars was true, and now that he was on the cusp of becoming an exemplar, it was even truer.

He didn't know how long it would be until Ava approved his exemplar status, but once she did, he would be in a completely different world than he currently existed in. He could sell his apartment, he could take a job doing something exciting, he could completely change his life.

And as Roman stood there in front of the group of poor souls, poor souls no different than he'd been just days ago, he simply ran out of lies to tell. The lie that had been unfolding, the one he'd made up on the spot, had lost its manufactured veracity.

It had petered out, crashed into a wall, drowned in its own bullshit. Died.

And this was how Roman found himself standing there, a captive audience in front of him, unable to continue his lie. He tried to excuse himself, but Bill stopped him, the big man stepping before him and telling him he should finish.

"Interesting story," Bill said under his breath, clearly pissed off, "and now you have to finish it."

Bill didn't usually bully people at these meetings, but Roman had seen him step up from time to time when the situation called for it. And he never would've thought of questioning Bill before, or getting in the big man's way, but now that he had power—now that Roman was on the cusp of being an exemplar—a small part of him imagined animating the podium and having it attack Bill.

Of course, he swallowed this down before he could act on it.

You're too close, he reminded himself.

"Sorry, everyone," Roman said as he stepped back up to the podium.

"Where was I? That's right, the telepath, the multiplier's friend. Has anyone in this room ever had their mind flayed by a telepath?"

He looked around to see everyone shaking their heads.

"It isn't pretty, and aside from attending these meetings—just kidding, Bill—it was one of the worst things that's ever happened to me. All this to say: I was caught with my pants down."

Roman gulped, pausing for more emphasis.

"I suddenly saw everyone, all the multiplier's clones, as some type of demon ghosts. I was running

370

around, screaming and breaking things, punching at anyone and anything in my vicinity. And this was in a resort full of exemplars, so needless to say, my mania got shut down very quickly.

"In the end, I was arrested. I had three ribs broken, all the bones in my right arm shattered. There was a Type II in the room next door, an aggressive one at that, and that's on top of the psychological attack the telepath levied on me. The point of my story is this: Be who you are, and don't try to be anyone else, lest you end up at an exemplar resort having your bones snapped by a brute of a man who has deemed you hostile."

Roman stepped back from the podium.

"Thank you for that." Bill placed his hands around the sides of the podium and looked out at the few who had gathered at the Heroes Anonymous meeting. "Roman is right: you should only be who you are, and no one else. Also, Roman, stick around after. I want to talk to you a bit more about your story."

Chapter Forty: Reopening the Past with Fists

"You really are something," Bill told Roman, the former still with that weary look on his face. The Heroes Anonymous meeting was over, and Sam had stuck around to put up the chairs, whistling quietly as he stacked them.

Bill and Roman sat at the back of the stage, their feet dangling over the side. Bill had offered Roman a little tea, some herbal stuff from the North that he usually drank after the meetings.

"I just wanted to keep things interesting. No one wants to hear my sob story."

"I've told you this before," said Bill, "but part of the process is you telling your sob story over and over again. It's that repetition, that verbalization that ingrains the message in your psyche. I know it sounds stupid, but that's really how it works, and while I appreciated your story, I don't think it did your case justice."

Roman grimaced. "I don't think there's anything that can do my case justice. Laughter may be the only medicine here, and by laughter I don't mean making fun of it—I mean just laughing at our humanity, the humanity of an exemplar versus a non-exemplar. That's what I'm getting at."

Bill took a sip from his tea. He stared into the liquid for a moment, watching it settle. Roman didn't know much about Bill's backstory, which made the fact that the big man was reprimanding him sort of ironic.

"You know how long I've been running these meetings?"

"A couple years, right?"

Bill snorted. "A couple years, my ass. I been running this meeting two or three times a week for the last decade."

"Haven't you paid your dues to society?"

"There's a lot about my life that I haven't really told anyone, Roman, and I don't know why I feel like telling you right now—maybe it's because you've been coming to this meeting for quite some time, and you still haven't learned your lesson. So, I have a new lesson for you."

"What's that?"

"What do I look like to you?"

"What you mean?" Roman looked Bill over, trying to decipher the meaning behind his question. Bill towered over most people. He was the biggest non-exemplar Roman had ever seen, and his muscles and shaved head only made him seem bigger and tougher.

"You know I'm a naturalized citizen of Centralia, right?"

Roman's eyes lifted in surprise. "You never said anything about that."

"Well, you've mentioned plenty about the fact that you work for immigration, and you can't tell I'm from another country?"

"You and I both know it's not that easy to tell."

"Yeah, maybe that's true. In the end, we are all just the same. An extension of the same person—at least that's what I believe. Anyway, there's a reason I'm here in Centralia, and it has to do with my background and experience. I'm from the Western Province, and when I tell you I've seen things a person can never unsee, I have a feeling you'll believe me."

"I definitely believe you." Roman had only heard of some of the devastation in the Western Province. He'd seen it in the faces of some of his appointments. Whenever they spoke of the West, there was a flicker in their eyes that carried with it unbelievable trauma, suffering, unadulterated anguish.

Roman started to back away. He had enough of his own problems; he didn't want to let Bill put his likely terrible backstory on his shoulders, too. But that wasn't Bill's intention, which became clear as he continued speaking.

"There's always more to a situation, I realize that, and what I'm trying to tell you is just that."

"Got it."

"My situation is pretty—well, it's prettier now, but it used to not be so pretty. You see, you and I share a similarity."

Roman locked eyes with the strongman. He couldn't tell what he was thinking; Bill's eyes were sunk so far into his head that it was hard to read anything in them.

"You don't have to share anything."

Bill smiled at him. "What makes you think I was going to share something? You're free to go; you and I can talk about it later."

"No, it's fine, I was just giving you an out."

"Well, like I said, you and I have a lot more similarities than you may think. So when you're ready to really open up, which will require me telling you my story, you let me know." Bill started to laugh. "You know where to find me."

Roman arrived home via a teleporter to find the place smelling of boiled meat.

"You cooked?" he asked Celia, who was wearing one of, well, Celia's old aprons over her superhero get up.

"We were hungry," said Coma. "And we figured you would be hungry too."

"But you two don't eat, right? I mean…"

Roman tried to think of whether he'd ever seen Coma eat. He was sure he hadn't, and it was only when Coma started laughing, throwing her head back, her eyes covered by her black mask made from his necktie, that he realized what she meant.

"I get it, I get it," he said as he sat down at the table.

"You have to have energy for us to have energy," Celia told him, a flirty smile on her face. "So I made you some stew. You really need to get some groceries. It's like you have no food around here. What do you normally eat?"

"I usually eat out at places. Since…" Roman didn't want to say the next few words, so he didn't, and Celia and Coma didn't press him.

Coma knew about his soon-to-be deceased wife. He'd told her just a little, not a lot; it was a hard conversation to have. Plus, like Celia, she knew some things about him, things she had intuited about his past.

"We really want to get some new clothes," Coma told him as he took his first bite of the stew.

Roman nodded. The stew was surprisingly good. "Where did you get this recipe?" he asked Celia.

"I found a recipe book in the kitchen. It's okay to use those recipes, right? The book said 'Celia's Recipes,' so I figured it was okay to use them."

The words struck him like a powered fist from a Type I, but Roman took another bite and let the taste of his wife's cooking satiate him. He hadn't expected that answer; it had been so long since he'd tasted the flavor of Celia's soup, and now he was ashamed he'd forgotten it.

It just went to show him how much he'd been eating out over the last two years.

"Like I was saying, we want to go shopping for some new clothes."

"Right," Roman told Coma. "I think it's a great idea. How about this? Let's go after I finish eating. You two need clothing, and I'd like to go out."

The two animated dolls glanced at each other and back at Roman, grins spreading across their soft faces.

"Great," Roman said as he took some small-denomination bills out of his wallet.

He laid the bills on the table and focused on changing their numbers to higher denominations. To make sure they looked perfectly like the higher-denomination bills, Roman went into his room and got one he kept for good luck tucked between the pages of a leather-bound book.

He set it on the table and made sure the ink looked exactly like it, both sides, checking his replicas for authenticity. Once he was finished, he returned the original bill to the book.

"Now we have some money to work with. What kind of clothing do you want? Let's start there."

As the two thought, Roman finished the rest of his soup, drinking it straight from the bowl. He wiped his mouth on a napkin and took the bowl to the kitchen, where he quickly washed it.

"Well, what have you decided?" he asked as he dried the bowl.

"I like the clothing style I have," said Coma, "but I just want to try some different varieties. Maybe some distinct colors. And some new masks. You like it too, right?"

Roman grinned. "It's not bad."

"So that means it's good?"

"Sure. And you?"

Celia tilted forward on her feet and dropped her elbows onto the countertop. She placed her head between her hands and smiled. "Superhero stuff is fun. I want some more superhero stuff. It's in fashion to wear exemplar clothing."

"How do you know that?"

"You had a couple comics in your bathroom," she said. "They were quite interesting. Lots of nude women, too…"

Roman started to laugh. "All right, and that settles it. Let's go to one of the garment markets."

As he set the clean bowl down, Roman mentally ordered a teleporter. A tall, lanky man appeared moments later, a sphere of yellow energy oscillating around his body. He had an odd pair of sunglasses on, with yellow lenses, but he was still in the Centralian-government-sanctioned clothing.

"Hello," Celia said to the man.

"Hi," he said, the tone of his voice clearly indicating he wasn't used to people actually talking to him. For about the thousandth time, Roman thanked his lucky stars that he hadn't been given the job of a teleporter.

Being a mule just wasn't his thing.

Coma and Roman joined the teleporter, and they were all about to leave when the man pointed out that Celia was still in an apron. She blushed, took off the apron and draped it over a chair.

"Okay, I'm ready," she said, her cheeks still red.

The four appeared in a yellow sphere, which quickly dissipated. The market was bustling, paper lanterns suspended in the air to provide light.

"Thank you," Celia said before the teleporter could disappear completely.

"Since both of you have clearly defined styles, it should be relatively easy to get some custom things made. I'm going to actually leave you, Coma, with the seamstress, while I take Celia over to the superhero section. Can you handle that?"

Coma smirked. "I won't let you down," she said, batting her red eyes at him.

"I'm sure you won't."

He brought Coma around to the area that specialized in ruffled dresses and assorted Loli accoutrements. A woman greeted them, definitely a Type IV Class C by the way swaths of fabric floated around her, and she bowed slightly at Coma.

Coma explained what she was looking for, pretty much more of the same, and Roman gave the woman several of the bills from his wallet. She took them readily, the smile on her face stretching even further up her cheeks as she realized how much he'd just given her.

"I'll be back in a bit," Roman told both Coma and the seamstress.

"See you soon, Coma, and get something cute and sexy," Celia said as she waved goodbye to the other doll.

The superhero part of the garments market was filled with both exemplars and non-exemplars, which made it hard to distinguish between the two. There was security here, mostly for the non-exemplars' sakes, and most of the main shops were busy. Roman eventually found a place that didn't have many customers, a new shop that specialized in superhero-styled clothing from other countries.

As he'd done with Coma, he let Celia explain what she wanted, cringing slightly as she told the tailor she wanted to look like some of the exemplars in Roman's comics, complete with a strange head piece.

"They're men's magazines," he started to say as he handed the tailor a stack of cash.

"Interesting magazines, lots of great pictures," Celia added. "But anyway, back to what I'm looking for. Something that fits, something that is tight, something that makes me look powerful, and preferably not something that just plays off the color of my hair."

The tailor, a short man in an impeccable exemplar overcoat, merely nodded and led her into the shop.

Three mental messages came to Roman at about the same time he was walking back to find Coma.

The first was from Nadine, telling him that his wife was still fine, that she was being artificially kept alive by some of her contacts, and that the telepath with the dream-walking ability would be available tomorrow night.

Roman paused at this message, the crowd moving around him as he considered it, and he felt guilty for not being there now.

But what could he do? He'd gone through this guilt before, and for the first two months he'd spent nearly every night in the hospital. She wasn't going to wake up, the doctors had told him that. Only a healer could do it, and healers were hard to come by.

No matter how he tried to frame it, he felt guilty.

The next message was from Harper: *You really like playing hard to get, don't you? Kidding. Just seeing what you're up to. Work has been really busy lately, and I've barely had a chance to breathe. Anyway, now that the weekend is here and I can catch my breath, let's meet up. Invite your friend, too; that was fun.*

Roman imagined the telepath that was tasked with sending this mental message to him, and he wondered briefly how many messages telepaths came across daily that left them either confused, disgusted, amused, or some combination of the three.

He messaged Harper back as well, telling her he would contact her if he had any free time. It was the right thing to do.

A message from Paris came to him, and as it played out in his head, a bitter look spread across Roman's face.

You did a good job the other day with Ian, but I've asked you to gather more information, and you haven't contacted me about it. I don't want to make this a blackmail situation, but since that is what it is, I'll be frank with you: If you aren't providing daily information to me, information that you feel would be pertinent to what I am interested in, then you will be in violation of our agreement.

Roman shook his head. He'd had enough of this shit. Paris's message continued:

I am assuming someone in immigration, someone who works for the government like yourself, would know what happens to a person who is found guilty of treason. From the info I've gathered, you have a pretty pathetic life. Your wife is practically dead, you live alone, and you spend your free time womanizing and attending Heroes Anonymous meetings. You contribute nothing to society, you have no real skills or assets aside from your good looks, and you'd be one of the first to go if the immigration office ever downsized. Let's not add treason to your list of accomplishments.

"I'm done with this shit," Roman whispered to himself as he saw Coma ahead, waiting for her clothes to be manufactured.

385

The animated doll smiled, her red eyes softening when she saw him. Roman had a brief flash of what he should do next, but it was just a small nugget of realization. Paris needed to go, and with Celia and Coma around, as well his ability to animate other things—if anyone could make her disappear, Roman could do it.

It was odd, contemplating murder, and he nearly ran into a woman carrying two large shopping bags as he tried to figure out his next step.

"Sorry," Roman said, pushing past the woman, his thoughts returning to Paris.

And if he did this, if he tried to take her out, he would have to have his mind wiped from any future telepath that needed to look into it for government purposes. This was possible, but it wasn't cheap. Nor was the procedure readily available.

Maybe Nadine would know of something…

Roman had a feeling that once he became an exemplar, or an official exemplar, they would put him through another background check similar to the one he'd done when he'd started the non-exemplar administration level. He'd definitely need Nadine's help at this point, and that would require revealing his power.

Perhaps he could do both at the same time: reveal his power and tell her about Paris, asking to have his mind-wiped. It would likely be no sweat off Nadine's back; a dead spy from a different country would matter little to her.

Paris had made a mistake not getting closer to him; had she gotten closer to him *before* trying to manipulate him into serving her, it may have been harder for Roman to make the choice he was planning to make.

We can meet whenever you'd like, he finally thought back to Paris. This would give him time to see his wife one last time and prep for the fight that lay ahead.

If he died fighting Paris, at least he'd get to see Celia first.

"What about my new mask?" Coma asked. It was a masquerade-style mask rimmed in gold, and upon further examination, he saw its fabric had been stitched together with red thread.

She had two new outfits in boxes that had been wrapped with purple paper, which was customary in this particular market.

"What now?" Coma asked. "I want to wear my new clothing."

"What if we went back to my, ahem, *our* place and changed? Then we could go out for a drink."

"We can't drink," Coma reminded him.

"True, but you can show off your new outfits."

Roman had his reasons for picking the seedy bar a dozen streets to the east of his building. He had a reason for wearing a stylized cape, popular with non-exemplars, and his own mask, something he'd found in a closet that he'd used at a costume party ages ago.

It was common for non-exemplars to wear masks when they went out. It was considered fashionable, sexy, and while Roman didn't normally wear a mask, he thought tonight would be the best time to strap one on, especially since he was planning to test his powers.

"It's great to finally get out of the house," said Celia, who wore a sleek, silvery outfit with a circle cut in the fabric over her breasts and a headpiece. Her epaulets matched the blue lines running down the sides of her long leggings, the material thin enough that Roman could make out the line of her boy shorts underneath.

Coma was also wearing her new clothing, a ruffled brown dress with a corset that exposed a good amount of cleavage. She was in a pair of Celia's red heels and white pantyhose offset by the darkness of her dress.

Roman had a lot of money on him—counterfeited money, of course, but enough to live the life of a big spender for a few hours. Which was what he wanted. A distraction, some time with the two living dolls, anything to bury the guilt raging through him.

He knew, even as he led the ladies into the seedy bar, that he would need to see his wife tonight; he felt stupid for even *thinking* he should be doing anything else, yet here he was.

Roman had come to this particular bar for a reason, and considering he had only a day and a half to get Celia, Coma and himself up to speed, he would need for this to go down rather quickly.

And it did.

Roman had barely taken a sip from his first cocktail when a large man approached him, sized up the masked immigration advisor, grunted, and told Roman to meet him outside.

"At least let me finish my drink," Roman said over the live band playing a popular song about Centralian independence.

Roman finished his beverage, wiped his face with his sleeve, and nodded for Celia and Coma to follow him out to a converted court behind the club. There were lights on at the top of the court, and the stands surrounding it were half full with bookies taking bets while one of the bar's waiters handed out drinks.

The man who had called him out stood in the center of the court, his fists at the ready. There were no rules at this particular fight bar about exemplars versus non-exemplars; it really was a "fight at your own risk" type of place.

"You have any friends?" Roman asked as he approached the man. Celia and Coma stood behind Roman, watching the proceedings with indecipherable looks on their pretty faces.

"Why are you asking that?"

The man was a head taller than Roman, scars running up and down his right eye giving him limited vision. Roman could already see the activity around them, bets being placed, mostly against Roman, few people going for the underdog.

"There are three of us and one of you."

The man snorted. "I don't know what you pulled out of the red-light district, mister, but these two bitches have never fought a day in their life." He grinned from cheek to cheek, showing Roman his missing teeth.

"Last chance," said Roman as he took off his overcoat. He rolled up his sleeves and loosened his hands, mostly for show. He would end this quickly.

It'd been a while since Roman had come to this club, and last time he'd left with a couple broken ribs.

That had been right after the incident with Celia, and Roman had been angrier than he'd ever been in his entire life. What made it even harder was that his rage had mostly been aimed at himself. He'd tried going to the gym, exercising more outside, and taking personal days until he got in trouble with Selena.

Nothing worked, until he got his ass kicked.

And he couldn't forget that man that had pinned him that night, striking him in the face, Roman taking the punishment and knowing he deserved it. He'd tried to fight back in the beginning, but it quickly became clear that the guy knew what he was doing.

So a few broken ribs, Roman took those—and in his head, he equated them with what he had put Celia through, and that she would likely never wake up again.

The things he did to forget only etched what had happened deeper into his memory.

Still, like sex, fighting had a high to it, a numb feeling of euphoria that Roman enjoyed.

While these fight bars were frowned upon by the Centralian government, no one did anything to stop them. The clubs paid their taxes, they allowed citizens to let their aggressions out, and as long as nobody died, officials generally turned the other cheek.

"I don't know what you're paying these ladies, mister, and I don't know what kind of sick shit you're into, but if my last statement wasn't clear, I'm not fighting them. You on the other hand…"

"I don't really think you have a choice."

Coma stepped in front of Roman, baring her teeth as she brought her fists up. If the man was a head taller than Roman, he was two and a half taller than her.

The man's shadow moved over the petite woman wearing gothic Lolita clothing as she approached.

The thing was, while he hadn't demonstrated it last time he'd been to this particular fight bar, Roman actually knew how to fight. He'd grown up fighting, mostly in torn-down places like this, but for a spell, in his early twenties, he'd taken it pretty seriously.

Celia had changed all that.

She hadn't allowed him to do it, and he'd listened to her, one of the only people who could ever get through to him.

"You need to get out of the way, little lady," the big guy said.

Rather than respond, Coma pulled her fist back and drove it into his stomach. The man stumbled backwards, fury wrinkling his brow.

"Please hold these," Celia said as she gave Roman her high heels.

The crowd around the abandoned basketball court had started to grow in size.

The people that came knew there would be crazy fights, but usually those happened later, after more drinks.

This was a rare treat: two hot women fighting a beefy brawler.

The man swung at Coma and she stepped aside just in time. She brought a fist into his ribs, and he managed to crack her in the back of the head with his elbow, sending her straight to the ground.

Roman saw his power dial flash as panic lifted in his throat. He calmed himself with a deep breath, not yet ready to make his attack.

"Sending your women to fight me!? Come on, you fucking coward!"

Celia kicked at the man, and he blocked her first kick with his forearm. She backpedaled, got her balance, and charged forward, where she was quickly laid to the ground by the man's big fist. It was a cringeworthy punch; it only reminded Roman that they needed much more work, and they didn't have a lot of time to do it.

Well, Celia anyway.

Within seconds, Coma was back on her feet trading blows with the man, which was causing some commotion in the crowd. She stood her ground even though his punches had started to rearrange her body— no blood, no broken bones, but they were actually *indenting* her skin, something entirely new for Roman and those watching to see.

He saw now that they had unlimited stamina, but they weren't as strong as he would like them to be, and because they had no real bone density, it became very clear that they were not human.

The crowd had noticed it too, and people were already whispering that Roman was an exemplar.

Roman called both women back to his side, where placing a hand on each of their shoulders was enough to reform the parts of their body that had been dented by the man's powerful knuckles.

I can heal them too, he thought as he eyed the man.

"I'm sorry you two had to go through that," Roman said under his breath. "I will finish this now, and we will learn from this. There's a reason for doing this, and it'll make more sense sooner rather than later."

Celia locked eyes with Coma, and they both looked up to Roman.

"Are you sure you don't want us to handle this?" Coma asked. "I can keep going."

"The part of you that was able to fight—that was part of me."

Roman stepped up to the man and raised his fists.

"Finally, the man that has two bitches fight for him decides to step forward. I've been waiting for this."

It was going to be too easy; the competitor in Roman didn't like this fact. But he'd come here to see how well these two skills of his meshed, his fighting ability and his newfound powers.

Roman knew the action he planned to take against Paris would put him on a collision course with people who wanted him dead. He wanted to be ready; he also wanted to see the real Celia.

He needed to make this quick.

The man's belt began tightening around his waist.

He dropped his hands to it, trying to figure out what was happening. It didn't take long for the belt to slither around the man's body like a snake, where it wrapped around his neck and quickly tightened, his face turning red.

This got the attention of a couple men on the sidelines, men who worked for the club and were there to make sure the violence didn't turn to sudden death.

Roman showed everyone his palms, and the belt fell to the ground, the big man wrapping his hands around his throat as he coughed.

"You're… you're a fucking exemplar."

"We can end this here," Roman told him.

There was a reason Roman wore a mask, and that reason had presented itself.

A guy with white hair, orange eyes, and a mask could be any type of exemplar, as many of them had odd features. Not that he thought anyone would rat him out—that was a punishable offense in a place like this. But he wanted to play it safe.

Which was also why he stepped back, allowing the man to decide if he wanted to take this any further.

"Step aside," Roman heard a booming voice say.

Emerging from the shadows was a huge man with red skin, his forearms covered in fragmented bits of bone-like armor.

Roman recognized him immediately: Ian Turlock, the man whose immigration paperwork he'd changed using his abilities.

Ian was clearly drunk, evident in the way he staggered and the glaze over his eyes.

He didn't recognize Roman, which was a damn good thing, because this was the exact type of challenge Roman had been looking for—a way for him to truly cut his teeth.

Not wanting to get involved with two exemplars, Roman's original opponent disappeared into the crowd, cursing under his breath that he'd been tricked by the superpowered.

"Are you ready?" Ian took off his shirt, revealing a muscled body covered in bone and keratin armor.

It was disturbing to look at, and as Ian loosened up, the protrusions began to grow from his forearms.

He punched his fists together, slapped himself a few times, snorted and spat.

Ian nodded, indicating he was ready.

"Coma, take care of Celia." And without saying another word, Roman powered Celia down. Coma caught her just in time, holding the limp sex doll in her arms.

A few in the crowd gasped; others simply placed more bets.

It was a cheap trick, but it had worked with the other men, so Roman went for it.

The ground beneath Ian rumbled. Rather than lose his balance, the towering man caught himself and exploded towards Roman.

If it hadn't been for Coma, Ian's attack would have taken Roman's head off.

Coma pressed forward just in time, leaving Celia to fall to the ground.

She shoved Roman out of the way and took the brunt of Ian's hit, squeaking as she flew backwards into the stands.

"Coma!"

The wooden planks ripped off the frame of the stands, morphing together and forming a tripod, which galloped over to Ian and began striking him with its wooden legs.

Ian blocked the attacks with his arms, his protrusions tearing through the wood, showering the air with splinters.

Roman tried rumbling the ground again, which only seemed to piss Ian off even more, the big guy clearly able to adjust his balance on a dime.

Since Ian wore pants, Roman animated his pants, which tore off his body and tried to strangle him. Even while being beaten by the tripod, Ian managed to rip his attacking pants to shreds.

"I thought you wanted to fight me!" Ian, now in his boxer briefs, smashed what was left of the wooden tripod and moved towards Roman, murder in his eyes.

Roman pulled all the concrete up, paying no attention to his power dial, and slapped it against Ian, wrapping him in it like he was rolling him up in a blanket. He twisted the ends of the concrete, temporarily preventing Ian from escaping.

The red bar on his power dial flashing, Roman stumbled towards Celia and Coma, realizing that Coma had actually been split in two by Ian's punch.

"Fuck," he cried out, then grabbed her lower half and dragged it over towards Celia and the rest of Coma.

One more glance at the crowd, their cries for death, and back to Ian, who was seconds away from breaking free of the concrete that enveloped his body.

Roman called a telepath; he was in over his head.

Chapter Forty-One: Two Assets in One Week

Nadine always checked over her shoulder. It was a habit, a paranoia with true implications. Once she was sure she wasn't being tailed, she knocked on the door and waited for the slit to open.

She was greeted yet again by Oscar's dark-purple eyes.

"Long time no see," said Oscar as he let her in. As always, he stood in the shadows, his presence felt but hardly seen, the communicator likely in some of Centralia's finest clothing.

"I can't find you. Where are you?" Nadine joked with him.

"You always have to make a comment when you come in here, don't you?"

"I think it's the shadow act. It's a little… much?"

Oscar stepped out of the shadows and Nadine saw that as usual, he wore a three-piece suit, an emerald cravat that matched his pocket square, and a pair of polished shoes with golden buckles.

"I never tell you how to do your job," he said, walking across the room to his seat. Nadine followed and sat next to him. She caught a glimpse of his necklace as he sat down, the one that granted him telepathic abilities, a way to communicate with the East that wouldn't be picked up by Centralian authorities.

This was one of the interesting things about man-made exemplar-granting jewelry. In a way, it was even more powerful than many exemplars themselves, especially the stuff from the East. This was precisely the reason that any of Centralia's network of telepaths looking for secret messages could not find Oscar's communications.

It was also the reason Nadine's power-canceling Zero Ring worked so well.

She glanced down at the ring while Oscar got into place, slowing his breath as his necklace activated. Her ring was silver, with a single blue gem on it, which acted as the absorbing factor. These rare gemstones were only mined in the East, and it was by accident one of their scientists had discovered their absorption abilities.

The scar on Nadine's side would have led to her death had it not been for the ring. She'd received the scar in a battle with a super that could morph his arms into long blades. He had reached her skin, that was for sure, but the scar stopped adjacent to her navel because she had instinctively activated the ring.

It was a painful injury to heal from, but if it hadn't been for the ring…

"I'm ready," Oscar announced.

"Great, I'll start with what I uncovered using the abilities of Lisa Painstake, the Type IV, Class D who is now one of my assets…"

Nadine went on to explain about the high number of prisoners from the East, much higher than their estimated numbers. The problem was the reporting, as many of the families hadn't come forward to the Eastern Province authorities and told them about their missing loved ones.

Yet another thing that Nadine didn't like about the East: its citizens were paranoid to the point that they didn't report issues to their government, fearing the government was behind the issues. And true, maybe the Eastern Province government from fifty years ago had been more authoritarian, but the government now had a single focus, and that focus was getting ahead of Centralia.

Once Oscar had transmitted the information, including estimated numbers and other details of Nadine's work, he sighed miserably, dropping his head into his hand.

"What is it?"

"That's just so many," he mumbled. "I believe it is three times more than we originally assumed. And no one has reported their disappearances. Predictable, but at those numbers, you'd think we'd know more."

The disappointment in his voice was twofold: Oscar had been assigned to Centralia for years, and he liked the place. Realizing that Centralia wasn't as squeaky clean as it tried to look on the surface always disappointed him. He also felt terrible for his countrymen, who could be any number of places now, from forced labor camps to early graves.

"I am working on a second asset," Nadine said, interrupting his moment of silence. "His name is Roman Martin."

Nadine went on to explain what she knew about Roman, how she'd stumbled upon his biggest secret, and that she had decided to leverage it.

"And you've already reported all this."

"Emergency reporting through an encrypted message. We have to use the dream-walker for this one."

She had never actually met this telepath, only heard of the woman's powers, definitely a Type I.

"Ah, Abby. Careful there."

"Is there something I should know?"

"Dream-walking can be complicated, that's all I'll say. Regardless, it is an interesting development, and you've managed to secure two assets in under a week." The dark cast an arc of blackness over his face, his purple eyes still shining bright. "The coincidences in this line of work never cease to amaze me. And you're saying none of the intel you received on Roman led you to believe his wife was in this condition?"

"There wasn't anything on it. Even the administrative records I was able to look through had nothing about it."

"And who put her in this condition?"

"Apparently, he did. Or it was an action he took, which is why he's currently enrolled in Heroes Anonymous—which, as you know, is in the records we've examined from administrative offices. From what I can tell, he would do anything for his dying wife, which gives us leverage."

Nadine gulped. She'd been at this job long enough to forgo feelings of guilt. Everyone had a skeleton in their closet, and exploiting that skeleton came with the territory.

That said, she wasn't proud of what she was doing. But she hadn't taken this job to be proud, she'd taken it to better her country, and eventually her family.

Even though she was never allowed to see them again. If it would better her country, and if it would help others, she was thoroughly prepared to abide by the Eastern Province's rules.

A message came in from Roman, telling her he wanted to see his wife tonight. She relayed this message to Oscar, who simply nodded.

"Now is the time to build bridges, to secure your assets indefinitely. You are doing well, Nadine, and I'm sure your handler is pleased."

Chapter Forty-Two: Trust by Default

"Are you okay?" Roman asked Coma, his hands on her delicate shoulders. The moon was out, adding a touch of pale blue to the streets.

He had healed her, and she looked just as beautiful as she had before the fight had started, but he wasn't sure if she was all right or not. This was the human in him thinking, not the exemplar. He had the power to animate inanimate objects, and this power had bloomed into several other incarnations, including the ability to return something to its original form, and the ability to manipulate ink and paper and whatever he'd like.

It was hard to process all this, as his power was only a few days old and continuing to offer him surprises.

"I'll be fine," she said, placing her soft palm on his cheek.

Celia stood near the two, a concerned look on her face. They were standing on a random street, a darker one, as Roman hadn't had a lot of time to pick a place to teleport. He'd just thrown out numbers of the streets toward the east, choosing the street near the restaurant he'd dined at with Nadine.

One glance at his power dial and he saw that the red bar wasn't as full as it normally was, which meant he was getting better and better at managing two entities.

His heart rate had gone down some as well, which had also attributed to the dial's current listing.

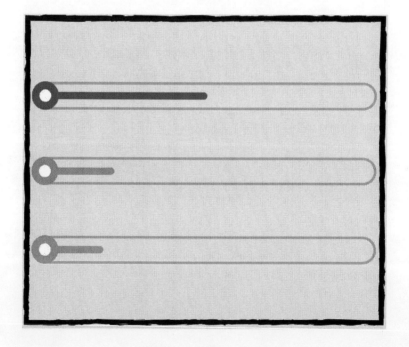

Things were going to be interesting once he got three dolls, and Roman had a feeling that soon he'd have a small entourage of them. The question then remained: what would he do with them?

And if they were taking bits of his personality every time he created one, what would happen if one of them took his darker side? And more importantly, or at least equally importantly, what would happen once he created an army? Would Centralia step in?

Maybe it was a bad idea to meet Nadine with the two, but he'd already briefed the dolls on what to say if they ever met anyone he knew. They were friends, that was all. Since no one could read their minds, and they looked entirely human, Roman wasn't too worried about Nadine's reaction.

Besides, if Nadine and Roman ever got any closer, or if she came to his home, they would be there and then he would have to explain them anyway.

He figured he should just get it out of the way now. He was tired of wearing a mask; and he had already cast the one he'd been wearing in the fight against Ian into a street-side garbage bin.

Roman ran his hand through his white hair.

He hadn't been injured in the last fight but he had come close to injury, which was a little unsettling, especially because an attack by Ian Turlock would definitely throw a wrench in his plans.

Roman shuddered as he thought of the man's flesh, the way his keratin protrusions jutted out of his arms. There were some weird powers out there, and Roman had seen a good many in his line of work, but Ian's was definitely one of the more gruesome.

A teleporter appeared and next to her was Nadine, who looked simply stunning in her tight gray dress, shawl, and her blond hair in a bun.

She smiled at Roman, her green eyes softening until she saw Coma and Celia.

"And these are?"

"Friends," Celia said.

"Friends of Celia," Coma said.

"I'm Celia," said Celia. "Not Roman's Celia. But Coma is referring to Roman's Celia. We are her friends. Good friends. Really good friends."

"I see." Nadine's eyebrow lifted, but not as much as Roman's would have had he encountered a similar situation.

"That's right," said Roman. "All of us are here to see her. We can discuss other matters later."

Nadine nodded, knowing all too well what he was referring to. "In that case, I will call a teleporter."

As they waited for the teleporter to appear, Nadine casually glanced to Celia and Coma, her face never quite showing that she was curious about the two.

Roman knew the situation was a little awkward, but he was fine with that. He had a strange desire to show them to his dying wife, even though she wouldn't be able to see them. Call it morbid, but it had taken some part of him to make the two, and he was proud of them. His new power truly was amazing.

A wave of sadness rolled over Roman, followed by guilt and shame that he'd gone out that night rather than go to her.

He swallowed it down just about the time the teleporter appeared, a female teleporter with emerald-green clothing, indicating she wasn't licensed.

Roman didn't pry, but he figured she worked for Eastern forces that were embedded in Centralia.

She lifted both arms wide; Roman and Nadine touched her right arm, Coma and Celia her left.

A prism formed above them, and they zipped into it, reappearing in a large waiting room with a nurse's station against the wall. A dimly lit space, not unlike the moonlit streets outside.

Roman stepped forward. "It's better than I thought. Dark, but cozy."

"Did you think I was going to have her put in a warehouse or something?" Nadine asked after the teleporter had vanished.

"I had no idea what you would do with her." He felt foolish saying it like this, so he corrected himself. "I mean, I didn't know what to expect."

"Do you trust me?"

"Sure."

Something about the way Nadine smiled at him made Roman feel like he should trust her, even though part of him knew it was a terrible idea.

"You trusted me enough to let me handle your wife's transfer."

"You're right, I trust you."

"Do you trust me?" Celia asked Coma, her voice just a hair above a whisper.

"I don't know. I never really thought about trusting you. I've never had to conceptualize trusting you. I trust you by default."

"Trust by default. Makes sense."

Roman paused for a moment, listening to them converse.

He'd been so wrapped up in his own bullshit that he hadn't really paid attention to the conversations they'd been having around him. It was something he wanted to do more of. The duo was entirely odd, alien—and judging by what they were talking about right now, they were oddly comical.

A nurse walked out from one of the rooms at the end of the hallway. She was short and stout, her hair

415

braided, her sleeves rolled up. From a distance, she looked like she'd be hard to deal with, but as she approached, a smile moved across her face that put Roman at ease.

"And you're the husband?" she asked.

"I am."

"Dr. Lobby," she said, extending her hand. "If you follow me, I will brief you on your wife's condition. I'm the type of doctor that likes to be upfront rather than beat around the bush. I hope that's okay. I don't want to give you any false hopes."

"He's aware of what's going on," Nadine told her, "and thanks, Leah."

"Great, then you know that her bodily functions are starting to shut down. It could take another day for her to completely pass, but she's on the way out. Is there anything spiritual you would like to happen while we have her here?"

"Anything spiritual?" Roman crossed his arms over his chest. He looked down at the ground, his brow furrowing. Celia had never been spiritual, nor had he. But now that he was in this situation, he wondered if the prayer, or possibly a priest, would be a good thing.

"We can arrange whatever you would like," Dr. Lobby said as she motioned him down the hall.

"I think we'll be fine," he ultimately said.

Celia and Coma stopped talking as they got in line behind Nadine, both judging the situation to be rather dire and adjusting accordingly.

As they entered the room, Dr. Lobby kept talking, going over vitals and other information she had monitored over the last twenty-four hours, but Roman had tuned her out by this point. His only focus was on Celia, who was tucked under a white blanket, her mouth agape.

He went to her immediately, taking her frail hand. It seemed cold, her skin pale, the veins visible on her arms.

This is your fault, a voice whispered at the back of his head, *your fault.*

"I need a moment," Roman managed to say, interrupting the doctor and Nadine.

"By all means," said Dr. Lobby as she made her way to the door. "And your, um, visitors?"

"They stay," Roman said. "Thanks."

417

Nadine shut the door, leaving Roman and the two dolls with Celia.

"It's been almost two years," he began to tell his wife. "Two very long years. And as you know, as I told you, I've done a lot of terrible things. Things I'm not proud of. I wish there were a better place for me to make these confessions besides the hospital. I mentioned to you a few days back that I had won a superpower. That's my luck, right?"

He tried to smile at his comatose wife, imagining her response.

"It was entirely by coincidence, you know. Kevin would have had this power if he hadn't tried to commit suicide due to his wife cheating on him. And here I am, the biggest cheat of them all, judging Kevin's widowed wife." Roman laughed bitterly. "I guess we all make mistakes; I guess we all have to scratch the itch. But I'm going to make a difference."

Roman looked up to Celia, focusing all his energy to the center of his forehead, hoping that she could hear him—if not with her ears, then telepathically.

"I've been granted this power." He bent forward a bit and brought her limp hand to his lips. "And I think it

418

is a better power than I could've ever imagined. They said I was a Type II, but I believe with time this may be a Type I, and maybe even a Type V. Funny, remember that time I ranted about the fact that there was a Type I, and it was considered the most powerful, but there was a hidden type, Type V, which is actually more powerful and makes no sense numerically? That still bothers me. Types I and II are powerful, III not so much, IV not powerful at all. Then Type V is the ultimate power."

He stopped speaking for a moment, and relaxed his grip on her hand. He was squeezing too tight, and he could see that now.

"Anyway, sorry to ramble. The point I'm trying to make is that this ability I've been granted is incredibly powerful. I've already discovered some things about it that would shock you. I know you can't see them, but here's one of the things I've been able to do. Coma, Celia, named after you, of course, please step up."

"Hi, Roman's Celia," said Coma. There was an inflection to her voice, something that told Roman she felt empathy.

"It's nice to finally meet you," said Celia, sniffing back a tear. Roman wasn't sure if she could cry or not, but she sure seemed sad.

"So this is my power," said Roman. "And I don't know its limitations yet. I'm sorry you're not here to see me changing this way, not able to see me become more powerful. Not that power even matters to me— but I'm going to make a difference with it. I don't know what the difference is, but…" He took a deep breath. "I promise you."

The thought came to Roman: Would he live up to the promise he'd just made to his wife? Would the womanizing slacker with a dark secret be able to turn his life around and contribute to the greater good?

He shook his head, realizing the answer may be nuanced. Centralia had good guys, but oftentimes, the good guys were bad guys good at branding. Not that Roman hadn't seen true heroes before—they did exist. But he had this feeling he would find out that exemplars and non-exemplars, even with their separate-but-equal status, lived similar lives.

He bent forward and kissed Celia on the cheek, noticing that Coma had gone to the other side of the bed to hold her other hand. Celia the doll simply stood off to the side, wiping her face every now and again, her purple eyes bulging with sadness.

It was hard for him to really come to grips with what he had created.

He was giving these two dolls life, and he knew he would give life to more. But with the creation came great responsibility, and watching them fight for him earlier and get injured only added to the gravity of this realization.

"I promise to do better, Celia," he said, internalizing it. "I know you won't see me later on, but you will be surprised. I will do better. I will make a difference in this world. I will use my power in a way that will make you proud."

Roman thought for a moment that Celia's face twitched, that she was acknowledging him. He'd experienced this several times before, and each time her action had given him false hope.

He dropped her hand and stepped away. Roman would spend the rest of the night in the room with her. He would go over his plans, steel himself, and power both the dolls down so he could be alone.

The next day would come, and Roman would be ready for it.

He wouldn't beat himself up any longer over the past, over the mistakes he'd made. It would be hard, and there were times when these feelings would come to the surface, but he would fight them.

At some point in the night, Roman began to feel lonely. Unable to fit on the bed with his wife, he gave life to Celia the doll. She approached him and crawled into his arms.

He sat now in the single chair in the room, Nadine and the doctor not disturbing him, Coma powered down with her back against the wall.

Roman held on to Celia the doll, his eyes closed, imagining she was someone else.

It helped. Roman had come into this world alone, and now that he could give pieces of himself to his creations, he would never be alone again.

"What are you thinking about?" Celia whispered, the only other sound in the room being an ink pen scratching on a piece of paper, monitoring his wife's vitals.

"The past, and the future."

"What about the present?"

Celia pressed back, a strand of her red hair falling into her face. She swept it aside and offered Roman a soft grin, a grin that reminded him of the way...

He swallowed that last thought. "The present dies every minute."

It was time to move on. Sure, there would be a period of mourning, but as he said, the past and the future were all that mattered.

And for Roman to ever make good with himself, and with what had happened to his soon-to-be deceased wife, the future was his only refuge.

"Rest, if you can," said Celia, hugging Roman. "You deserve it."

"I don't deserve anything."

Chapter Forty-Three: Will the Real Kevin Blackbook Please Stand Up?

"You're late," Paris told Ian Turlock.

The dark-haired Western Province spy stood a block away from Kevin Blackbook's brother's sizeable home. The mansion was in the Amor District, where the wealthiest non-exemplars lived, and while his home wasn't the largest she'd seen in Centralia, it was definitely one of the newest and nicest.

"Sorry," said Ian, a not-so-sorry smile on his face. "I got in a fight, and I had to teleport home for new clothes."

Paris sighed, the slight hint of alcohol reaching her nose. She took in Ian's form: big, red, wearing all black, his necklace the only thing gleaming on his hardened, crusty body. She liked having a typical strongman around, but his appearance made him stand out, which was a terrible thing. "Why are you fighting?"

"Men are supposed to fight."

She rolled her eyes. "Spare me the macho bullshit."

"It wasn't a fight I could get in trouble for. I was at one of the fighting bars, and like I said, men are supposed to fight."

"Kevin's security has been handled, and we were supposed to be in twenty minutes ago. Now we are running out of time before the next security apparatus arrives."

"It still bothers me that they share the same name."

Paris paused. "What?"

"Our Kevin, and his brother, also Kevin. Just confuses me."

"Why is this important right now, of all times?"

Ian burped. "Yeah, you're right. Their parents should have handled it years ago. Let's do this." The big man turned towards Kevin's gate, stomping down the street, oblivious to everything around him. He was a terrible spy—but then again, he wasn't a spy, just more or less a muscled mule for spies from the West.

Still, Paris was glad the district was quiet, and the only thing on the street was an occasional trolley.

The two stopped in front of Kevin's gate and slipped inside. It was already open, from the earlier siege, a siege Paris hadn't taken part in but had overseen, and after they were in the courtyard, she was sure to make sure the gate was locked behind her. It was attention to detail like this, a sense of cunning, that had helped Paris move through the ranks.

"All right, I'm bringing his brother here, and the girls."

"As long as they don't get in the way."

"What's that supposed to mean?" Paris asked. "The whole point of coming here is to leverage Kevin against Kevin."

"Why the hell did their parents give them the exact same name?"

Rather than respond, Paris fired off a mental message to Turquoise.

The Western Province teleporter appeared moments later with the two cat girls surrounding Kevin, all of them in matching superhero outfits. Turquoise had her hair in pigtails, her large cat ears peeking out from her locks. The outfit she'd chosen—a black spandex piece with armor up and down the sleeves—showed off her hardened nipples and seemed entirely impractical to Paris.

Obsidian had on a similar outfit, except the colors were reversed.

Where Turquoise had light, blue-green hair with a black outfit, Obsidian had her black hair in a ponytail and wore a matching turquoise outfit. There were some differences, including the fact that the bottom portion of Obsidian's outfit nicely framed her ass, and Turquoise had white tennis shoes instead of boots, but they were clearly going for the duo look.

Kevin's outfit was a combination of the cat girls' colors. A typical superhero getup, a turquoise triangle across the chest with black weaving throughout to slim the fat man down.

He was also wearing a fucking mask, a black one, with glittery turquoise around his eyes.

Paris dropped her head into her hand as Ian snickered at their getups.

This was her fault; she'd given Kevin permission to wear exemplar clothing. And as long as he did what she wanted, the fat bastard could wear whatever the hell he wanted.

"We're at my brother's place?" Realization and confusion came to Kevin all at once as he tried to figure out what the hell was going on.

"You know what to do," she told Ian, curtailing his laugher.

With a grunt, Ian approached Kevin, a menacing look cracking across his chiseled face. The cat girls scrambled to get out of his way as he dropped one hand on Kevin's shoulder, leading him forward.

"We're going to pay a visit to your brother, and you are our leverage."

"Leverage?" Kevin tried to cover his shock by coughing. He coughed for a good fifteen seconds until Paris told him to shut up, Ian nearly clapping him on the back.

"I thought… I thought I was one of you, now," he said, looking to Turquoise and Obsidian for support. Both their ears were down now, the two cat girls showing obedience to Paris's demands.

"One of us?" Ian chortled. "You?"

"You will be one of us if you do what we ask you to," said Paris, ready for all this to be over. Security would be here soon; timing was important. "What you need to know is we've brought you here as a hostage."

"A hostage?"

"That's right." Her frown turned into a look of understanding. "You're serious right now, aren't you? You actually thought we didn't know the difference between you and your brother? Have you ever even seen your own brother? He's fit, successful, professional. You're a fat slob, a lowly immigration administrator."

"Advisor," he whispered.

"Same difference. Do you seriously think the Western Province is dumb enough to confuse the two of you?"

"They said I was Kevin Blackbook," Kevin said, nodding at the cat girls.

"I can't believe I really have to go over this," Paris mumbled to herself. "You are Kevin Blackbook, and so is he, your brother. He's the one who has political power, your brother, not you. *You* are a fat piece of shit. We're only using *you* to get to *him*."

"He's not the real Kevin Blackbook?" Obsidian asked. Turquoise looked like she understood a little more what was going on, but not much.

Kevin cleared his throat. "But I thought you thought I was Kevin Blackbook."

"You are Kevin Blackbook, dammit," said Paris.

He shook his head. "Ah, you led me to believe you thought I was my brother. Am I following this correctly?"

"Paris, we need to wrap this up," said Ian, squeezing his big paw around Kevin's shoulder.

"Thank you, and you're right. Fuck all of this. Now, there are couple ways we can do this, Kevin. You can either play along, or I can instruct the cat girls to poison you."

Kevin might not have been particularly bright, but he wasn't that stupid.

He'd figured out that the cat girls were able to poison him with their bodily excretions. Their poison made him delirious, susceptible to things he wasn't proud of. But most of those things had ended in pleasure in some way, even if the pleasure came from an object being inserted in him by Obsidian, or a little scratch torture.

The truth was, Kevin really had been starting to enjoy the two, with or without their poison.

No matter how sadistic they were, there was a sweetness to them, and he really wanted to know more about them. They hadn't opened up yet, but he could tell that they would, as long as he stayed alive.

And this was also on his mind as he looked at Paris. He needed to prove to her that he could be useful, because he had the itching feeling that Paris would just as easily kill him as keep him alive.

Kevin nodded, ignoring the pain from Ian squeezing his shoulder. "I'll do whatever you need me to do, and if there's a way I can help with your leveraging, I'll do it."

"Good, because if you don't, we will kill you in front of your brother."

He gulped. "Got it," he said, his reply barely audible.

They approached the entryway, and Kevin wondered for a moment how they had gotten the security detail to leave.

Kevin's brother didn't have a family—he'd always been too hard of a worker for anything like that—and even though the house was large, it was empty, devoid of life in a way that made it feel small.

"I can tell you right now that he's upstairs," Kevin said in a faint voice. His brother usually worked until late every evening. If he wasn't in his office downtown, he was definitely in his home office.

"Get him," Paris told the two cat girls.

Obsidian and Turquoise dropped to their haunches, their tails lifting into the air. They scurried up the stairs, their heads bobbing and their ears flitting as they made it to the second level.

They turned right, and a few seconds later there was a brief sound of a struggle.

"We're good," Ian said once the sound had died down.

Paris moved up the stairs followed by Kevin, with Ian close behind.

They turned left and entered a large office to find Kevin's more successful twin brother cowering behind his desk. Turquoise was crouched on the desk, perched on it and overlooking Kevin's brother, hate in her eyes. Obsidian was on his left, and every time he tried to move, she hissed or lightly flicked at him with her tail.

"Thank you, girls," Paris said.

"What's the meaning of this?" Kevin looked nothing like—well, Kevin. The successful brother was fit, with a full head of hair, good skin, and even though he was at home, he was still in the suit and cravat he had worn that day.

"Kevin?" He gulped when he saw his twin brother. "Why are you wearing that outfit? What's the meaning of this? Get away!"

He pushed his rolling chair toward Obsidian, who scrambled over it, and used the chair as a springboard to tackle him. She leapt off him again, this time cornering him from the other side, a sinister smile on her face.

"As you can see, we have your brother. And unless we get answers and assistance, we will kill him."

Both Kevins cried out as Ian punched a hole in the brick wall, leaving a small crater and sending up a cloud of debris.

"Kevin, are you okay? What happened? I thought you'd died! Your funeral was supposed to be this weekend…"

"You wouldn't care if I died or not," said costumed Kevin, feeling emboldened by the way Turquoise was looking at him. He liked the cat girls, and he would say whatever he had to say to keep them around, even if he was just a pawn in their game.

"That's not true! This is about your wife?"

"My wife?"

"Yes, is this about Susan? Don't touch me!" he cried as Obsidian took a playful swipe at him.

"Why would this be about my wife?"

"I'm sorry, Kevin, I'm fucking sorry!"

"What are you sorry for?"

The color drained from his brother's face. Kevin could see a sheen of sweat on his brow, and he watched as his brother loosened his cravat, his hands shaky. "She came on to me, I swear! I didn't mean for it to happen—it was at a party, about a year ago. We don't see each other that often. Just, like once a week. Sometimes twice a week if I'm feeling stressed."

Kevin's heart dropped. It was hard enough see his brother cowering, but to hear him confess to screwing his wife filled him with a mixture of anger, shame, and jealousy that he didn't know how to manage. "You've been fucking Susan this entire time?"

"Yes! I'm so sorry, please... please don't let them kill me!"

"This isn't about that," Paris finally said, glaring at the government official. "This is about healers."

Kevin, who had just whipped his cravat at Obsidian, lowered his hands. "Did you say healers?"

Paris nodded. "I'll be quick about this. The Western Provinces need more healers. Centralia has been holding out on these healers. We were promised a dozen, and they never came. Because Centralia is

435

waging their war in the West with rebel groups, you should be providing healing to those caught in the crosshairs. But you aren't, and of the branches in the Centralian government, your branch is the one that should be providing them."

"This is about healers?" he asked, his chest moving up and down.

"Have some compassion," costumed Kevin said to his brother, going with whatever words came to him first. "These people are suffering—I know for a fact they're suffering. I have advised so many exemplars from the Western Province. I know what they're going through over there; I've heard it firsthand. So help them, dammit. You are supposed to help them! That's your fucking job as a diplomat. All the war that Centralia has brought to the other countries—your one job is to help them."

Kevin was getting worked up. He felt his heart pounding in his chest, his hands shaking as he raised his voice even more.

"And another thing—did you just say you were fucking my wife? What the fuck is wrong with you? What is wrong with all of Centralia? Why would you do something like that? You're my brother, dammit! Why is everyone fucking my wife!?"

"I'm not fucking your wife," Ian started to say.

"It just happened," Kevin blurted out. "We were at a government function, she was there with some flying superhero she was doing PR for, I don't know his name. Anyway it just happened. She wanted to compare sizes—her words, not mine. You're bigger. There. Want to hear that? But I have more stamina. Fuck, this is not the conversation I want to be having right now. Please tell these cat girls to leave me alone." He started sobbing. "They're scaring me!"

"Do you want us to do something to him?" Turquoise smiled as costumed Kevin started to nod.

He brought his hand to his chin, considering this for a moment. Finally, with a flick of his wrist, Kevin gave his orders. "Take his eyes out."

"No!" his brother cried.

Ian let go of Kevin's shoulder. He brought his arms over his chest, interested to see where this would go.

"I need more answers before we do something like that," Paris said.

437

"You Westerners are too desperate!" Kevin said, a look of sternness splashing across his face. "It's you who brought the war, and now you want assistance from the very people you are fighting against. Look at you right now—you're here in my office, both of you, *all five of you*. And you're asking about healers? Look how you operate! What type of government is funding these types of operations when they could be funding recovery and hospital assistance?"

"That's not what this is about. And you and I both know that the rebels aren't from the West, at least not entirely." Paris paused, letting her words sink in. "This visit is about the fact that we need actual healers. Recovery and hospital assistance won't do anything when the hospitals have been destroyed and there's nothing left to recover. We need healers. Healers."

Costumed Kevin nodded. "Give us healers, you fucking asshole!" His heart was racing; he'd never felt more alive in his life than right now, coming face to face with his brother.

"Don't we all need healers?" his brother asked, a wicked smile forming on his face. "Haven't you figured it out yet? Is your intel really that terrible?"

"You're not answering our questions," costumed Kevin told his brother. "Turquoise, take one, *now*."

Kevin tried to cover his face, but Turquoise's tail grabbed his free wrist, pulling it to the side as she used the momentum of his swipe to circle around, latch on to his back, and drive her clawed fingers into his right eye socket, ripping it out.

"Fuck!"

She hopped away before he could slam his back into the wall, his only defense against her.

Obsidian moved in and took his legs out from beneath him, slamming his bloodied face into the edge of his desk.

"Fuck!"

The sound was sickening, and costumed Kevin felt something rise in his stomach. But he kept it down, so tired of being bullied, overshadowed, belittled. Sick of people fucking his wife.

For her final act, Turquoise returned to her perch on his desk, throwing Kevin's eye over her shoulder.

"There are no healers," Kevin said, sobbing now as he tried to get back to his feet, blood oozing down his face. He glared over at his twin brother and the company he'd chosen. "All of you are dead. I will make sure all of you die. Fuck!" He brought his hand to his face again. "What did you do to my eye? I can't fucking see. Can't see…"

"What do you mean there are no healers?" Paris asked.

"We killed all—all of them but one," Kevin said between gulps of air. "They're all dead. It's a terrible thing; they could fix my eye. It wasn't supposed to be like this. It wasn't supposed to be like this!"

"They're all… dead?"

Paris looked to Ian and then back to Kevin's bloodied face.

"Wasn't supposed to happen that way; it was an accident. We were… there's only one left. So that's your answer. Now how about my fucking eye? Look what you've done to me!"

"Take the other one," Kevin instructed Turquoise, again surprising himself.

"No, that's enough," said Paris. "Keep it at one eye; I want him to be able to look at himself and remember what happened this evening. And good job, Kevin. We may have a use for you yet."

Chapter Forty-Four:
Hospital Confessional

"I'm sorry, Roman," Nadine said, a sorrowful look on her face.

Roman stood by Celia's bed, his two animated dolls on the opposite side of the room, their heads hanging.

Morning had brought a cruel surprise. Her form now pale, her shaved head leaning to the side, her mouth open.

Celia was dead.

"Nothing anyone could have done," Roman said, not able to fully form his words.

Nadine placed her hand on Roman's shoulder. "I'm so incredibly sorry."

"Nothing anyone could have done…"

He tore his shoulder away, waiting for the emotion to hit him.

It didn't, and try as he might to experience the anguish he should've been experiencing in that moment, it never came.

Roman was too wrapped up in the moment to realize this, but a part of him had made peace with Celia.

He had promised her to do better, to use his power to help others, and he had confessed everything, every single one-night stand, from the first one to the very last, which had involved Coma.

He had said all those things last night. He'd told her how he felt. And the moment he'd told her was one he would never forget. He hadn't been standing by her bedside; no, he'd still been sitting in the chair, Celia the doll in his lap.

Roman had told her these things in a dream—a wonderful, entirely vivid dream.

Everything, even the details he had never gone over before, Roman had shared it all. Celia never said anything, but there was a look in her eyes that only strengthened his resolve: He would make something good out of the power he'd received.

"We can talk about our arrangement later. I will say this: I couldn't deliver, so I don't expect you to deliver."

"What?" Roman asked Nadine, still unable to take his eyes off his dead wife.

"Like I said, we can talk about it later. Now is not the time. I just wanted you to know that."

"No." Roman turned to Nadine and locked eyes with her, his orange and hers green. "I need to know more about what it is you do."

"It's fine; you don't have to be involved now. I want you just to…" Nadine glanced down at her hands, the ring on her finger. "I want you to forget about it. Forget this ever happened. Be here with your wife, and make good on any promises you've made to her."

"What led you to become who you are, and where do you see it going?"

"Are you asking why I'm a spy?"

"What drove you to do what you do?" he asked, his voice barely above a whisper.

Nadine looked at him curiously for moment. The two women standing in the corner were incredibly silent, neither of them looking at her. "Are you being serious right now?"

"Yes, I need to know right now. I need to know who you are, and why you do what you do."

"For my family," Nadine said, barely able to contain the words as they burst from her lips.

"What happened to your family?"

"They are still alive, but I'm not able to see them."

"That seems unnecessary."

"It's for their own good. By joining the Eastern Province, I knew what I was giving up. I also knew what they were getting."

"And what's that?"

"A second chance. The Eastern Province is very poor, as you know, and my father's business failed because of sanctions put on the East by Centralia. By signing up, I was able to better serve my people, and provide my parents with a comfortable life. Their brains have been wiped, but I know they're happy, safe, secure. If you're asking why I do what I do, that's why. For them."

"And how do you feel about Centralia?" he asked, his eyes twitching.

"If you had asked me that years ago, when I was newer at this and just working on the border, I would've told you that Centralia was a terrible evil. But asking me now, I see there are many forces at play here. Sure, there are some totally iniquitous practices by the government, but they are also the only government that gives aid to the Western Province—not much aid, but at least they're doing something. And..."

"What?"

"I've never admitted it, and I have gone to great lengths to stop any telepath from discovering this thought."

"You can fully stop a telepath?"

"It's part of our training. You would be surprised at how telepaths actually operate, but yes, it's possible to control surface thoughts."

"Okay, what were you going to say, then?"

"I like living in Centralia. The place has grown on me. I hate to say that, and I can't tell you how much I hate that aspect of myself, but I like it here. There's still suffering, but the suffering is invisible. You can be yourself, and there isn't much surveillance on its own citizens. I like all these things about Centralia. Plus, it's peaceful."

"It is peaceful. Aside from the occasional superhero crisis, there aren't many dangers here."

"It has been getting harder and harder to do my job."

"Your work at the immigration office?"

No matter how much he stared at Celia's dead body, part of him thought she'd come back to life, smile, become herself again.

But she was gone, he knew it. And even though he felt terrible, he needed to do something to change the course of the rest of his life.

Nadine shook her head. "Well, yes, that's part of it, but my actual job is to gather any intelligence I can."

"Step outside with me," he finally said. Roman glanced over to Coma and Celia. "I will be back in a moment. Please keep an eye on her."

"She's safe with us," Coma said, coming alive, her eyes flashing red.

Roman and Nadine stepped out of the room, to a quiet spot at the end of the hallway.

"I really shouldn't be saying any of this."

"We've come this far," said Roman. "And all I'm asking for is clarity."

"I'm embedded in the Fast Travels Department, and the point of my assignment is to be there as long as possible, even if I approach retirement age. Doing so, I can naturally move up the chain of command. You realize now that by me telling you this, I've given you information that could cost me my life and the lives of my parents. It's not something I would ever normally tell someone."

"We'll talk about that later. What is it exactly that you were wanting to get from me?"

"Centralia is holding hundreds of Eastern Province residents in jail, people taken from the province."

"Taken?"

"From what I can tell from the data I've uncovered, your government is illegally kidnapping people and putting them in jail to serve hard labor charges here in Centralia. That's what I'm aiming to solve at the moment. This was something that came as a surprise to everyone in diplomatic forces, and those working for the Central Intelligence of the Eastern Province. What is Centralia trying to do? Why are they taking her people?"

"So people are just disappearing?"

"Yes."

"And you have evidence of this?"

"I have the prison records that have listed all their names. All this has been relayed back to my government, disappearances confirmed."

"And how would I have played into that?"

Nadine brought her hand to her face. "I always try to look at things from all angles. Maybe there is something you could have uncovered through the immigration side of things, and you'd know if people were being called in for visa-related issues. I was hoping you could find a trend."

"You shared your secret with me, and now I'm going to share my secret with you." Roman glanced back to his wife's room.

"Come again?"

"Please, follow me."

"Coma, Celia?" he asked as soon as he entered the room.

"Yes, Roman?" asked Coma.

"Step out into the hallway."

Celia and Coma joined Roman, Celia's high heels clicking against the floor as she walked. Roman instructed them to take a seat at the back of the hallway, in a small, dimly lit lounge.

There was a nurse at the opposite end of the hallway, going through papers related to one of the other patients.

The two dolls sat next to one another and looked up at Roman for further instruction.

And in that instant, they were lifeless.

Their heads came forward, their arms fell to their sides, their knees relaxed.

"What did you just do to them?" Nadine asked, looking to her Zero Ring. She placed her thumb on the bottom of the ring, ready to activate it at a moment's notice.

"Recently—as in earlier this week—I received a superpower."

"You what?" Her eyes went wide. "How?"

"Through a Hero Ticket."

Roman turned to the drapes over the window that looked out onto a dark, brick building.

By focusing on them, he caused the drapes to roll themselves up and then roll themselves back down. He then very carefully cast his focus on a picture of a lovely meadow hanging on the wall. He was able to quickly elongate the frame and change things around, creating a new picture entirely as the paint swirled together and reformed the original image.

"That's a new one for me, to manipulate ink. I guess all this is kind of new."

"You're a Type…?"

"My trainer thinks I'm a Type II, Class A and C. I believe I may be a bit higher than that."

"And what is your power?"

"I guess I should've said that in the beginning. I have the ability to manipulate inanimate objects. With the dolls, I have given them part of my own being. They are intelligent, and they operate and look just like you and me."

It'd been several days since he hadn't had one of dolls attached to him in some way, draining some of his power. Roman felt the difference now; he felt like he could construct the building with little more than a thought.

"You won the lottery?"

"Actually, someone else won the lottery, and I happened upon their ticket. I never played the superpower lottery. I didn't think it was possible to actually win."

"So you're in training now, and once you pass training, you will be an actual exemplar," she said, astounded.

"Exactly. I won't have to come to the administrative offices anymore, which was why I was a little disgruntled at the retreat. I'm basically just biding my time, waiting to get the go-ahead to take an exemplar role. No one knows about my power, either, aside from Coma and Celia."

Saying their names brought them back to life. Celia ran her hand through her red hair, bringing it over to one side, while Coma adjusted her mask, her bright red eyes shining for a moment.

"Welcome back," Roman told them.

"It's good to be back," said Celia.

"This is absolutely not what I was expecting this morning."

"What were you expecting?" Roman asked Nadine.

"Well, as you might have put together by now, I dozed off out in the waiting room. I woke up when the doctors ran past, after you called for them. I figured you'd be a wreck, no offense or anything, and that this day would be pretty much shot. And now, I've confessed something to you that I haven't told anyone, and you have now told me that you are close to being an exemplar—also a dangerous confession. This was not what I was expecting."

"Well, it wasn't what I was expecting, either. But what I said earlier is true: I will help you. I want to use my new powers for good, and people disappearing from their own country, taken by another country, is clearly a bad thing. And I know there will be times in the future where there's a blurred line between good and evil, but this is clearly something that's wrong, something that needs some investigation. And I have the power to help you out."

"Thank you, Roman, and it doesn't need to be said, but your secret's safe with me."

"Same." Roman extended his hand, and Nadine took it and shook it.

I'm doing this for you, he thought to his deceased wife. *For you, Celia.*

Chapter Forty-Five: Dead to the World

Nadine decided to take a teleporter home.

It was a lovely day out, warm, with a breeze blowing in from the north, and she made the instant decision to crack her windows when she got home. The breeze reminded her of the weather in the Eastern Province, where it was always a bit cool, no matter which season of the year.

While she could have walked a couple blocks and caught a trolley, she was tired, and she hadn't slept so well in the waiting room last night.

And talk about a wild morning.

She needed time to process what Roman had told her, and more importantly, how she could use it to her advantage. Having an exemplar with a unique ability would prove useful to her cause.

A smile took shape on her face.

It had been a Hail Mary to confess everything to Roman, to put that much trust in an asset.

And it had actually worked. It was risky, sure, but he had also put faith in her to keep his secret, and now they held each other's secrets, both of them in a Catch 22. Nadine from a couple of years ago would've been worried about this. As it stood, she was fine with how things had turned out; not only did she have an asset, she had a powerful asset, and he seemed determined to help her.

Hell, he seemed genuine, and even if he wasn't, even if all this was a ruse, she could adjust accordingly and move forward.

So, a win-win situation.

A red prism of light lifted from the street as the teleporter appeared.

He was an older man with a long gray beard, and as soon as he made eye contact with Nadine, the two of them zipped away.

They reappeared in her living room, both rising from the ground again, the teleporter leaving without saying a word.

Removing her shawl, Nadine stepped out of her heels and relaxed onto her couch for a moment. She yawned, happy that she didn't have to go in to work today.

Sleep started to come over her, but she also had to use the restroom, so she figured she would go to the restroom, change, and actually sleep in her own bed.

Truth be told, Nadine fell asleep on the couch half the time, mostly due to the fact that she'd never had a couch growing up, and she found the piece of furniture rather remarkable.

As she stood, she felt a slight pinch at her side, where her scar was located. It had long since healed up, but every now and then, if she moved in a particular way, she would be reminded of the time she'd almost been killed by that Type II.

Nadine stepped into the hallway that separated her bedroom from her bathroom. She paused, thinking she'd heard a floorboard creak in her room.

You're hearing things, she thought as she moved into the bathroom.

Once she finished up, Nadine opened the door and crossed the threshold into her bedroom.

Later, when trying to piece together what had happened, she would recall seeing a large man with red skin smiling at her. She would remember something striking her in the stomach, something slamming her into the wall, something dragging her out of her bedroom as she blacked out.

Nadine's next memory felt like a dagger giving birth in her skull cavity. Dragged up a flight of metal stairs, her thoughts came to her in a flash: red man, stomach, knocked out, pain.

The red man was still with her, ahead of Nadine now, dragging her by an ankle.

She'd been trained for a variety of things, but even with extensive training, there was only so much a human could take.

Nadine let the moment of shock pass, doing as she'd been instructed in her Capture Preparedness class. She began by trying to get a sense of where she was. It was a large building, with an open space in its center.

A slight draft.

A warehouse, she thought as the side of her head slapped against another step. Her vision was blurred around the edges, and smacking against the metal stairs wasn't helping.

"Almost there, little princess," the red man said with a cruel laugh.

Nadine tried to reach her arms out to get some leverage, but something was wrong with her arms. They were numb; it felt like a million tiny needles were pricking her every time she tried to move.

I can't activate the Zero Ring, she thought, which spelled bad news for the Eastern Province spy.

The ring was her trump card; it had saved her ass before, and not being able to use it meant she was at the mercy of the red man.

Nadine strained her neck, trying not to hit her head on the next rung. She was scared, but she was alert enough to steel herself and wait for an option to present itself.

They reached a doorway and stopped while the red man spoke to someone.

"Keep moving, this isn't for you to see," the man said, and Nadine turned her head the other way, pressing her cheek against the ground.

The last time she'd seen Kevin Blackbook, he'd been standing on the edge of a building threatening to jump.

Now he stood ten feet away from her, wearing a black-and-turquoise superhero outfit. Desperation splashed across her face, desperation that was quickly muted as the red man dragged her into a room, her cheek scraping against the floor, her mouth naturally coming open and leaving a trail of spittle as she was moved across the threshold of the door.

"Get on the bed," he told her. When Nadine didn't respond, he lifted her by one arm and forcibly placed her on the bed.

Not able to sit up, she fell to the side, her body going limp again.

Thoughts fired inside her head. She'd learned in training that most puzzles had solutions, and even though she knew this was just a saying to placate agents caught in rough places, she took this concept to heart, hoping that an opportunity would present itself.

If not, maybe she'd get lucky.

And if neither of those things happened, she'd simply die.

Images of her father and mother flashed in front of her mind's eye.

I will stay alive for you, she thought to them. Seeing the red man return to her with a wet cloth in his hands did little to calm her fears.

"Paris will meet with you later," the man told her. "For now, it's time to sleep."

He pressed the cloth over her mouth and soon, Nadine was back in the Eastern Province, running through a field outside her home. The air was crisp, and her mother and father were not far behind her. She was happy, carefree.

Dead to the world.

Chapter Forty-Six: Flame On

Roman didn't know how Ava would respond to his request.

He didn't know her schedule, nor did he know if she worked weekends, which was why he was relieved to quickly receive a response from her.

I'm on my way.

"She's coming," he told Coma, who stood to his right. Celia was at his left, and the three of them were under an awning attached to the gym he'd been training at all week.

"Sounds good." Coma placed her hands on her hips and watched a trolley pass, something registering across her red eyes.

"We should ride a trolley soon," said Celia, speaking for her counterpart. "That would be interesting."

"It's not as interesting as teleporting, but it is a little easier on my stomach," Roman admitted.

Everything was in its right place. He'd been waiting for the sadness to hit him since leaving the hospice, but it hadn't. It wasn't that he didn't feel remorse; no, remorse and guilt were still ever present. It was more that he felt determined to make good on his promise to his wife—to leave his mark on society.

"You have another one," Ava said as soon as she appeared out of thin air, a stringy teleporter with long white hair behind her. The teleporter nodded and flitted away.

"Yes, yes, I do. Her name is Celia."

"Nice to meet you, Celia," said Ava as she approached the doll clad in superhero clothing. She extended her hand and Celia took it. "I like your hair."

"I like your hair too," Celia said, her red hair a shade darker than Ava's fiery locks.

"Very interesting," Roman's teacher said under her breath. She turned back to him. "And you're sustaining them both?"

"I am."

He showed her his power dial and her eyebrows rose.

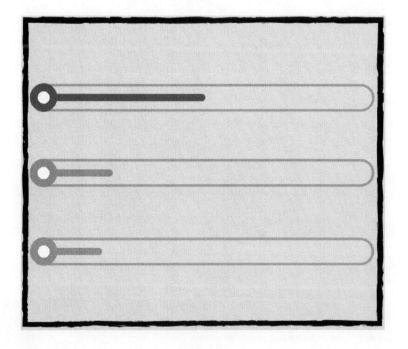

"Impressive. And you're using a bit less energy than before."

"It is starting to feel normal, supporting two additional lives."

"We like being alive," added Coma.

Ava chuckled. "I'm sure you do, even though you are extensions of Roman. So you called me here for training, correct?" she asked, turning back to Roman.

"That's right." He ran his hand through his white hair and offered her a toothy grin. Roman was pretty sure he looked a bit crazy at the moment. He was in the same outfit from last night, and his eyes were bloodshot, but he felt good regardless—energized, despite the fact that he hadn't slept much and had eaten hospital food for breakfast.

"Then let's get started, and your dolls are going to need to change as well."

"We can't fight in this stuff?" Celia rotated her left hip forward and looked down at her superhero outfit.

"Maybe you can, but *you* definitely can't." Ava nodded to Coma, who was still in her gothic Lolita getup, the tops of her bosom exposed. "I'm assuming that part of your attack strategy going forward will be to use them, correct?"

"Correct," said Roman. "I mean, I'm still working on an overall strategy, but yes, I believe they will be part of it."

"Then they should change, and we should see if there isn't some way you can imbue more power in them. I don't know. This is all new territory for me, but it is something we should work with. I'll ask the guy I have assisting me with your case."

"The one who did the research on my abilities?"

Ava winked. "That's the one. Let's get inside and get changed. I'm guessing you're really in the mood to train, considering that you've called me on my day off."

"Yeah, I am. There are other things, too."

"Oh yeah?" Ava asked as she opened the door that led to the gym. "What's that?"

"I'll explain once we get inside."

Ava stood before Roman, stretching her hands over her head. She was lean yet curvy, her tight athletic clothes straining to cover her breasts. Celia and Coma wore similar outfits, and it was strange for Roman to imagine that the three of them had gone into the locker room together and all changed at the same time.

This wasn't a sexual thought; rather, it just reminded him that the two dolls were exceedingly autonomous, which he was still getting used to.

"All right, before we begin, you said you wanted to tell me something."

"I have a question for you," Roman said.

Ava raised an eyebrow at him. "I'm all ears."

Celia snickered.

"Was that funny?"

"I was just imagining you as all ears." The red-haired doll looked to Coma for support. Coma, who was still in her mask, thought about how this would look and shrugged. "It would be funny, right?"

"Strange more than funny."

"Moving on," said Ava. "What's your question?"

"Is it possible that someone like me, a non-exemplar who is on his way to becoming an exemplar..."

"So you think you're exemplar material, huh?"

"You know what I mean. I plan to do everything in my power, no pun intended, to get your approval. I don't care how long it takes me."

Ava stretched her arms wide, grabbed one of her wrists with her opposite hand, and bent to the left, sighing as she stretched out her side. "I'm listening…"

"I want to do something different with my power. I don't want to have a menial job like the teleporters, or some Type IV Class C tasked with cleaning the water supply."

"Those are very important functions in Centralian society."

"I realize that, but if possible, I want to use my power to help people."

"You want…"

"Yes."

"…to be a superhero?" The smile on Ava's face cracked as she finished her statement.

"Something like that. I mean, yes, exactly that. I want to use my power to help people. To live a different life than I've lived up until this point."

"You keep saying that, but I don't think you realize what it entails, nor the training you'd have to go through. Especially at your age. Those tasked with hero work start very young."

"That's why I'm asking you if it's a possibility. What would I have to do? I have the endurance, and the stamina. I'm not worried about those types of things, and I'm not saying I couldn't improve those abilities. I also think that if I improved my strength and stamina, I would be able to create more of them."

Ava considered the eager look in her student's eyes. She'd seen it once before, but she wasn't self-aware enough to realize it was the same look she'd given her sister when Ava had trained to be a hero.

"How would I do it? How would I become a hero? I know that there are things Centralia is dealing with all around the globe, and I would like to be part of them."

The words were spilling out of Roman's mouth now. He felt obsessed with what he was saying, determined to make things right. He wasn't thinking about the fact that he'd just made a deal with Nadine, that he was actively committing treason. All he could think about was helping others, whatever that meant.

It was entirely unlike him.

"What is it?" he asked, noticing a sadness behind Ava's eyes.

"It's not uncommon for someone to want to be a hero after they've been given a power, but I don't think you understand what a hero is tasked to do here in Centralia. It's by no means an easy life. The training is difficult—believe me, I know—and you have to train with the group that they put you in, which can be difficult, especially given your half-powered background. I suppose you could convince them you're forming your own group, but that would be a whole different round of paperwork and approvals you would need to get. The point I'm trying to make is: it's not easy."

"I didn't sign up for this because it was going to be easy."

Ava laughed. "You didn't sign up for this. You were granted this power—you won it."

"No, I didn't." Roman looked from Coma to Celia, realizing he'd said too much. They knew it, too; they shared some of his memories in a blurred way. It was odd, but he could tell by the way they glanced back at him that they knew what he was thinking.

"Then how did you get it?"

"How good are you at keeping a secret?"

"By asking a question like that, I get this feeling that you already know the answer." Ava turned her palm around, and a spark of fire appeared in it, then disappeared. She did it again, Celia watching her intently this time, her fists at her side.

"I mean, the people that granted me my powers, your sister and the council, seemed to know. So I guess it isn't that big of a secret. It all started when my coworker tried to commit suicide..."

Roman quickly caught Ava up.

It wasn't as long of a story as he'd anticipated, and while telling it, he realized that he was sort of a dick for what happened. Well, maybe not a dick, because there was some luck involved, but he could've done more to stop Kevin from trying to commit suicide.

And then the poor guy wouldn't have been killed in the hospital, whatever happened to him.

Since he was on the truth train, Roman figured he would tell Ava more about his ability, and the fact that he'd discovered he could modify documents. He explained this to her as well, leaving out the part about Paris and Ian Turlock.

By the end of tonight, Paris would no longer be in the equation anyway.

The spark of fire in Ava's hand disappeared. "That is quite a story, Roman Martin. From what I can tell, you haven't done anything that was illegal, per se, but it is a strange way to come about a power. Especially considering you were attacked by a super who could manipulate shadows."

"Hazrat, I'll never forget him."

"Right, which led to you getting the lottery ticket, which led to you getting the ability you now possess. And I have to admit, this new extension of your power has me interested. Moving ink around is something that could be useful in a variety of ways."

"I'll be honest, I wasn't going to tell you about that, but I had some epiphanies last night and I'm trying to change the way I operate. It's important for me to be clearer with you, to have a clean slate."

"Well, then I will have the same attitude towards you," Ava said, offering him a firm nod. "You are the twentieth or thirtieth person I have trained. Some of them had different types of powers, like the lady who could manipulate gases inside other people's bodies, which was a terrible power to have, to the person that could turn anything he touched into wood. You would think that was a good power, and it's useful for a construction company, but the training with him was brief—hell, most of their trainings have been brief."

"That sounds odd."

"It was. And what I'm trying to tell you is this: I think that there is a potential for your ability that neither of us have recognized. If that potential is on a team with other supers, then I will do everything in my power to get you there. Now, enough talk. Because you are trying to become a big bad super, I figured today's lesson would be a little more interesting."

"A big bad super?"

She pulled her hair back into a ponytail. "I want you to fight me. And you can use your friends, too. We can't, or maybe we shouldn't, call them dolls. That just seems wrong."

"It doesn't bother us," said Coma.

"I think it sounds cute," Celia added.

"Cute?" Ava looked from Celia to Roman. "Anyway, Roman, I want you and your *dolls* to attack me."

"You're just going to melt them."

Ava gave him a hurt look. "I promise I won't melt them. Although, in the future, we will train with higher stakes, and at that point, they could face those results."

"What about me?" he asked, loosening up his arms.

"I want you to attack me. And don't kill me. I don't know if that's what you're going for, but obviously, neither of us should try to kill the other. What kind of teacher would I be if I let that happen? I really should've laid out some ground rules."

Roman smirked. Ava was more bubbly than usual. There was something about her personality that he had really started to enjoy, likely that she didn't take things too seriously.

"Okay, first, try to take me down. Just try to bring me down to my knees. And I didn't come in on my day off just to take a sick day tomorrow. Although that doesn't sound so bad."

"How'd you get this job anyway?"

Ava cocked an eyebrow at him. "Do you want to go on a date or something? You sure have a lot of questions for a guy who called me to train."

"I don't..." Roman gulped.

For once, he was feeling a little apprehensive around her. This wasn't normal for him; normally he felt in control when he spoke with women he was attracted to. "Sure, we can have a meal later. Not today—I'm already taking up too much of your time. But later."

"Did you just ask me on a date?" Ava's hand flared up, the flame dancing in her palm as she turned it around.

"I thought you asked me on one."

She rolled her eyes. "We'll deal with that later. It's time to get started. Try to take me off my feet, and I promise not to melt your dolls."

Roman simply rumbled the floor beneath her, like he'd done the previous night against Ian.

Ava shot her hands out, stabilizing herself. "That's kind of cheating. I guess I should have said this a different way: let's really try not to bruise each other too much, but still actually go at it."

"If you say so…"

Roman nodded at Coma and Celia, sending his two dolls forward. They advanced quickly, and as they did, he pulled some of the metal piping from the space heater that ran along the bottom wall of the gym.

Like a snake, the heating coils slithered toward Ava, who simply blasted them back with fire.

"Okay, this place is going to need some repairs after, but we have a budget for that. Let's do this!" she cried, fire flaring behind her pupils.

With an eye on his power dial, Roman lifted the ground beneath Coma into the air, giving her a perch to jump from. He realized as she jumped down toward Ava just how much of an extension of her psyche belonged to Roman.

As he would have done in a similar position, Coma came down with her knees bent, fists back and ready to take Ava out. Instead, she crashed into a column of hot air Ava had erected around her body.

The air suspended her, and Ava stepped forward, actually able to spin Coma around. Celia too was swept up by a column of hot air.

"Let me down!" Celia cried out, punching at the air. Coma simply spun, an angry look on her masked face.

"Oh, come on," Roman called over to Ava.

"It's a tactic!"

Roman glanced around the gym, looking for something he could use to attack Ava.

Hating to do what he was about to do, but knowing it would have some effect, Roman focused on Ava's tight clothing.

He began to melt her clothing down, until it formed into a puddle on the ground, leaving her standing in her bra and panties.

Of course, by this point, Ava had dropped Celia and Coma to cover herself, which gave the two dolls the time they needed to corner her.

"That's fucked up!" she said as she blasted both of them back, the explosion at their feet sending the two dolls high into the air.

Ava's eyes again glared with fire, and her red hair actually turned to flame as she levitated into the air, fiery snakes twisting up her arms and legs as they formed armor.

She torpedoed towards Roman, who was barely able to bring the ground up to create a wall to protect himself. His power dial flashing, Roman dropped his control over Celia so he could focus more power on controlling the artificial wall.

He backpedaled, the floor beneath him writhing as Ava tried to burn through the barrier he'd erected, smoke filling the air, the crackle of fire reaching his ears.

She's going to get through that, he thought as he glanced up at the ceiling.

The ceiling extended down like a person stretching backward with their arms wide, forming a bowl over Ava. The building's structural integrity was starting to go, evident in the creaks, and the fact that the ceiling was starting to shift.

One of them was going to have to give.

Roman raised his hands into the air and let the floor down, returning the ceiling to its rightful position.

478

A flaming bolt of fire zipped towards him, Ava's burning fist stopping inches away from his face.

"Your attack was to strip me of my clothing?" Ava asked, her chest heaving up and down. She floated a few feet back and righted herself. She was completely covered in flames now, her eyes yellow orbs of fire.

"I was trying to throw you off guard! Please don't burn the shit out of me."

The flames fell off her body, all but a swathe of fire that formed a bathing-suit-like covering over her lady parts.

"What should I do?" Coma asked, her fists still at her side. Celia was near her, standing with her head bent forward, dead to the world.

"Hold on a second," Roman told her.

"I have to admit," said Ava, "that was an interesting tactic."

"And I was literally just trying to throw you off guard," Roman said, his hands coming up. "There are other things I could have done; I could have used your clothing to strangle you."

"Interesting, but I'm still offended."

479

"I'm sorry…"

"You know what? It's fine. I'll just keep this form. And it's too bad, because I like wearing my athletic clothing. They look good on me."

"Yeah, they do, but the flame-suit is cool too," he said as she floated another foot back or so. "I can still fix your clothes, if you'd like."

"And let you see me in my bra and panties again? Actually, I'd be naked, so the answer is no."

Roman had noticed that engulfing her body in flames had burned off her bra and panties. If he looked hard enough into the flames over her chest, he could almost see her nipples, or at least he imagined he could see them.

"Like I said, I'm sorry."

Try as he might, Roman couldn't help but grin as she floated back to the other side of gym. And try as he might, he couldn't help but get a glimpse of her ass as the fire raged off her skin.

Old habits die hard, he thought as he re-animated Celia.

Roman wiped the sweat off his brow.

His shirt was off, his muscles tense, and as he stood opposite Ava, his shoulders moving up and down as he took in big gulps of air, Roman felt better than he had in a week.

It was two hours later, and they were still going at it. The gym was destroyed, but Ava assured him that would be okay—that these gyms had Type IV duplicators on hand whose job it was to repair the facilities.

Ava was at the halfway point between the ceiling and the floor, her body still covered in flames. Roman was impressed by the fact that she could maintain this unnatural condition for so long. For Roman's part, he'd had to again de-animate one of his dolls, Celia, as he'd been afraid of maxing out.

Truth be told, he probably could've gone longer with both of them at his side, but he was trying to play it safe, and Coma was the better fighter anyway.

"Have you tried forming an armor yet?" Ava asked.

"I would tell you if I had."

"You didn't tell me about your ability to modify documents and move ink," she said.

"It was a surprise," Roman said, slicking his hand back through his white hair. He was sweaty; one glance to his right and he saw Coma sweat free, her hair a little frazzled but looking good otherwise.

"Well, I want you to try it then. See if you can make armor out of…" Ava looked up at the rafters. "That should work, the steel."

"Got it," Roman said as he glanced up at the object he would need to animate.

His first order of business was bringing the steel down, which he did simply by focusing on a few of the pieces he deemed not as important as the others. The steel dropped to the ground, rattling the floor a bit.

It snaked over to Roman, changing to the consistency of a putty, and once it met his legs, it began to slither up, similar to the way he'd seen fire overtake Ava's form.

His first attempt was a little bulky, but he reset his breath and kept playing with his armor until he was able to form a movable steel defense around his body, with hunks of metal jutting off his forearms, mirroring the spiky protrusions that defined Ian's.

He tried moving his arms and noticed they were a little stiff. Focusing on the metal that had formed under his armpits, Roman imagined it being more porous, even opening up a small space to give him some room for mobility. He did the same between his legs, and at his most important joints—shoulders, elbows, wrists, knees, ankles.

"It's not bad," said Coma, who had walked over to him as he'd been forming the armor. She placed her hand on his arm, and he looked to her, returning her soft grin.

With her red eyes behind the mask on her face, Coma, like most supers, looked like she was keeping a secret, that she held a mystery. She was different in her athletic gear, still sexy but also fierce.

"Let's try this." Roman used some of the steel that had gathered at the backs of his shoulders to scale up his neck and make a mask. To give his head the space it needed to look around, he made sure the metal on his neck was ribbed, so he could move his chin around and look left to right.

Once he'd finished his armor, Ava started clapping, flames bursting in the air every time her palms met. "Bravo, bravo, now of course, that would do nothing against someone like me, because I would simply melt that steel around your body. But it is very interesting."

"It seems like everything I do is interesting to you."

A curious look came across Ava's face. "Have you tried doing anything with water?"

"No; I didn't know if that was in the parameters of my abilities," he said, his skin warm beneath the armor he'd created. "It never really crossed my mind that I could do something with a liquid."

"Remove your armor and follow me."

Roman did as instructed, his armor falling to the ground. He glanced up to the ceiling to make sure he didn't need to send the steel back, and once he saw that the structure was sound enough, he just let the material rest on the floor.

"Can you get Celia?" he asked Coma.

She nodded and moved over to Celia, who stood perfectly still, her head bent forward. Coma lifted the other doll over her shoulder, her hands just below

Celia's ass, and glanced to Roman, letting him know she was ready to move.

Roman and Coma followed Ava into another room, where they found a long hallway defined by its white paneling. "One thing the general public doesn't know about this facility is that it is a lot larger than it seems from the front of the building. It's an optical illusion, created by one of the Type III exemplars Centralia employs."

Roman looked up at the place.

"An optical illusion from outside."

"Really? How many buildings are like that?"

"More than you'd think."

"Good to know," he said under his breath. "Buildings can be optical illusions."

"That they can, and this should be the perfect place for our next test." Ava, Roman, and Coma entered another gymnasium, this one with a giant pool in its center. Coma set Celia down, making sure she was able to support herself.

Ava turned to Roman, a mad grin on her face. "I want you to animate this water, and then if that's

485

possible, I want you to try to create a water-based armor."

Chapter Forty-Seven:
Kevin Doubles Down

"We have to do something," Kevin told Obsidian.

He'd hardly spoken to Nadine—hell, he may have spoken to her just once, in the canteen on the bottom floor of their building. But he did feel a sense of loyalty to her, and seeing a coworker being hurt nearly snapped him out of the whole "I want to be a super villain" schtick.

At the very least, it made him hate Ian Turlock.

And sure, Kevin still wanted to be a super villain, but he didn't want to be the type of super villain that attacked innocent people, and the fact that he was staying here in this warehouse, and that she was now here, clearly in duress, had really done a number on him.

Kevin, Turquoise, and Obsidian were lying on a mattress in one of the back rooms of the warehouse.

Kevin was too big to really go at it with either of them, but they'd had sex, his throbbing proof of Kevinhood only able to go a quarter of the way in.

Neither seemed to mind, and considering that it had been one of the most exhilarating experiences of his life, he didn't mind either. The more accustomed Kevin got to their three-way sexual situation, the more normal it felt to him.

In fact, he couldn't understand why he'd ever had a different type of life with the opposite sex. It was natural. The three of them were always either going at it or teasing each other, or they were doing weird stuff to him that he accepted because, well, it was interesting.

Felt good, too.

He hadn't thought of his wife, Susan, in the last twenty-four hours—*the cheating bitch*—and a big part of him was glad that he'd tried to commit suicide, which had somehow ended up with his death being faked, which had somehow ended up with him in the throes of passion with two mad-sexy cat girls.

It was definitely not a life he ever would've predicted; mild-mannered Kevin had never even been to one of the strip clubs in the red-light districts. But now that he had taken a dip on the wild side, becoming a prince of debauchery, his previous life felt like nothing more than a fleeting image.

It was amazing to him how quickly one could go from "good" to what society deemed as "bad." All one had to do was take the leap of faith. There was nothing stopping anyone from doing anything they desired except morality and societal norms. Kevin knew what he was experiencing was a perversion of this, but it was a perversion he felt comfortable with, possibly the most comfortable he'd ever felt in his life.

That said, seeing Nadine in the other room had definitely caught him off guard.

"What do we have to do?" Obsidian asked, turning to him. She placed her hands over her breasts, her ears perking to attention. He could see her black tail as well, moving in the air ever so slightly, as if it were riding on an invisible wave. Turquoise lay on his other side, on her stomach, her tail lightly tickling his hairy belly button.

"How loyal are you two to Paris?"

It was a simple question, but he knew their answer would dictate how the next several days played out, and quite possibly the next several hours.

"Why are you asking us that?" Turquoise moved onto his stomach. She crossed her arms, giving herself a prop to press her body up.

"I like both of you, you know that, right?"

"We know," said Obsidian, who still lay on her side. "What's your point?"

"That lady in the other room, you know who I'm talking about, right?"

"We know. Paris is going to kill her when she returns."

"That's the thing," Kevin told Turquoise. "I don't want her to die. She's a friend of mine."

"A friend of yours?" Obsidian purred.

Kevin nodded, his jowls bouncing up and down. "We used to work together. She seemed like a nice lady, and I don't want her dying. I don't want her involved with this. In fact, I want to rescue her."

"Rescue her?" Obsidian sat up and looked to Turquoise.

"Before you both say anything, I just want you to think about something for a moment: you two are essentially mules for Paris. She doesn't seem to really care about you, and she just tells you what to do and when to do it. You're clearly powerful, strong, and fast, plus your poison power."

One of Turquoise's ears lowered. "You know about that?"

"I've worked with a lot of exemplars, and what you release through your... um, orifices... is a neurotoxin. I get that now, and it's kind of nice, actually, but I could see how it would be quite powerful and cause a lot of trouble if anyone were to actually fight either of you. You are both from the Western Province, but you weren't trained as spies. Am I correct?"

The two cat girls exchanged glances.

"What I'm saying is, from what I can gather, she's paying you. Is that right?"

"It's right," Turquoise finally said.

491

"And she's not paying you that much. So what she is doing, then, is exploiting your powers. And just hear me out—I think the three of us could do better. Much better. I know that may sound crazy, and that I don't technically have an ability, but stranger things have happened, and I think with you two, I could really…"

"Really what?" asked Obsidian.

Kevin cleared his throat. "That remains to be seen. People have suddenly received abilities before; haven't you heard of that? And then there's the lottery. I loved to play the lottery. I was hoping to get a superpower, and I didn't get one, but now I know you two."

"And we could be your superpower," Turquoise said. "Is this what you are suggesting?"

"It is indeed what I'm suggesting. I would treat you better, and once we figure out what it is we want to do, whatever that may be, I'll figure out a way to make it happen. It sounds crazy, I know, but that's what I'm trying to say here. I know a lot about the inner workings of the Centralian government. Plus, we could start by exploiting what my brother knows."

Kevin couldn't see himself in the mirror, so he was unable to witness the crazy look in his eyes. Nor did he realize that for some very odd reason, the crazy look resonated with Turquoise. Obsidian, not so much, but she had always just gone along with what Turquoise did anyway. And even though the two cat girls weren't related, oddly enough, Turquoise played the role of an older sister at times.

"What I'm saying is that we free her, get her out of here, and then let her go on about her business. Then the three of us escape. What do you say? Will you join me?"

Turquoise squinted at him. "Paris is going to be pissed..."

"Paris has enough on her hands, and we can figure a way out of here, get underground. I want to fight the system. I want to stop what my brother has done—why did they kill healers? And the others, and the people that..." Kevin sat up, which moved Turquoise off his stomach.

He started huffing, barely able to get the words out.

"What is it?" asked Obsidian.

"I'm sick of being who I am. I want to change everything about myself. *And it starts now.* I'm making the decisions that I think are right, not what society tells me is right—not what Paris thinks I should do. And I hate to say it because I like both of you, but not what you two think I should be doing. I'm taking charge of my life, for the rest of my life."

Turquoise smirked. "So you really want to do this, huh?"

"That's right, but we will need to wait until Ian leaves. Paris is gone, and I'm guessing Ian will either be joining her soon, or he'll go out. He's not going to stay around here all night. He seems restless."

"He's supposed to join her; Paris has already told me. We're supposed to watch the woman as well, or at least I am," said Turquoise.

"Good, then that settles it. We're going to rescue Nadine. Agreed?"

Turquoise looked from Obsidian to Kevin. "Agreed."

"Obsidian?"

She smiled, her black ears pressing forward. "Sure, why not?"

Chapter Forty-Eight: Water Boy

~~⌒⌒~~

The water lifted out of the pool forming a large eagle, its wings flapping and sending droplets of water to the surface of the pool.

Roman concentrated even harder, moving the flying beast made of water higher into the air, spinning it around, keeping its form in place.

"It worked!" Ava floated on the opposite end of the gym, fire licking off her body. She had a smile on her face, her eyes burning yellow as she watched the water creation touch back down.

"Water Mimicry," Roman mumbled. When breaking down Class Cs, he'd seen words like hydrophysiology and hydrokinesis thrown around, and all could be used to describe what he was currently doing.

In fact, the usual verbiage he used, something like a Type II, Class C, was simplified. It could get much more complex than that, but most didn't bother. If they needed to investigate what class an exemplar was, they could simply look for the details on their ID.

Roman watched the eagle made of water fly a bit higher. His ability to animate inanimate objects was something entirely molecular, its possibilities seemingly endless. A quick look at his power dial and he saw that the middle bar was pulsing. He turned his palm up, and the water lifted in a column that fanned out at the top.

There was another thing he wanted to try, but he could give that a shot later, after he did what he'd come here to do.

Roman pulled the water toward him, forming a sluicing suit of armor over his body. The water moving over the fabric of his clothing felt incredibly odd, almost as if he were being massaged with his clothes still on.

Ava zipped over to him, a trail of flames following her.

"Are you ready for this?" she asked, a supernova of energy moving over her body.

"As ready as I'll ever be."

Ava bulleted into the air and spun backwards, careening toward Roman. Realizing this would be like any fight, albeit one that involved elemental forces, Roman did what he normally would if an attacker advanced on him in this way: he sidestepped her attack at the last minute, chopping her in the back with his water-encased hand.

The air filled with steam as the two forces met and Ava landed and lunged for Roman, who again blocked her next strike.

His fists at the ready, the water had come up and over his head, forming a moving mask that felt strange against his skin.

"He's a good fighter," Coma said, reminding Roman that he was controlling the water *and* giving the doll life.

"Coma, can you go stand next to Celia? I'm sorry, I just want to try something."

Coma understood immediately what he meant.

The masked doll stepped next to Celia and spread her legs a bit to support her body, and once she did, Roman stripped her of her power.

He felt a surge of energy come to him. "You really want to take this to the next level?" he asked Ava, feeling the water beneath his feet start to lift him into the air.

"I was hoping you'd ask that."

He blasted backwards, propelled by water spraying from his heels. He noticed that the surface of his armor had changed in porousness, which made him think it was bringing in the natural moisture in the air and using that to fuel the suit of water.

Once he was in a good position, Roman brought his arm back and fired off an arc of water at Ava, who blocked it with a huge fireball, both their attacks sizzling out.

He was a little shaky, not able to get his footing as well as he wanted, but he was getting more used to being suspended in air, his stomach doing somersaults as he dove forward, protected by his shield of water and a slide-like water chute he'd created.

Roman hit the end of the chute and smashed into Ava, steam billowing off their bodies as they cracked into the ceiling.

It was a bold move, one Ava hadn't been ready for.

The two tumbled towards the empty pool below, steam smoking all around them, Ava trying to right herself and Roman, a wild look on his face, trying to drive her down.

She pressed away just in time, her fist connecting with Roman's cheek. Thrown off his trajectory, he slammed into the side of the pool, getting the wind knocked out of him even as his armor protected his body.

"Are you crazy!?" Ava shouted at him.

"Maybe?" Roman blasted off again, a column of water spraying out of his feet.

He felt the air around him begin to change. The water surrounding his body started to boil and soon, he was free-falling to the ground, no longer able to control the boiling-hot water heating up his skin.

A gust of balmy air stopped him from the fatal fall. It lightly set him down, Ava now hovering directly over him.

"Let's be clear," she said, a grin whipping across her fiery face. "I'm still the teacher here."

"Yep, that's right." Roman pushed himself to his feet. "I got ballsy. I just wanted to know the limitations. Speaking of which…"

He focused on some of the fire flickering off her feet. The fire began to twist in the air toward him, curling as it stopped just before his finger.

Ava lowered to the ground and approached Roman, hardly able to contain the look of surprise on her face. "I mean, it makes sense," she finally said.

"Yes, it does." The fire twisted into the air over his palm.

"But you aren't an absorber, nor a mimic."

"It must be molecular," he said, honestly. "It seems like if I have the ability to see it, I have the ability to modify it, and by 'it' I mean anything."

"There are other things we should try later," Ava suggested.

"Is this before or after we have dinner together?" he asked as what was left of his water armor dripped to the floor.

"You are really pushing your luck with me, you know that?"

"Sorry, just trying to make a joke."

She rolled her eyes. "It wasn't a bad joke, but it wasn't good either."

"I'll take mediocre."

"As I was saying, we should try other substances later."

"Like what?"

"Anything and everything we can think of. So far, I've seen you modify love dolls, wood, metal, water, fire, ink—and I'm sure there are some things I'm missing."

"They're not love dolls, they're sex dolls."

"Ha! Okay, if you'd prefer I call them that."

"Just joking," Roman said, a yawn coming to him. He was starting to feel tired. He'd gotten little sleep the previous night, and was planning on a nap when he got home. Roman knew it'd be foolish not to recharge before meeting Paris.

"Well, I don't know about you, but I'm ready to actually enjoy my day off. What do you say? Let's call it quits for today, and reconvene two days from now."

"I have a meeting then," he said, referring to his Heroes Anonymous class.

"After that. And we can order food if it gets late. How's that for a date?"

Roman smiled at the flaming woman, enjoying the tension between them.

"Sounds like a plan."

Roman wasn't expecting to see Harper waiting for him when he got back to his apartment. The young waitress with her long neck, short brown hair and her eyes spaced far apart seemed genuinely happy to see him, and he felt bad that he'd been blowing her off.

"Harper," she said, looking to Celia, who stood next to Roman in her superhero regalia.

The teleporter that had transported them cleared his throat and disappeared in a fizzle of energy.

"Celia," said the doll.

"Hey Harper," said Coma, who looked at the woman with a mischievous grin. If Harper was thrown off guard by the women with Roman, she didn't show it.

"We should talk."

Coma and Celia naturally stepped away. The two moved to a newsstand on the street corner and checked out the magazine rack.

"Yeah, sorry if I've seemed a bit out of the loop." Roman placed his hand on the back of his head.

"It's fine," she said, reaching her hand out for his.

"I've gone through some serious stuff over the last few days," he blurted out. "And right now might not be the best time to be around me."

"What are you saying?"

"I'm saying that there are big changes coming in my life, and at the moment, I'm trying to sort out the pieces."

"What kind of serious stuff have you been going through?" she asked, concern in her eyes.

It was on the tip of his tongue, and Roman knew that he was trying to force himself to turn a new leaf, but try as he might, he wasn't able to get his confession out. Thinking of telling Harper that his wife had just passed, and that they'd been seeing each other while she was in the hospital only reminded Roman of just how depraved he'd become.

No, he wouldn't be able to come clean about this to Harper—not yet, anyway. He liked her, and she had a dominating sexual energy that he enjoyed, but Roman also didn't want to be with someone he'd have to lie to constantly. And that wasn't considering his newfound power, yet another secret.

"I can't really tell you what I've been going through," he finally said.

"Is it something I did?"

"No, absolutely not. You're incredible. Really. I just need some time to process all this right now, and figure out how I should go about my life moving forward. Sounds crazy, I know."

"So you're breaking up with me?"

"I never said that."

"Sorry, that assumes we were together." Harper ran her hands down the front of her pants and then crossed her arms over her chest. "What I'm trying to ask is: do you still want to see me?"

"I think the bigger question is if you still want to see me." Roman sensed Celia and Coma behind him, their presences always known. It was odd that Harper hadn't mentioned them, but then again, Harper really seemed like a cool person, one who wouldn't immediately pass judgement.

"That's why I'm here," she finally said.

"Even with what you already know about me, and the fact I can't be honest with you?"

"Yes," she said, hesitation in her voice.

Roman nodded, offering her his best smile. "Give me some time, a week or so, and let me see how things are shaking out. I'm totally attracted to you, you know this; and aside from that, I think you're a great person. I know this isn't the answer you wanted, either, just to be clear. But I have a lot going on. I need some time to sort it out, and I don't want any of my issues backfiring on to you."

"Okay."

Harper stepped toward Roman and he lifted his arms, bringing her into a hug. "I'm sorry for all this."

"It's not your fault."

"No, it really is my fault. All of it."

And for a moment, Roman thought of inviting her up for a nap—nothing fancy, just a nap. But he knew better, or at least, he was trying to know better. And he was by no means looking to curb his sexual drive; he just knew now wasn't the time.

Chapter Forty-Nine:
Kevin's Future Power Play

"Let me see her," Kevin heard Paris say to Ian.

He was lying on the floor mattress with Obsidian, who was back in her costume. He had part of his costume on as well, his black pants, mostly because it was a little warm in the bed and the fabric of the shirt had been making him sweat.

"We have to hear what they're saying," he whispered to Turquoise, who sat in the corner of the room performing some religious ritual he'd seen her do a few times now. Now that he was around them all the time, he'd noticed both of them performing these rituals, chanting in a strange tongue he'd never heard before.

Turquoise finished her mantra and stood, her tail perking up. She nodded Kevin over, and the heavy man got off the bed as quietly as he could. He snuck over to the door and placed his back against the wall, trying his best to careen his head around without bringing attention to himself.

He was breathing a bit too heavily to hear Ian and Paris's discussion, so he held his breath for a moment, listening as she spoke.

"…I haven't decided if we keep him as an asset or not, to be honest," she told Ian. "He helped you get your paperwork done, but there's just something off about it all. I don't know how reliable he is, or if he will jeopardize what we're trying to do here."

"And Kevin?"

Paris paused for a moment. "He clearly has a terrible relationship with his brother, which could prove to our advantage. But he is expendable, as are the girls if it comes down to it."

Kevin's fists tightened; he was about to prove to her just how expendable he was. No longer able to hold his breath, he let out a short squeak of air, which caused Paris and Ian to stop speaking.

A bead of sweat appeared on his temple.

He felt Turquoise wrap her hand around his, her nails protruding ever so slightly as she pressed them into his knuckles, releasing her neurotoxin.

He was growing more and more familiar with the way it felt when the high came over him. It felt good, calming him almost instantly. He let his heart settle as Paris and Ian continued speaking in the hallway.

"We can deal with them later. Nadine as well. We're supposed to be meeting him soon, and I want things to be set up."

"So you want me visible or not?"

"Not. Which is why I've asked him to meet me in another warehouse, not far from here. Plenty of places for you to hang in the dark, just in case I need some muscle. Then again, maybe our conversation will go well, and I won't be needing your services."

"Fine by me," said Ian. "Are we going now?"

"Yes. Meet me downstairs; I need to speak to Turquoise and let her know we're leaving."

Kevin wasn't a fast man, but the time it took him to get back to his bed was impressive to say the least, especially when considering his girth and how far away the mattress was from the door. He had just bounced onto it, waking Obsidian (who screeched loudly and clawed him), when Paris entered the room.

"I see you two are keeping Kevin entertained," she told Turquoise, who still stood by the door.

"Yes, Obsidian is very entertaining," she purred.

Picking up on what was going on, Obsidian began to lightly claw at Kevin and giggle. "Kev, Kev, Kev…"

"We're leaving now," Paris said, cringing. "And you're in charge of our hostage—*both* our hostages. It won't be long before we return."

With that, the slender woman turned away, disgust evident on her face at seeing Kevin shirtless.

"If we're going to do this, we need to do it now," Kevin said. They'd heard Paris and Ian Turlock leave about five minutes ago. It was now or never.

"Where will we take her?" asked Obsidian.

"To a hotel or something. I don't know." Kevin drummed his fingers on his chin. "She's not staying with us, that's for sure. We've got to get just about as far away from here as we can if we do this."

Turquoise's head bobbed left and right as she considered this. "Okay, you can carry her."

"Definitely."

"Good, then I know a teleporter who will help us." She grinned up at Kevin, her tail lightly flitting against his arm.

Kevin put his shirt on, stretching it over his fat body and adjusting his pants.

They checked the hallway once more, and after they confirmed it was clear, the three moved into the room where Paris was keeping Nadine.

Kevin was nervous, his palms sweating, but he was also feeling bold. And besides, Paris and Ian were gone, so he was able to combat his nervousness using logic.

"Nadine!" Kevin rushed over to the woman and lightly slapped her cheek. "Remember me? It's Kevin, from the office. Remember?"

Nadine's eyes were glazed over, her expression indicating she was pretty much dead to the world. A glint on her finger caught Kevin's attention, and as he stared down at the woman, he began admiring her ring.

"Get her," said Turquoise, approaching from his left.

"Sure. I'm taking her ring, too, as a souvenir," he said as he lifted Nadine's hand.

"Your first rescue," Obsidian hissed. "A good day to remember."

Kevin slipped the ring off her finger and shoved it onto his pinky.

It was a tight fit, and there was a strange notch on the bottom part of the ring, which he started to explore almost immediately. Kevin's thumb naturally pressed into the notch on the bottom of the stolen ring—*just as Turquoise's teleporter appeared.*

The female teleporter stumbled forward, nearly colliding with a wall.

"What's going on?" she asked, her hand now on her stomach.

Kevin turned to see both cat girls also bending over, their eyes bulging. His thumb found the bottom of his ring and he pressed it again.

The three exemplars returned to normal.

Kevin's bushy eyebrows lifted as he put two and two together. Before the cat girls and the teleporter could respond, Kevin pressed the ring again, noticing the three of them start to react.

He turned the ring off, realizing he now had some leverage.

"What's going on?" Turquoise asked.

"I felt it, too," Kevin lied, his thumb still fingering the bottom of the ring. "Maybe Paris put a trap in here or something. We should go, now."

"A trap? How is that possible?"

The teleporter, a gray-haired woman in an orange leotard, looked to Turquoise and Obsidian. "Are we safe to leave? This place is giving me the creeps."

"We are now," Kevin said as he hoisted Nadine over his shoulder. "First, take us somewhere far from here, then take her somewhere equally far."

"After this, we're even," the teleporter reminded Turquoise.

One of her ears folded forward a bit. "Definitely," she finally said.

Kevin joined the three, Nadine slung over one shoulder. As he got into position, his thumb flitted against the bottom of the ring again. He had an idea of how he would make this work, but for now, he just needed to get to safety.

He could execute his power play later.

Chapter Fifty: Goodbye, Roman Martin

～ᴐ

Roman's dreams were muddled, filled with images of what had transpired over the last twenty-four hours, a bird's-eye view in some of them as he watched himself sob by Celia's bedside, as Celia's spirit lifted from her body, as she placed her hand on his head.

These images moved to himself battling Ava, the sheer power he'd felt as he learned more about his ability, and the moment in which he realized he was dreaming and tried to animate the dreamscape, it came tumbling down like a house of cards, turning into lava as it reached his feet and was absorbed by his skin.

Roman awoke from his nap in a sweat, Coma curled at his side, Celia at the edge of the bed, staring at the wall.

"Were you sleeping?" he asked Coma out of instinct.

"I don't sleep," the red-eyed doll told him, her mask still on her face. "You were dreaming, though."

"Scary dreams?" asked Celia.

While Coma was still in her ruffled outfit, Celia had stripped down to her bra and panties, and as she stood, Roman's eyes fell to her ass. Both dolls were perfect in every way, flawless beauties.

"Get dressed, Celia."

He knew he wasn't going to go along with Paris's plans, and he'd have to move quickly if he wanted to put an end to all this.

But can you kill someone? he thought as he dressed, going for black clothing and an overcoat that gave him plenty of room for movement.

It wasn't something Roman had ever contemplated before, but he'd been in enough fights to know it was something he was capable of. Back when he used to brawl, there were times when he or his opponent had been beaten within an inch of their life.

All Roman had to do with Paris was step over this line—finish it.

And then what? he thought as he looked at himself in the mirror. *Then you're going to all of a sudden become a hero, after you've murdered someone in cold blood?*

Roman knew then that if he pulled this off, there'd be one more skeleton he would need to stuff into his closet, literally.

Only then could he move forward.

And there was little he could do by this point anyway. It had come to this, a good part of it his fault, and getting rid of this future obstacle would make things much easier for him in the long run.

He'd have to see about getting his mind wiped after that, but he figured Nadine would know someone.

She'll understand.

Roman bent his head forward and brought water up to his face, animating it as soon as it touched his skin and forcing it to scrub him until he felt clean.

He was ready. Whatever the hell that meant.

Roman used an unlicensed teleporter, a woman Nadine had put him in touch with in case he ever needed it. She was short, her hair braided, and she looked skeptically at Roman as he approached her with Coma and Celia at his sides.

A series of blinking lights swirled around them like fireflies. Roman and the dolls took shape in a dark warehouse. Paris stood a few feet away from him under a grimy skylight, clearly annoyed to see he'd brought guests. She was in different clothing now, no pencil skirt; what she wore looked more like an exemplar outfit.

"I told you to come alone," she said as the unlicensed teleporter disappeared.

"They go where I go."

Paris considered this for a moment. "That's absolutely unacceptable. You can't just show up with some..."

"Friends," said Roman. "I want to make sure you understand where I'm coming from."

"And you need friends to do this?"

"Yes."

Paris's dark eyes narrowed on him. "You know, Roman, I've thought of several options regarding how I should handle this. I could expose you for what you've done, which would bring charges of treason against you, or I could simply finish it now."

"I thought we were going to work something out," Roman said, one eye on his power dial.

"Why do I get the feeling you didn't come here to work something out?"

"I worked for you last time, for Ian—that worked out."

"True, but only through threat. I don't want to have to threaten you when I need something. When I need something, I need it then. No exceptions."

"That's why I think it's best if we part ways." Roman glanced down at his power dial. He knew he'd probably have to de-animate one of the dolls, but if he could keep them both active, he would.

"And I was right again. I wish I could retire on how many times I've been right. Goodbye, Roman Martin, I believe your fate has been decided."

Her tongue flew out of her mouth, only to meet a wall of concrete that Roman had already called up from the ground.

The concrete formed a series of hands that grabbed hold of her tongue and yanked her to the ground.

Paris was shocked, sure, but she'd had enough training to react accordingly, and this reaction wasn't what Roman had been expecting. As he continued to grow a concrete wall around her, Paris's arms *elasticated*, growing six times the length of her body, and pulling her up and over.

As she landed, Paris twisted in the middle, her top half going to the rafters above and her bottom half running to the right.

Roman realized at that instant what he was up against, as her body returned to its normal size yet her arms remained six times larger than her form, her hands growing in width.

Her clothes torn away, Paris was now in a custom training bra and a pair of dark-blue tights that seemed to be made out of a polymer that stretched with her body.

"Looks like someone has a secret," she said, and this was when Ian Turlock stepped out of the shadows, the big man flexing his muscles as more protrusions tore from his skin.

"I know who you are," Ian told Roman.

"Of course you do; I'm the one that did your paperwork."

"Not that. I fought you last night, you and your two lovers."

Paris looked from Roman to Ian. "You knew about this?"

"He was wearing a mask last night; I didn't recognize him," the big man said, cracking his knuckles. As he cracked them, craggy spikes tore through the skin on his forearms.

"Celia, Coma, I want you to distract him," Roman said under his breath. "I will handle Paris first; it'll be easier that way."

Roman was over the fact that the two dolls were dispensable.

Now that he knew he could heal them up quickly, it bothered him less that he was sending them to their doom. Coma was the first to respond, her fists lifting to the ready, the small muscles on her frail arms pulsing.

Seeing her response, Celia also lifted her arms, a little unsure of herself as she had been before.

Roman would train them—he vowed to do this when he saw them step in front of him—but for now, he needed to pick off the easier of the two targets, and then focus on Ian.

"It's a pity you're going to die here tonight alongside your whores," said Paris. "Your power, which I'm assuming deals with taking control of ordinary objects, would be useful for our operation."

"I told you, I'm not going to be a cog in your machine."

Paris's torso elongated, her shoulders expanding back, her arms loosening as they lengthened. She launched herself at Roman, moving over the two dolls, who ran toward Ian.

Paris was fast, and before Roman could respond, the Western spy had wrapped around his body like a snake.

Roman could feel her starting to squeeze him tighter, his muscles starting to ache, his organs starting to press into one another. He had one arm outside her grasp, the one that had been up when she'd latched on.

Her neck four feet long and curved, Paris gazed down at Roman, a faux sadness in her eyes. "It's too bad, Roman Martin, you would have been very helpful in what we are trying to do. I've done this before; it shouldn't hurt for much longer," she said, her grip on his body tightening.

Roman called all the concrete in his vicinity to his right fist and then swung it at her, causing her to scream out and loosen her hold.

He hit the ground and moved to the left, briefly checking to see that Celia and Coma were still engaging Ian.

The two had gone for a pester-and-dodge strategy, knowing full well that they wouldn't be able to do anything to him. The big red man swung at them both, trying his best to grab one, but they were quite fast, and they moved around his punches with ease.

"You're going to regret that!" Paris said, a hoarseness to her voice now.

Roman went for the first item he could spot, which happened to be a pipe jutting out from the wall. The pipe came down, spilling water onto the floor. Noticing his power dial flashing, and feeling his heart palpitating, Roman curved the pipe into a wheel, which he sent off in Paris's direction.

Paris's legs simply elongated, and the pipe went between them.

The taste of blood in his throat, Roman retracted power from Celia and Coma, leaving them stranded in front of an increasingly furious Ian.

Now in full control of the water spewing out of what was left of the pipe, Roman formed armor around himself and blasted it at Paris, the water wrapping around her throat and pouring into her mouth, choking her.

Her arms and legs flailed as the water lifted her into the air, drowning her. And he would've finished the job, too, if it hadn't been for the large metal ball that struck him in the side.

His water armor protected his body, but the impact also knocked the wind out of him, forcing him to release his hold on Paris, who came crashing down to the ground, her arms drooping to her sides, a soggy mess.

What was that? Roman thought as he tried to piece together what Ian had flung at him. He saw both dolls lying on the ground now, tossed aside by Ian. It only took him a second to notice the steel ball zipping back to Ian's hand, his silver necklace flashing.

Now that Roman knew the culprit, assuming it was some type of magnetic ballistic weapon tied to the big man's necklace, he was prepared when Ian pulled his arm back to throw the metal ball at him.

Before he could let the ball go, which he held by putting two of his fingers in the holes of its metal surface, Roman animated Ian's ball of metal.

It quickly engulfed Ian's hand, spreading up his arm.

Using his other hand, the big man tried to peel the liquid metal off his forearm. He struggled to get it off, keratin spikes tearing through the metal, his muscles tensing as he tried to get control.

Figuring it was now or never, Roman called the concrete to his fists, followed by the metal, which coated his concrete fists and glinted in the soft light of the warehouse.

"That's how we're doing this?" Ian growled.

The fighter in Roman nodded, his water armor sluicing around him, his concrete and metal-laced fists twitching.

If someone had been standing outside the abandoned warehouse, they would have felt the two men collide. If someone had been standing three blocks away from the abandoned warehouse, they too would have heard the sickening collision, Ian's gnarled knuckles against Roman's concrete-and-steel-covered fists.

Roman fought his heart out, for Celia, for his own life, and for the future life he hoped to create for himself. He dodged all of Ian's blows, connecting several times with Ian's chest and once with the side of his face.

Ian's luck changed when Roman moved in for another punch, missed, and Ian managed to headbutt him.

Roman went down, everything around him fading to black. With his last spark of consciousness, he poured as much energy as he possibly could into Coma.

Chapter Fifty-One: Unholy Alliance

Celia dropped her soft hand to Roman's cheek. They stood in a meadow covered in ultraviolet flowers, the sky a starless vacuum of darkness.

"Celia," he started to say, tears welling in his eyes. Her hair was back, the color had returned to her skin, and she looked healthy, happy.

"Roman," her voice came as she moved up to kiss him on the cheek. "You're almost there."

Roman gasped, his eyes bulging open. He was lying in a puddle of water, his head pounding. He rolled to his side, breathing heavily, not able to fully comprehend what he was seeing.

Coma was going toe-to-toe with Ian, the masked doll dodging his advances, responding with quick punches and kicks. She moved faster than Roman had ever seen her move before, her attacks actually hurting Ian, evident in his grunts and the way he was nursing his ribs.

Roman felt the pressure of a thousand needles pricking into him. His arms and legs were numb, and once he was able to turn and look at his power dial, the realization came to him.

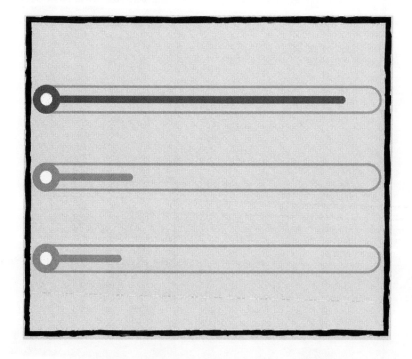

Roman was closer to dying than he'd ever been.

And part of him was fine with this.

Roman had never been a religious man, but seeing Celia in his dream-like stupor made him feel as if he could really go to that place, the meadow of ultraviolet flowers, and be there with her for the rest of eternity.

You're almost there.

That was what Celia had said to him in his brief vision, and it must have meant something. Had she meant he was almost there—almost reunited with her? Or that he was close to defeating Ian?

Roman spat blood onto the concrete flooring of the warehouse. His entire body pulsed and went numb again, red flashing across his pane of vision.

It was as if his heart was the size of a throbbing watermelon, cracking against his rib cage, bullying his lungs and other organs, shaking his entire body.

Coma cried out as Ian struck her, sending her arching backward.

Now or never.

Animate inanimate objects.

Affect things at their molecular level.

Red is dead.

Roman took the power back from Coma, feeling his breath return to him.

His limbs stopped pulsing, and as Ian brought his foot back to punt Coma across the room, Roman focused on the protrusions jutting out of the man's body.

Ian stopped moving, a look of discomfort spreading across his face. His protrusions quivered and started to shrink, but they didn't just grow back into his body—some of them began curving towards his red skin, piercing his hardened epidermis and pressing through.

He doubled over in pain as a giant spike tore out of his back, blood spraying into the air. Ian dropped to his knee, more protrusions reversing their course and cutting into his skin, tearing through his tendons, shattering his bones.

Ian was a bloody mess by the time Roman finished.

He was also dead.

It took Roman a good ten minutes to catch his breath and finally get to his feet. Once he felt he was able, he re-animated Coma, who stood immediately, her head bent forward in an unnatural position as she came back to life.

He opened his hands to her and the masked doll moved to him, wrapping her arms tightly around his waist.

"You saved me."

Coma didn't respond; she merely hugged him, the incarnation of Roman's more aggressive side softening in his trembling arms.

He still felt like his energy had been drained from him, and while his power dial showed that he was running close to normal, it certainly didn't feel that way.

"Thank you," he said again, nuzzling the top of his chin in her dark hair. She felt human, her skin warm, her shoulders heaving up ever so slightly as she breathed.

It was incredible; she was alive because of him, and Roman was alive because of her.

They remained like that for another touching moment, one Roman would always recall when he recalled this scene.

Eventually, he animated Celia, whose first comment revolved around how disheveled everyone looked. Her second comment was a bit more gruesome. "And he's dead," she said, squinting at Ian, who lay in a bloody mess on the floor.

"Let's finish this," Roman said. While he caught his breath for a moment longer, Celia and Coma arranged Paris's arms and legs so they were spread wide.

Roman turned the concrete beneath her wrists and ankles into liquid and sank her hands and feet deep into the concrete, pinning her to the floor. Focusing on her face and her dark hair, he quickly created a concrete band around her neck.

At that point, Roman waited, crouching next to Paris, biding his time before she awoke.

He wanted to know why she'd gone to all this trouble before he killed her, before he buried this part of his life, sealing it away in concrete.

Eventually, she blinked her eyes awake, and as she came to realize she'd been pinned, Paris tried to elongate her torso and break free from Roman's clasps, slapping her back against the floor in the process and ultimately failing.

"What do you want?" she gasped, the concrete band around her neck tightening.

"I need to know why."

"Why? What happened to Ian?" she cried, true fear in her eyes.

Her panic was momentary; she soon regained her composure, a trained soldier at heart. The West had more money than the East, less than Centralia and the South, and equal reserves as the North. Paris's training had been extensive; she knew that any window of opportunity for her to get out of this was quickly dwindling.

"Red man is dead," said Celia, her weight now tilted to her right hip.

Paris's throat quivered, her eyes readjusting as she strategized on what might happen next. "And why did you keep me alive?" she finally asked.

"I need to know why."

Paris tried to read the look on Roman's face, the meaning behind his action, what he could possibly hold behind his orange eyes. The man she'd met at Heroes Anonymous was not the same man that crouched before her, blood streaked through his white hair, two seemingly innocuous doll-like women standing behind him.

"Why?" she asked, still not comprehending what he wanted to know. "And where did you get this power?"

Roman ignored her last question. "Why are you doing what you do? What are you hoping to get from the Centralian government?"

A million thoughts fired off in Paris's head, all centered around the fact that she only had one chance to phrase what she said in a way that would appease Roman. She didn't fancy for a moment that Roman would spare her life; he'd already killed Ian, an impressive feat to say the very least, and nothing about the way he now stood over her, killer instinct written large on his face, told her he'd let her live.

"Healers," she finally said, going with her current assignment.

"Healers?"

"The Western Province has been ravaged by war for decades, especially in the borderlands. You probably already know this."

"I do."

"And we need healers." Paris tried to laugh, to lighten the situation as best she could. "Sounds crazy, I know. I should clarify: the extent that I've been assigned with turning immigration advisors to gather data on healer numbers sounds crazy, not the fact that we need healers—that's no laughing matter. Centralia doesn't want refugees, doesn't allow refugees really, and so we have to do something about those caught in the crosshairs of this war. So, healers. And from what we've uncovered, *Centralia has killed all the healers.*"

"That's why you chose me? Healers?"

"The plan was more complex than that. It was actually about your officemate, Kevin Blackbook. His brother, of the same name, works in the Centralian Diplomatic Forces, which you probably know."

"Aware. Kevin's twin. What's that have to do with me? Kevin's dead…"

Paris held her tongue for a moment. If Roman didn't know, then she wasn't going to be the one to tell him. "Yes, he's dead. Unfortunate. We wanted to use Kevin as leverage to get his twin brother to give us the info, which we weren't able to do because of his death. We found another way, and from what we've been able to gather, Centralia has killed all but one healer."

"I've never dealt with paperwork for a healer. Pretty sure Kevin hadn't either, and if he had, it was years ago."

"That's because there are no more healers, like I said. Well, according to what we've been able to uncover, there is one, and your government has them."

"Only one?" Roman immediately thought of Celia and watching her wither away. "Are you saying there is only one healer left in the entire world?"

Paris shrugged as best she could with her neck pinned to the floor. "Could be, or there could be more. This has changed the nature of my operation. What was once an operation to secure more healers to use in the West has now become an operation to uncover what has happened to all the healers."

Roman glanced to his fists and noticed they were clenched tight. He thought of Celia, the fact that she could have been cured if they'd had a healer. If there'd been a healer available, she'd be with him now, alive, happy.

His knuckles grew red as he squeezed his fists even tighter. Someone was to blame.

"What do you think happened to the other healers?" he asked through gritted teeth.

"I don't know," said Paris, desperation flickering behind her dark eyes, "but if you let me go, we can work together to uncover the truth."

Epilogue: New Horizons

Nadine gasped.

Life came back to her in the form of a deep gulp of air. Her lungs expanded, pressing against her rib cage, aching.

She coughed, rolled to her side, and coughed even harder.

She had no idea where she was, but she could quickly figure this out with a mental message to an Eastern Province teleporter. She couldn't quite remember what had happened, but she did recall being attacked in her apartment, and a brief moment in which she'd been dragged up a flight of stairs.

Nadine cursed herself for not contacting a teleporter then, knowing that her training had failed her in some way.

But wherever she was, it was quiet, and oddly enough, it felt relatively safe.

She was in an alley, definitely an alley in Centralia based on its cleanliness alone, and as soon as she sent a mental message to the teleporter, she also asked them to confirm her location.

Nadine was somewhere around 100th and 51st Street, not too far from her home country.

The teleporter would be there any moment, and he would take her to Oscar, the man who operated the secure communication channel. He would find a telepath who could piece together what had happened to Nadine, and why she'd ended up here. Then again, these types of telepaths, the ones with the psychometry skill, were hard to come by.

But it was pretty easy for Nadine to piece together a big part of the puzzle: someone had saved her.

The teleporter had just arrived when Nadine discovered that her Zero Ring was missing. She panicked, looking around for it, and even had the teleporter, a male with spiked hair, help her search the alley.

Nothing.

So this wasn't as clean of an escape as Nadine would have liked.

There had been a trade-off.

539

If only Kevin could find some grapes.

The former immigration advisor felt like a king, an exemplar, a cut above the rest. And with the Zero Ring on his pinky finger, that was exactly what he was.

More powerful than he had ever been, with confidence he had never experienced, Kevin now had a thirst for revenge, a desire to see to the deaths of his enemies.

The only thing was, Kevin didn't have that many enemies.

Sure, there was the flying exemplar who had fucked his wife—that guy was definitely going to get killed. And there was his brother, who had used his influence to deny basic healing rights to the Western Province, but he'd be a better pawn than a target for death—at least for now.

There was also his wife, Susan, whom he would also have to kill, and possibly a few of his coworkers who had never been that nice to him. He remembered some of them from the rooftop, and he'd probably need to take out Selena too, just because she had always been a bitch to him.

The ring he'd stolen from Nadine granted him the power to bring supers to their knees.

And in the few hours that had passed since he'd saved Nadine's life, Kevin had formulated a plot as to how he would go about doing this, how he was going to get the revenge he sought.

For now, there was Turquoise and Obsidian, both of whom had started to treat him even nicer than they had before. He could already tell the difference in their eyes when they looked at him, the respect, the way they waited on him, the mantras Turquoise said under her breath as she took Kevin in.

Their dynamics had changed. He was their leader, and he would treat them better than Paris ever had.

Another thing he'd noticed was that their neurotoxin excretions didn't work on him when he wore the ring. A pity, because he liked the intoxicant.

Regardless, it was probably better this way.

Kevin had been reborn, and his rebirth was going to cause a lot of deaths.

And that was what he felt as the sun came up the next morning, his eyes on the horizon, both cat girls asleep on his chest, their ears flickering ever so slightly.

If only Kevin could find some grapes, he would ask Turquoise to feed them to him.

No, he would *tell* Turquoise to feed them to him.

There was nothing particularly special about the room Roman sat in.

He'd been to the Human Resource offices before, when he'd been a new hire as part of a mandatory training. The HR offices were on the second floor, with windows overlooking the small pond next to the administration building.

An office with a view—what he wouldn't give for that.

Roman had already received a funny look from the receptionist when he'd entered, a woman in her early forties who wore a designer scarf. Ultimately, she hadn't asked why he was so bruised up, and he hadn't offered any explanation.

But he knew the question would come, and he was ready for when it did.

"I'm Dante," a bald man in glasses said as he stepped into the room. He was dressed in a pressed overcoat with embroidery over its front pocket and matching black slacks.

"Roman Martin."

Dante kept up his fake smile as they shook hands, as he took in Roman's face and the fact that his hand was bandaged. What he couldn't see were all the small cuts and abrasions covering Roman's body, the scabs that had formed, and the various bruises he couldn't recall acquiring.

Fighting was hard on the body—Roman knew this. And he also knew from his past experiences at the fighting bars of Centralia that smaller injuries usually made themselves known after the fight.

"Nice to meet you, Roman. I see that you are…" Dante hesitated.

"It's not what it looks like. After what happened, I needed to blow off some steam. I went to a fighting bar. The steam is gone, but now I'm a little worse for wear."

"I see. Nothing illegal about that."

"Exactly."

"Please, sit," said Dante as he took a chair in front of Roman. "Do you have the paperwork?"

"Sure do." Roman opened his shoulder bag to retrieve several pieces of paper he'd made that morning regarding his wife's death.

It wasn't that he couldn't have obtained the paperwork—no, Roman had slept in, and he hadn't felt like taking a teleporter across the city to obtain a Notice of Death. Besides, as he was seeing now, the HR guy didn't really question any of the paperwork, focusing instead on what had led to Celia's death.

"And she was like this for the last two years?"

"Give or take."

"That's so long."

"It was excruciatingly long."

"And what was the cause of the coma?"

"Trauma."

"Please elaborate." Dante scribbled some notes down on a piece of paper.

"I'd rather not."

The HR representative looked up at Roman and frowned. "I can only approve your bereavement leave request if I have adequate information. This is completely confidential; nothing that is said in this room leaves this room."

"I've just lost my wife. This is the evidence of me losing my wife. If you need more information, you can view the archives via our office's telepathic record keepers. It has been the worst weekend of my life, and there isn't anything else I'd like to say about it."

"Okay, Mr. Martin, that's fine," Dante said as he scribbled some information down. "Now, regarding your employment here, is there anything you'd like to report to me while we are having this one-on-one meeting?"

"What do you mean?" Roman asked, an idea coming to him.

"Have you had any issues with your immediate upper management or anything company related that you'd like to discuss? If so, now is the time."

He considered this for a moment, focusing on a decal pinned to the HR guy's lapel. "If I felt management was abusive, what would happen?" Roman finally asked.

"Well, if it is their first or second offense, they'd be put into mandatory Inclusion Strategy Training. In fact, one of the workshops starts later this week and goes into the weekend. It is a comprehensive course that requires the use of an empath with mood-adjustment capabilities for those who prove to be difficult to reach."

Roman did his best to suppress a grin.

Dante looked at him over the rim of his glasses. "Is there someone in upper management you'd like to discuss?"

"As a matter of fact, there is. And this same person also made a comment about my deceased wife that I'd like to have filed."

All in a day's work, Roman thought as he made his way to his favorite bench next to the office, the one in front of the small duck pond. Coma and Celia sat on the bench, both looking out at the water, thin smiles on their faces.

"How did it go?" asked Celia, looking up at him with her soft purple eyes.

"It went well. I'm off for the rest of the week, and somehow, I got my boss in trouble."

Coma smirked. "Was that intentional?"

"They gave me an opening, and I took it."

The masked doll shrugged, her breasts bouncing up and down as she did so. Roman glanced at the ducks in the pond, one of which had lifted out of the water, flapping its wings and causing quite a commotion with the others. It was a bit chilly, but not too bad, a breeze blowing up from the south.

"What are we doing now?" asked Celia. "I could look at the ducks forever, if that's what you'd like. It would be nice to go swimming, too."

"We can't go swimming here," Roman said, cracking a grin. He would continue to find this out, but Celia the doll always had something cute to say.

"Then what are we doing?"

"I have a Heroes Anonymous meeting later today, and I'll meet with Ava before that."

"Will we see Harper?" asked Coma.

"Is that what you'd like?"

"It's what you seemed to like."

"I don't know." Roman turned away from them. "I need to get my, well, for lack of a better phrase: *ducks in a row.*"

Celia tilted her head at the ducks in the pond. "Do ducks usually line up in rows?"

"No idea, but you know what I mean. We do need to kill some time, though. The red-light district won't open for at least another hour."

Roman saw another duck lift out of the water and figured he'd go for it. Focusing on the water beneath a black duck, Roman physically lifted the duck, the water spraying around it as if it was attempting to nest at the top of a fountain.

The duck beat its wings for a moment, and Roman let the water drop back into the pond.

As the two dolls laughed, an idea came to him that he'd been meaning to try. He turned Coma and invited her over to him.

Roman willed his ability to Coma. At first, it didn't feel like anything was happening. Then he reached this strange threshold that he could sense, a threshold he could press through, and once he did…

Roman glanced at his power dial, and he saw that for once, the green bar had raised.

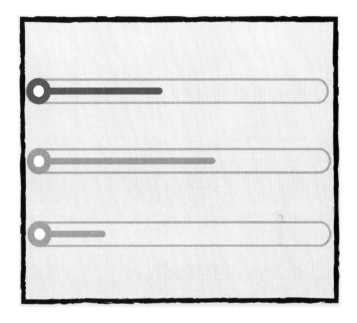

What he had experienced before was mostly activity in the red and bottom blue bar. This was something else, something new, and what Roman said next would change the course of his afternoon.

"Can you feel that?" he asked her.

"I can feel… something."

"I want you to try to do what I did with the water, try to lift it up."

"Lift up the water?" Coma looked to Celia.

"I bet you can do it," Celia said, a smile on her face.

Coma spread her fingers and stuck her hand in front of her body. As she did so, the surface of the pond began to tremble, droplets pushing upward.

"Good!" Roman said, clapping. "Try harder, focus even more."

Coma closed her red eyes, and a small pillar of water began to lift from the surface of the pond. It fell back down immediately as she let out a gasp of air, her mouth agape.

"You can do it," Roman told her, breathing heavily himself.

Coma tried again, the water lifting out of the pond and annoying the ducks.

"Hold it just a little longer," he told her, and after she'd held it for about thirty seconds, Coma released the water.

"I have a superpower now?" she asked Celia.

"It sure looks like it!"

A couple approached the pond, two men from one of the different departments. Rather than stick around,

Roman nodded for Celia and Coma to come over to him, instantly calling his power back, too. "Let's get out of here; we can play with this later."

He went ahead and ordered a teleporter to take them to a diner near the entrance to the red-light district.

They appeared outside the diner a few seconds later, and after a short wait, the three were seated in a small booth with a view of the entrance.

Roman couldn't help but smile as his coffee came to him and he looked across the booth at the incredibly gorgeous living dolls who sat before him, Coma with her black hair, mask and ruffled clothing, and Celia with her red hair and tight superhero outfit.

As they spoke of lighter things, of plans for the week and places they'd like to visit in Centralia, Roman kept a watchful eye on the red-light district.

Eventually, he saw the person he was looking for, a young woman with light-gray hair in a tight dress. Roman remembered her name instantly—Emelia, the empath with violet eyes who had sold Celia to him.

He waved the waiter over. "Can I get my food to go? Something has come up."

"Did you see her?" Coma asked as the waiter left to the kitchen.

Roman nodded.

"Great, I'm excited to meet the next one."

Celia placed both elbows on the table, so she could rest her face in her palms. "I wonder what you will call her. Perhaps we can name her."

"Do you have a name in mind?"

The two dolls looked at each other and shrugged. "We'll have to meet her first," Celia finally said.

Coma nodded. "Agreed. Let's meet her before we name her."

"Fair enough," said Roman, "fair enough."

The end.

Back of the Book Content

Reader,

I really hope you enjoyed this book. It is my second foray into superhero fantasy, the first being my best-selling series, Cherry Blossom Girls.

I plan to expand more on Centralia and the rest of the countries in House of Dolls Book Two, which I plan to release in December 2018. I also have plans of growing the world and fleshing it out through other series related to House of Dolls. The first likely series will be a book about Heroes Anonymous, but don't hold me to it. I'm still floating this idea.

Yours in sanity,

Harmon Cooper

Other Books by Harmon Cooper

I have written over thirty books. Here are some of the highlights!

My best-selling Superhero Harem Adventure about a sci-fi writer and the superpowered women who are trying to kill him. Fun content, adult read!

A fantasy harem adventure inspired by *Pokemon Go!*, *Scott Pilgrim vs. The World*, and the *Persona* family of video games. Check out this Amazon best seller!

What if Ready Player One was a multi-part epic? Gritty LitRPG action, gamer humor, fantastic fantasy worlds, and a killer MC.

(This one is related to Monster Hunt NYC)

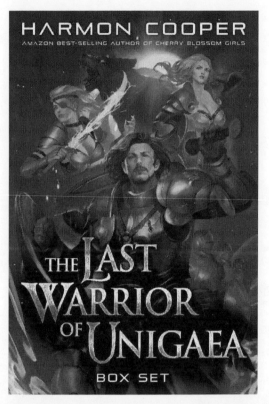

If you love dark fantasy, RPGs, Witcher, Punisher, or Mad Max, you'll love this powerful gamer trilogy about a man and his wolf companion.

(This one is related to Monster Hunt NYC)

Tokyo, Japan meets online fantasy gaming and South Park-styled humor. Yakuza, goblins, action, intrigue - add this book to your inventory list!

(This one is related to Monster Hunt NYC)

Made in the USA
Columbia, SC
18 December 2018